MAGICIAN'S CHOICE

RISE OF MAGIC
BOOK 1

STEFON MEARS

Thousand
Faces
Publishing

Also by Stefon Mears

The Rise of Magic Series
Magician's Choice
Sleight of Mind
Lunar Alchemy
Three Fae Monte
The Sphinx Principle
Double Backed Magic
Mercury Fold (forthcoming)

Cavan Oltblood Series
Half a Wizard
The Ice Dagger
Spells of Undeath

Power City Tales
Not Quite Bulletproof
No Money in Heroism

Standalones
The Hireling
The Captain's Cat
Save Whiskers!
The Ogre of Threepeaks
Between the Cracks
Sects and the City
Prince of a Thousand Worlds
Devil's Night
Portal-Land, Oregon
Stealing from Pirates
Fade to Gold
With a Broken Sword
Twice Against the Dragon
The House on Cedar Street
Sudden Death
On the Edge of Faerie

Short Story Collections
Spell Slingers
Twisted Timelines
Longhairs and Short Tales: A Collection of Cat Stories
Dangerous Space
Confronting Legends (Spells & Swords Vol. 1)
The Patreon Collection, Vol. 1-8 (Vol. 9, coming soon)

Nonfiction
The 30-Day Novel and Beyond!

Spells for Hire Series
Devil's Shoestring
Zombie Powder
Spirit Trap
Dragon's Blood

The Telepath Trilogy
Surviving Telepathy
Immoral Telepathy
Targeting Telepathy

Edge of Humanity Series
Caught Between Monsters
Hunting Monsters

Jumpstart Duchy Series
Into the Torn Kingdoms
The Dragon's Gold
The Gift Castle
The Deadly Feast
The King's Test
Triumph in the Torn Kingdoms

Published by Thousand Faces Publishing, Portland, Oregon

http://1kfaces.com

"All I ask is a tall ship..." is quoted from "Sea-Fever" by John Masefield

Trade Paperback ISBN: 978-1-948490-98-6

MAGICIAN'S CHOICE

The year is 2025
Six decades after the Rise of Magic

1

Donal Cuthbert frowned at the tourism sign above the customs station and said to the agent, "In a few weeks Bran might be the first human to set foot on Ganymede, and I'm not even the five millionth man on Mars."

"Passport" replied the tired woman whose skin bore the red tint of a local. Official speculation had it that the spells adapting Mars to human life might also adapt human life to Mars. The agent tapped Donal's passport with her badge. It chimed legitimacy. "Who's Bran?"

"Bran Cuthbert. My brother."

"*The* Bran Cuthbert is *your* brother?" The agent paused, giving Donal's passport a second look. "You must be very proud. Without men like Bran we wouldn't be on Mars today." She touched Donal's distressed leather messenger bag with a baton enchanted to detect contraband, then twirled the baton in a circle over Donal's head. No sound of alarm came. "Anything to declare?"

"IIX courier package for delivery in New Leningrad."

She consulted a list. "Everything's in order. Any checked bags will be in baggage claim in thirty minutes. Welcome to Mars."

Donal looked over the spaceport foot traffic as he left the customs area: busy, but less so than San Francisco. Maybe a thousand travelers instead of tens of thousands. He took a deep breath and started into the spaceport proper. He got two dozen steps past the waiting area when a half-meter-long dragon made of sinuous, wingless smoke whirled a wide circle around him and zipped away. Donal stopped. That had to have been someone's familiar. His contact?

Wait, was that sulfur he smelled?

Fire roared. With a crack like a boulder shattering, a garbage can ahead and to Donal's right exploded into flame. The shock wave threw Donal at least two meters. He landed in a crumpled heap. Others in the crowd weren't so lucky. Donal spotted four charred bodies, then panic made the crowd a mob.

A silent mob. The explosion had consigned Donal to a world of dreamlike silence. Travelers milled and ran every direction. Donal clutched his messenger bag. Adrenaline froze him. Run away? Try to help? What should he do?

A hand grabbed his wrist. Donal was yanked to his feet by a beautiful Chinese woman with red skin and a light gray business suit. Her lips moved in rapid speech, but Donal shook his head and tapped his ear. She grimaced, craned her neck to look past him, then turned and dragged him sideways through the chaos in a broken-field run. She shoved him against a side wall. Donal's body lit up with dozens of aches that promised bruises from his fall. The woman glanced back, watching something over her shoulder. As far as Donal could tell, customs had locked down, sealing away the gates and docking bays. Travelers pushed every direction, a mass of confusion.

Travelers, but not everyone. A handful of men moved through the crowd, seeking something. Donal fished through his pockets. Where was his tuning fork?

The woman towed Donal along the wall and through a door marked, "Employees Only." Then they stood in a hallway that led straight back into the port or away on a curve. Along the opposite wall was a series of closed doors labeled in code.

Donal found his tuning fork, struck it, and waved it past his ears while chanting words he could not hear. Warmth flooded his ear canals, then heat, then sound popped back into his world. He could hear muffled screams and panic just beyond the door they came through.

"Better?"

"Yes." He held the tuning fork between them. "Who are you?"

"Just shock then. Good. I'm Tai Shi Li Hua, your liaison on Mars."

"I.D."

"About time you asked for that." She handed him a business card that identified her by name as the Regional Director of Corporate Security for 4M. She fidgeted, impatient, while Donal tapped it with his tuning fork and checked the soft orange glow against what he saw when he waved the fork in front of her: a perfect match. Donal glanced to double-check, but she rolled her eyes and said, "We need to get moving."

"What's going on?"

She ignored the question. "Pinyin-Lung," she barked, and a spirit dragon puffed into being, the one Donal had seen near customs. Donal noticed an echo of resonance between them and concluded it was her familiar. Tai Shi Li Hua gave the dragon orders in Chinese, and turned back to Donal as it flew off. "I have just arranged for private transportation, but we cannot meet it here. My agents will collect your luggage. Do you have a familiar?"

"No." The comfortable subject helped Donal recover himself. He had a plan for binding the perfect familiar as part of his graduate studies. "I..."

"What is this, your first assignment? Stick close to me, then." They flattened against the wall as a crew in uniforms rushed past and out into the chaos. She flung a spell after them, a false trail deception if Donal read it right, then looked back at him. "Tell me the package is secure."

Donal gripped his messenger bag and the liaison smiled. She must have realized that his spells had made the bag too innocuous to notice. He smiled back. "The package is secure."

John Jacobs, captain of the helioship *Horizon Cusp*, crouched with one knee on the Martian ground as though he bowed before a king. He closed his eyes and picked up his customary handful of local dirt. He rubbed the rough soil through his fingers. He held it to his nose and smelled its tang. He opened his eyes at last and looked at the dirt. Dark. Red. Gritty. Mars. He stood.

Jacobs hoped to finish his day's business in time to refill his books with different novels, but he would not skip his personal gesture of gratitude for another safe voyage, another immaculate landing. He wiped his hands clean and sighed into the distance at the Barrier, where the blue sky above New Leningrad became the yellow sky of Mars. Was yellow the natural color or an effect of the Barrier? Jacobs could never decide if he wanted to know.

The spaceport's architecture was typical for Mars: a Mediterranean feel, all curves and arches, reds and tans and browns and open air buildings with plants that were sprayed, not watered. Jacobs did not dally for the art display: the story of humans on Mars told in curving, twisting red-brick statues carved by "local" artists who had been born on Earth, some fifty-six million kilometers away.

Jacobs left the tourist area of the spaceport for the smaller section dedicated to businesses run out of the port. Warehouses, shipping lines, and a handful of passenger lines like his own, Starchaser Spacelines.

Jacobs entered the office, but before he had time to greet the receptionist he heard his partner's voice. "John? That you?"

"It's me." Jacobs poked his head into Zoltan's office: spotless as a magazine ad for an executive suite, done in red oak as an homage to the planet. On Earth, Zoltan's office was brown, green and blue, on Earth's moon it was gray and blue. "What are you doing here, Zoltan? I thought you were heading back to San Francisco with Yoshi."

"Good thing I didn't. The *Beamrunner* didn't make it. Yoshi, his crew, and almost all of his two hundred eighty-seven passengers: dead."

"What happened?"

"We're still trying to find out. Zuglodon attack maybe."

Jacobs sank into one of the guest chairs across the desk from Zoltan. Yoshi was in his forties. Half Jacobs' age, and a decade younger than Zoltan. Too young. "Whiskey."

Zoltan broke out a bottle of bourbon, Butcher's Block. He poured them each a double. Jacobs raised his glass and said, "To Captain Yoshi Hirohito, taken home too soon by the stars. May his name live on, and may his spirit light our way whenever we sail the black depths."

The Butcher's Block burned on its way down, in Jacobs' mind a perfect choice for the occasion. Sixty-seven years he had sailed the seas, the skies and space, ever since he was a lad of eighteen, before even the fall of technology and the rise of magic. He had buried too many friends.

"How many dead men have you toasted?" asked Zoltan.

"I've lost count."

"You might be toasting our business next."

Jacobs noticed that his partner looked half-dead himself: bowed and rumpled like a poorly folded map. He waited for Zoltan to continue.

"Seventy-five cancellations in the last twenty-four hours. At this rate we'll be lucky to book a fifth of the *Horizon Cusp's* berths for your next flight. Then there are the lawsuits, insurance problems, Mars and Earth are both investigating—"

"They can't blame us for—"

"They do, John."

Jacobs held out his glass for a refill, then slammed down the bourbon. He savored the burn against the unfairness of it all. In sixty-seven years he had never lost a ship, and now his business might be ruined over something he could not have helped. "I was going to retire next year."

"You've been saying that since I met you."

"I had a place picked out in Mazatlan."

"Your attention please," said a voice over the loudspeaker in the corner. "There has been an incident in the public area. Please proceed to your assigned safe zone in a calm, orderly fashion. There is no cause for alarm."

No cause for alarm? Jacobs gritted his teeth. His business and his future were spiraling out of control. He faced the real possibility of dying broke and homeless, starving in a gutter somewhere.

DONAL RACED AFTER TAI SHI LI HUA AS THEY RAN TO THE RENDEZVOUS point. His breath came in gulps. Sweat stuck his collar to his throat. His bag rubbed against his hip. Side doors flew past. Still the hallway curved.

Donal's legs grew heavy. He pushed to keep pace. Sweat spread into his shirt. His muscles burned from the effort. His bruises throbbed in time to his heartbeat. Still the hallway curved.

And she does this in a suit?

"How ... much ..."

"Not far," the liaison said in a regular, conversational voice, "We're almost to the west employee exit."

Finally she stopped. Donal leaned forward, hands on his knees, and tried to steady his breath while his messenger bag dangled. He wiped sweat out of his eyes. The liaison looked crisp, as though she were ready for an interview. No, that was not quite true. Her nostrils flared at a steady rate, and her chest rose and fell in deep breaths.

Don't stare!

The door in front of Donal did not look different from any of the other doors they passed. He reached for the knob, but she stayed his hand.

"Wait." Tai Shi Li Hua closed her eyes and chanted briefly in Chinese while moving one hand back and forth: a seeking spell. "We lost the ones near baggage claim, but I can't be sure the streets are clear. Pinyin-Lung will tell me when it's safe to move."

"What happened ... back there?"

"Corporate espionage." The liaison shrugged. "Clumsy corporate espionage. Aetheric Dynamics must be hiring cheap labor." She looked him up and down. "We have a moment. Rest if you like."

"Look Ms...."

"Someone just tried to kill us, Donal," she said with one eyebrow raised. "Call me Li Hua."

Donal fell back against the wall and stared at Li Hua.

"Wait, that explosion was supposed to kill us?"

"No, I don't think even Aetheric Dynamics is that clumsy." She glanced back down the way they came. "I think the explosion was supposed to create confusion while their agents came at us from both sides and killed us before order was restored."

Donal rubbed his temples. Someone had tried to kill him. This was supposed to be the safer way for Donal to earn quick money, safer than the illegal option...

"Sloppy execution though," Li Hua continued. "They should have tightened their perimeter before triggering the bomb. Of course, it's not that easy. You have to keep out of the target's line of sight, and ... are you all right?"

"No one's ever tried to kill me before."

"Really?" Li Hua put a hand on Donal's shoulder. "Well, don't worry. I'll get you out of this alive. Besides, that attempt just activated the combat clause in your contract." She smiled, and it made her eyes radiant. "Look at it this way: you just got a pay raise."

"If I live to spend it." Donal tried to worry, to focus on the fact that his life was under threat, but her relaxed smile had infected him. Li Hua pulled out a compact and straightened hairs that Donal would not have known were out of place. She seemed to treat the whole encounter like a trip to the corner store; perhaps they were not in any real danger. Still, the combat clause was so named for a reason. "How can you be so calm?"

Li Hua laughed.

"Let's just say it's not the first time someone's tried to kill me." She glanced toward the door. "Come, Pinyin-Lung tells me our ride is here."

STARCHASER SPACELINES' "ASSIGNED SAFE ZONE" WAS A DOME-SHAPED warehouse some sixty meters in diameter. Two officers at the entrance greeted everyone and passed word that the investigators would soon conduct interviews. Camp chairs had been set-up before Jacobs and Zoltan arrived. Scattered crates served as tables. Jacobs wondered what use the warehouse filled under normal circumstances, that it could be converted so readily. Perhaps it stood empty. It did smell of must. Still, the arrangement far exceeded Jacobs' expectations. He estimated about fifty people stuck with him in a space that would not have felt cramped with twice that number. Much better than Kennedy Spaceport on Earth's moon, Luna, where Jacobs had once wasted six hours in an eight meter square interview room with some two hundred strangers while port security searched for a murderer. Perhaps a larger "safe zone" was a benefit of Mars' small population: New Leningrad had plenty of space and spent it freely.

Jacobs spotted the Starchaser Spacelines logo and he and his partner led their office staff toward the chairs below it, per official New Leningrad Spaceport emergency procedures. Jacobs sighed. Before he could figure out how to save their business, he had hours of paperwork to finish after that last voyage from Earth. Passenger lists, cargo manifests, crew passports and licenses, customs reports, star chart anomalies logged in transit, upcoming schedule, maintenance requirements, even the contents of the ship's lost and found: Martian bureaucracy made up for its small size with vast quantities of regulations and forms.

And now he had to waste time waiting for some official idiot to realize Jacobs did too much business in this spaceport to blow it up. At least, he used to.

The various companies present all seemed to gravitate toward their logos, and either engaged in small talk, speculated about the reason for the alert, or tried to continue their business. A few people flitted among the groups, either seeking or fomenting rumors.

Jacobs took a seat at the center crate-table of his designated waiting area. Zoltan joined him, but the sales and administrative staffs gathered at the other two crates and fell into easy conversation. Over the silence at Jacobs' crate he heard one of them mention that security would even provide coffee and a snack if the wait stretched past the half-hour mark.

Of course, good coffee would be too much to ask.

"At least port security is organized," offered Jacobs. "There's even talk of coffee."

Zoltan did not respond. His attention was fixed on a gathering two tables away, under the Taurus Insurance sign. Jacobs followed his gaze and saw a crowd of ten people watching a show of some sort.

"Let's see what's going on over there," said Zoltan.

They joined the crowd. A man near Jacobs' own age, dressed in a soft gray suit, stood behind a collapsible table on which he had lined up three small cups, face down. The showman had sharp features and eyes, a charming smile and short hair slicked back on his head.

"Now the question is simple," said the showman. "Which cup hides the ball?"

Something about the scene echoed in Jacobs' mind. Something he almost remembered from his youth.

A young Martian boy, perhaps too shy to speak, pointed at the cup by the showman's right hand.

"Are you certain?" The showman smiled. The boy nodded. "Are you quite certain?" The boy squirmed, less confident, but nodded again. The crowd seemed to hold its breath. "It's not too late to change your mind. No? Very well then." With a flourish, the showman lifted the cup. Nothing. "It was a good guess, my boy. Between the two of us, I thought it was there too. I bet it moved when we weren't looking." He lifted the middle cup, then the left cup, but the ball was gone. "Where did it go?"

The crowd murmured at the showman's apparent confusion, and the boy bent to look under the table. The showman leaned forward, looked at the boy, and said, "You clever lad! You had it all the time!" He plucked the ball from behind the boy's ear. The crowd applauded, no one louder than the child's parents, and the young Martian gaped in amazement.

Jacobs remembered now. He had once been that boy, dazzled by men in tuxedoes who sawed women in half and made volunteers disappear. Smooth men who lost their jobs when "real" magic returned.

The showman appeared to draw a deck of cards out of the air, and offered them to a woman in the crowd for inspection. Zoltan, however, must have tired of the show. Jacobs followed him back to their table. Near the door he saw a team from port security arrive and begin to interview people.

"Didn't like the magic show?" asked Jacobs.

"I was hoping for an opportunity," said Zoltan. "That wasn't even magic, just sleight of hand. Anyone could do it."

"They used to call it stage magic, and if you think it's that easy, you try it."

"All right, all right." Zoltan raised his hands in surrender. "My point is that anyone can learn to do it. Directed attention, the magician's choice...."

"The what?"

"Give the audience a choice between A and B, but arrange it so that whichever they choose, the result is the one you want: C."

"Why do you know so much about this?"

"Business school. It's good for marketing..." Zoltan started stabbing at the crowd with one finger. "Our answer is in that crowd, John, I just can't see it yet." He settled back in thought, and Jacobs envied his comfort. Zoltan looked so relaxed that his camp chair look might as well have been in front of a fireplace. When he turned back to Jacobs, Jacobs half-expected him to offer cigars and brandy. Zoltan said, "You're here more than I am. Does New Leningrad have this sort of problem often?"

Jacobs should not have thought of cigars. Now he wanted one. He would have to have one after dinner that night when he sat down to read. Not brandy with it though, whiskey would be better, something Irish.

"While I wouldn't call New Leningrad a quiet town, I wouldn't call it a war zone either. This is a standard evacuation procedure, and the tower didn't issue a terrorist warning when we docked, so I doubt that port security expected trouble."

Jacobs could see the security team more clearly now, only two tables away. A squad of five men and women who wore gray uniforms trimmed with dark brown and emblazoned with the insignia of the Martian Federation: twin moons over a stylized horizon. The security agents had the reddish tinge of natives and bore short, smooth clubs at their waists.

"Safety," said Zoltan. "Security. That's what we offer above and beyond our top accommodations. Starchaser Spacelines has never had an incident aboard ship!"

"And the *Beamrunner*'s accident?"

"Not a problem aboard ship." Zoltan began shaking one finger in the air as though he tapped an invisible table to keep time with fast music. "That was a hazard of space travel. Could have happened to anyone."

"Yoshi and his entire crew are dead. Hell, most of the passengers too. And you want to sell our safety?"

"Work with me, John. We need to focus on our clean record *aboard* our ships or we're...."

Zoltan let his words dangle as the port security team arrived. The agent in charge was a fit young woman with close-shorn hair. Her team fanned out behind her as she consulted a memoboard, held out an expectant hand, and said, "Identification please."

Jacobs handed her his captain's license while Zoltan presented his passport. She inspected each then verified their authenticity with a tap from her silver pinky ring. Jacobs did not see or hear any response to the check, but the officer seemed satisfied and returned their I.D.

"Where were you at the time of the attack?"

She sounded bored with the routine, which Jacobs assumed was either a deception or an indication that the real problem lay elsewhere, that this part of the investigation was a mere formality.

"I don't know when the 'attack' took place," said Jacobs, "but when the security alert came we were in our office." He waved a hand at their employees. "Everyone here will verify that."

The officer made a note on her memoboard. "And before that?"

"I just captained the *Horizon Cusp* here from Earth."

"I've been in the office all morning."

"That agrees with what I see here" she said. "You are both free to go. Public transit should be restored within the hour. All space traffic has been grounded until tomorrow, while we investigate." Jacobs thought he saw the first hint of real attention from her when she looked up again. "Have either of you spoken today with representatives of any of the following companies: Red Sun, Sandstorm Transit, Allied Enchantments or 4M?"

Jacobs stood to leave. He had no interest in local politics. He raised his eyebrows at Zoltan, who remained seated and asked, "Does it matter?"

The agent in charge studied Jacobs' partner.

"I wouldn't ask if it wasn't relevant."

"I met with a representative of Allied Enchantments this morning."

Jacobs shook his head and left quietly. One of the passengers from Earth had worked in the upper management of Red Sun. He had brought along six crates that customs had certified contained wine. That was more cargo weight than Jacobs liked to allow a single passenger, but the sales office had handled the details. The executive also brought two underlings, plus a personal secretary and a half-dozen bodyguards.

Jacobs had reported only the pertinent details on the cargo manifest and passenger list. If the locals had questions, they knew where to find him.

On his way out, Jacobs passed the showman, who entertained his audience by making a handkerchief dance. Jacobs wondered how he concealed the wire.

Li Hua threw open the exit door, and Donal saw about five meters of dirt between himself and the hard-packed clay of the New Leningrad streets. The ride waiting for Donal and Li Hua was a runner with tinted windows and six powerful legs. It looked like someone had hollowed out the body of a huge komodo dragon - two meters high and five long - strapped two more legs on the center section, and lopped off the head and tail. The runner waited at the curb with its rear passenger door open.

Donal bounced on his toes to convince his legs they could handle one more burst of speed, then he and Li Hua sprinted across the bare dirt while a gust of wind covered them in red dust. The driver, a scarred man dressed in black, snapped the reins as Donal and Li Hua scrambled into the rear bucket seats, and the runner took off at a swift, smooth clip before they had time to close the door. The runner's gentle side-to-side sway and the rhythmic ticking of its feet might have felt soporific under other circumstances, but just then even the soft leather of the seats pressed uncomfortably against Donal's aches.

Donal coughed dust and dug a tissue out of his bag so he could blow his nose and spit. He tucked the used tissue into a pocket by reflex - a magician did not leave ready-made magical links lying around. Donal's now-clear nose filled with the scent of the leather interior.

"Sitrep," snapped Li Hua.

"We're being followed," said the driver in a rasping growl that suited his cragged face. Traffic on the road was light: four-legged and two-legged runners alongside the occasional twelve- or eighteen-legged behemoth and even a riding horse or two. Horses had been out of fashion for over a decade, but finances did not always allow for fashion. Donal could certainly not have afforded a runner.

He spotted their stalker three vehicles back. It slipped between lanes like a saurian panther. Donal's stomach started to fold in on itself. People really were trying to kill him over the papers he carried. Maybe he should have taken that gig summoning malignant spirits to fix sporting events after all. It certainly sounded safer.

Panic would not help. First rule of magic: fear devours. He would have to fake confidence until he found it.

"More corporate espionage?"

"One in front too," said the driver. "They must have been ready for us."

"I'll take the one in front," said Li Hua. "Donal, get rid of our tail."

"But...." He could barely finish the word before she grabbed his shoulder and looked him in the eye. Her eyes were a soft brown.

"No one hires a Heirophant for pursuit," she said. "You're a Journeyman. You can handle this. Go."

Donal took a deep breath. True, he held a Bachelor of Arts in Thaumaturgy, and true he had taken a few self-defense courses, but this? He could see that Li Hua was already casting, calling a spell out of her earring and channeling forces to direct and contain it. Her gestures conveyed pure elegant efficiency.

Calm. Clear your thoughts. Take one smooth breath. Good. Now look - really look - again.

He counted two Martians in a runner teeming with spells.

Slow down. Compare.

Another deep breath and Donal realized that the pursuer's runner did not carry many more enchantments than any of the others around it. That meant that most of the spells he saw handled animation. Donal could handle that, given time. But the man in the passenger seat dug at something in his pocket. Whatever he wanted, it could not be good. Donal had to act now.

No good link, but at least I can see them. Wait, I can see them. That's it!

Donal brushed the local red dust from his shirt, pants, hair, and skin and cupped it between his hands. He mumbled a few words over the dust, then shook it gently, like a devout gambler praying over his dice. He chanted a few more words before he took a deep, deep breath and filled his lungs with as much Martian air as possible. He tossed the dust into the air between him and the rear window, his gaze locked on the following runner, and launched the spell with as much force as his lungs could manage.

A dust devil swept across the road and down on the pursuers, cutting off their vision. Donal heard great legs skid and clamber, the sounds of drivers fighting to maintain control and avoid collisions. Something crunched and crumpled, but his dust devil obscured the result.

"Not bad," said Li Hua with an approving nod.

Donal whirled around to find out what had become of her target, but saw only normal traffic: no sign of an accident or disabled vehicle, nothing.

"What happened to yours?"

"Oh, they won't be bothering us again," said Li Hua with an enigmatic smile.

As they passed a side street, Donal saw a runner on its back with its belly shredded, as though it had torn itself apart with its own claws.

Donal looked a question at Li Hua, but she only smiled.

2

JACOBS WALKED A SLOW, LONG PATH THROUGH SIDE HALLWAYS AND along the length of every arc of the outer business circles on his way back to the office. How would he break this news to his crew? The *Beamrunner* was bad enough. Many of his people had friends on that ship. But to have to tell them that Starchaser Spacelines was in trouble? Some of his men and women had shipped with him for almost a decade. They could find other jobs, but the *Horizon Cusp* was their home as much as it was his.

"I am very sorry, Captain Halford, but this flight is critical. My employer will require more experience."

Halford? Of the *Dawn Star*? Jacobs looked over at the speaker, a man with a Terran complexion - dark, without the ruddiness life on Mars seemed to overlay. He had dressed for the weather, though: light shirt and slacks, casual shoes. Most tourists expected Mars to be cold, like the first colony reports had described. The Barrier had long since corrected that discomfort.

The man turned and began to walk away from Halford. No time to fetch Zoltan, who was as good with people as Jacobs was with ships. Jacobs would have to make a sale himself for the first time in twenty years.

He quickened his pace to catch up. As Jacobs closed the stranger whirled with one hand reaching into his sleeve.

"Excuse me," said Jacobs, arms spread to display his empty hands. "I overheard you talking to Captain Halford. I'm Captain John Jacobs of the *Horizon Cusp*. You won't find a more experienced helioship captain than I am."

"Ah, Captain Jacobs. Half-owner of Starchaser Spacelines, I believe? Good, I prefer dealing with partners. My name is Imenand bin Zuka. I wish to enquire about chartering your ship for a private voyage to Earth, if we might speak somewhere privately."

Could it be that easy? Jacobs looked over this bin Zuka again. Casual clothes, but without a seam out of place or even a wrinkle. He spoke in an encouraging tone, but so did Zoltan — right up until he demanded stiff terms and a dozen concessions. Jacobs would have to keep one hand on the rudder. This might be a tough sale and an even tougher negotiation. Why did Zoltan have to get caught up talking to port security?

"My office is right this way."

A few minutes later Jacobs attempted a professional smile across his desk at bin Zuka. They sat in an office that Jacobs shared with Captain Gonzales when he was on Mars, and until recently with the late Captain Yoshi. On Earth Jacobs kept a private office, but in other ports he declined this as an unnecessary expense.

Untouched cups of rich coffee steamed on the oak desk's polished surface. His guest seemed content to sit, examining the room's spare decorations with an attentive eye: Jacobs' picture of home, taken from space on his first voyage to the moon, his commendation from the United North American States for captaining the first successful commercial passenger flight to Mars, Yoshi's helioship in a bottle, Gonzales' Nihonga painting. Apart from these touches it might have been a hotel conference room.

Jacobs stared at the helioship in a bottle. He would have to contact Yoshi's son about his father's effects. Jacobs almost lost time to thoughts of Rhonda and Carl, his own wife and son, both lost to him in the riots that followed the collapse of technology in the 60's.

He brought himself back to the present by scalding his lips with coffee. "So, what can Starchaser Spacelines do for you, Mr. bin Zuka?"

Bin Zuka turned his attention back to Jacobs. "My employer wishes to charter a ship for a private, ten-day trip to Earth, leaving three days from today."

"The standard Earth-Mars run takes seven days."

"That might not be sufficient time to conclude important negotiations."

Jacobs almost smiled before he realized that bin Zuka was not joking. He could not imagine why they would not be able to continue their business on Earth, but perhaps local laws or business rules made a difference. Either way, slowing his ship would be inefficient, but not worth losing a sale right now.

"That won't be a problem. How many passengers?"

"Thirty: two parties of fifteen."

Jacobs paused with his coffee cup halfway to his mouth and watched the deal drift out of a porthole and float toward the sun.

"The *Horizon Cusp* berths over three hundred."

"If I am pleased with the accommodations and crew, my employer will cover the cost."

"We do have passages sold on our next flight right now. I could isolate them from your party without much trouble."

"If we agree, I will ask you to cancel all other tickets for the flight. My employer will cover their cost, plus extra to apologize for the inconvenience."

Bin Zuka named a price, and Jacobs sipped his coffee while numbers spun through his mind. Running at less than ten percent capacity for full price would bring in enough profit to weather the *Beamrunner*'s accident. Zoltan could spin the cancellations, and giving the canceled passengers a bonus would help public relations. This deal might save Starchaser Spacelines.

"I've been captaining ships since they were made of steel and driven by electricity. You won't find a more experienced hand than mine. My ship's mage is a Magister and he has been fine-tuning the *Horizon Cusp*'s spells for five years. Our restaurants—"

"I am well acquainted with the reputations of your restaurants and the histories of your crew, Captain. I do my own research. Starchaser Spacelines would have been my first choice before the *Beamrunner*'s accident." Bin Zuka picked up his coffee and swirled it, but still did not raise it to his lips. "What I need from you are assurances of safety and privacy. You will be carrying passengers who are very important on Mars, Earth, and Luna. We cannot afford to risk a similar accident."

"Captain Yoshi was a good man," *forgive me Yosh*, "but he had never faced an attack at high space. I've survived three. I've even brought home a ship that floated dead in space. The *Horizon Cusp* is the ship you want, and I'm the man you want at the helm."

Bin Zuka set his cup down. He still had not drunk any coffee. He looked around the room once more, adjusted his pinky ring, then nodded. "I believe you are right, Captain. Are we agreed then, your standard fare, plus a bonus, to carry thirty passengers on a ten day voyage to Earth, set to leave three days from now?"

"I believe we are...." Jacobs stopped with his hand half-extended. "I almost forgot. There will be one additional passenger."

"My employer will pay—"

"I'm afraid this isn't a matter of cost. This passenger is a courier, and Starchaser Spacelines has a long-term contract with his firm. When we next leave port, so does he. But he can be berthed well away from your people. You'll never know he's there." Bin Zuka started to object, so Jacobs closed his eyes and added, "I'm afraid this obligation leaves me no room to negotiate. I understand if we cannot do business."

Jacobs held his breath and opened his eyes. Bin Zuka tilted his head in thought, but did not take long to reach a conclusion.

"Of course, Captain. My employer will wish more security in place then. Assume there will be forty passengers, apart from your courier."

"I'll have our sales people draw up the contract." Jacobs stood, hope rising in him for the first time in hours.

THE DRIVER STEERED DONAL AND LI HUA THROUGH A COMPLEX SERIES of turns through downtown New Leningrad while Li Hua chatted away as they drove, probably about sites of local importance because she pointed out the window at statues and plaques.

Donal could hear only the pound of his heart, feel only the squeeze of his pulse in his neck, arms and legs. He had just caused an accident, to stop someone from trying to kill him.

Someone had tried to kill him.

And the woman next to him, who now played tour guide, had likely murdered the people in that shredded runner. And smiled about it.

Snap out of it! Fret later, survive now. Has it occurred to you that this "tour" might be a way to shake potential pursuit?

"And that's the statue of Nicolai Gurdjieff, who led a private expedition to Mars over the objections of three governments back on Earth, and founded New Leningrad."

Donal looked at the statue. The artist had given him the faraway look of a visionary, but this Gurdjieff could not have been much older than Donal. And yet he had accomplished so much more. "He looks so young. Is he still alive?"

"No, I'm afraid he died of a heart attack shortly after the settlement was established. The common belief is that Earth had him assassinated by a Heirophant, but nothing was ever proven." Li Hua gave Donal a reassuring smile and squeezed his shoulder. "I will keep you alive."

Donal tried to smile back. *Take it easy. The immediate threat is gone. Try to enjoy the scenery.* He gazed out the window at the largest of the three cities on Mars. New Leningrad had to be at least fifteen kilometers across, with a spacious layout like an artist's dream of one of Scheherazade's tales. The roads were wide, surrounding broad domes and twisted towers all through the city center. Some of the buildings were even open to the sky, which was the blue of Earth inside the Barrier, and looked to be yellow beyond it. Raised dunes beneath small buildings implied underground construction.

By the time the view relaxed Donal, the runner had cruised past the city center and into a residential neighborhood. Unlike the greater Bay Area back in California, where Donal saw houses and apartments organized in rectangular blocks, the Martian blocks were circular, with raised dirt spokes leading from each dwelling to a central hub. Donal wondered what purpose the hub served.

He must have stared, because Li Hua said, "Hubs like that one provide water and power to their blocks."

Donal saw small stores mixed in among the private houses, but no buildings taller than about three stories. He thought about his reservation in a twenty-story hotel. He looked at Li Hua, who had just given an order to her familiar in Chinese. Donal said, "We're nowhere near the Romanov, are we."

"We're going to a safe house."

"Just what kind of business are you in?"

"The kind that makes money," she said with a laugh. "Let's get inside before we worry about more questions."

The "safe house" fit in with every other dwelling in the neighborhood, right down to the color scheme and the lack of visible doors or windows: a brown and tan one-story dome that stuck out of the ground like a half-buried egg.

Donal gazed at the tan horizontal stripe, just about head-height ... windows. The stripe was probably an illusion that made their windows one-way. If so, it appeared to be a common decoration on this block.

The runner went up the driveway and around back, where a three-meter-square section of dome slid into the ground to reveal an empty garage. Donal felt the tingle of detection wards as they cruised inside. The driver dropped Donal and Li Hua off, then backed the runner out again. The dome slid shut behind him. Li Hua preceded Donal into the house proper and handed him a permission token shaped like the 4M logo — a letter M with a numeral 4 drawn around the left vertical line — so he could follow her through a second, more dangerous set of wards.

The safe house might have looked plebian on the outside, but the interior overflowed with luxury: plush carpets and sprawling couches done in rich forest greens and deep mahoganies, paintings and statues that Donal thought looked old and valuable, and soft violin music with no apparent source. After the dusty red streets, Donal felt like he had entered a sybarite's cabin, except that most cabins did not have a broad spiral staircase leading to levels below ground.

Li Hua spoke with a pair of servants while Donal had his look around. She then beckoned him to follow, and led him down that dark wood staircase. On closer inspection, the unstained stairs shone almost purple. Donal wondered what kind of trees produced such a color.

As they passed the first underground level Donal saw a lap pool. The next level down had been closed off by walls carved from the same wood as the stairs. A thick-looking, mahogany double-door ensured privacy. Donal sensed yet more wards lining the door and walls. He examined their magic, and gave a soft whistle as he appreciated the spell work. These were complex wards. They did not just detect or shield; they could counterattack. Wards like these cost a lot to maintain.

"Do you like the wards?" called Li Hua over her shoulder. "I commissioned them myself. They're Heirophant-cast."

"Very impressive."

They hired a Heirophant, a Doctor of Thaumaturgy, to cast wards? Donal tripled his mental estimate of the maintenance cost. He suspected his number was still low.

The bottom floor had four doors, none as impressive as the double-door above.

"This is your suite," said Li Hua, pointing to a door, "but you have the run of the house, except for the few locked areas."

Li Hua turned left, but Donal saw nothing there except another closed door. He expanded his awareness and saw that her familiar had arrived, though he could not hear its report.

"I'm afraid Aetheric Dynamics isn't the only complication," Li Hua said to Donal. "Mr. Mancuso is still in Plymouth. You will have to hold the package for one more day."

"My ship leaves in three days. I can't give him any longer than that. He should have named a secondary recipient."

"The deal is his baby," Li Hua said with a slight shrug. "No one else gets to handle it." She glanced at Pinyin-Lung again, then added, "Rest for a bit, then meet me in the billiard room. You'll find it near the pool."

She started back up the stairs, and Donal entered his quarters. A quick glance told him the furnishings were as rich and fancy as the rest of the house. Donal shoved the door closed, and dropped onto the bed, exhaling with a tight whuf.

"Dagda," he implored the distant heavens, "I took the legal route, the moral route. Let me survive doing the right thing?" Explosions. Attempted murder. Chases. Safe houses. What would be next? Poison? Kidnapping?

Donal lay back, and a few breaths later the tension in his shoulders, chest and legs unknotted. A few breaths after that his bumps and bruises soothed and smoothed. His left arm slackened enough to let go of the precious messenger bag, which slid down onto the bed.

Puzzled by his abrupt sense of peace, Donal keyed his breathing to a meditative pattern and noticed the subtle use of Earth magic - elemental stuff from home, not some Martian equivalent - working through the mattress to spread comfort and relaxation. Donal double-checked to confirm it: gentle, intricate Earth spells eased physical and emotional tension and discomfort at a slow, steady rate. This bed had to have cost a fortune.

Donal sat up and examined his room while maintaining his opened senses. The air came from outside, but paintings on the walls filtered and freshened it: meadow scenes that did more than conjure images of home. The air even smelled like spring. The room's light was environmental in that way that only the rich could afford: no lamps, just light as gentle as the morning. The furniture was more terran mahogany, including the ornate nightstand and the huge writing desk. The wardrobe and bureau were vast, the latter topped with a large oval mirror; Donal mused that he could have organized all the clothes he owned in them and had room left for ten years' shopping. Donal could have bought his parents' house, furnishings, and woodworking business for the cost of the contents of this room.

The bathroom was appointed as finely, but it drew water from a common source for the building. Donal had half-expected fresh water conjured directly with more elemental magic. Perhaps even 4M had limits to its extravagance.

The Romanov could not have been nicer, Donal decided. But then, he had no view from three floors underground ... behind two sets of wards ... where the staff answered to a woman who smiled after killing. And Donal did not even have his luggage.

All this to earn fast money for grad school?

Well, if he wanted to live to see that fast money he had better find out more about this place, and that meant keeping an appointment in the billiard room. But first, he needed to hide the package unless he wanted to carry it with him. Donal reached into his messenger bag and withdrew the soft bundle, wrapped in tanned calfskin and sealed with wax. He slipped his tuning fork out of his sleeve, tapped it against the seal and listened to the ringing tone: clear, but with a hint of buzz. Donal frowned, closed his eyes, and chanted words of cleansing over the simple tool, then tapped it again against the seal. The note sounded pure this time, and the tuning fork and seal glowed with a matching soft orange light.

Everything remained in order. The package was still intact.

Donal sought through his room for hiding spots, and concealed the bundle behind a nightstand. Now for the shroud, and spells of deception were one of Donal's two specialties. By the time he finished blending the package with its surroundings and laid two false trails to other hiding spots where illusory packages waited, no one short of a Heirophant would have been likely to find the original. Donal grinned at his handiwork.

In his office aboard the *Horizon Cusp*, Jacobs met with his executive officer, Kristoff Tunold, a thin man who carried himself like a grizzly bear. Jacobs sat at his large, oak desk, but Tunold had yet to take one of the two guest chairs. Instead he stood with his arms crossed and frowned through Jacobs' summary of his meeting with bin Zuka.

"I don't like it."

Jacobs sighed. Tunold was the best executive officer Jacobs had had in the last twenty years, and would make a fine captain himself one day. He had good instincts, and a solid sense of when to say what he meant. He still had anger issues, but Jacobs had dealt with a few of those himself over the years and the last thing he needed right now was a yelling match with his Ex Oh.

"What's your problem, Mr. Tunold?"

"Where should I start?" Tunold paced the width of Jacob's office: from the middle of the room to the long, comfortable couch under the porthole, then back past the desk to the display of the sixty-seven ships Jacobs had served on. Jacobs had images of them all, from old fashioned photographs of the pre-Rise United States Navy destroyers and carriers to still illusions of the new airships and the more recent helioships. The ex oh stopped under the display and whirled on Jacobs, throwing his hands out in an angry shrug. "First, who charters a three-hundred-fifty-man passenger liner to carry forty people? We could fit the entire complement on our boarding shuttle. Second, why does a business meeting need that much security? And what kind of negotiations have to take place at space? For ten days? And—"

"Good questions. But the wrong ones."

Tunold stared at Jacobs as though expecting a trick. "The question is, why take the job?"

"Exactly."

Jacobs poured each of them a shot of Irish whiskey, fifteen year old Brigid's Own. He set Tunold's down in front of one of the visitors' chairs, stared at the man who was less than half his age, and waited.

Tunold growled out the rest of his steam and threw himself into the offered chair, which creaked in protest. He picked up his glass and showed more grace than Jacobs expected: he savored the honeyed smell of the whiskey before downing it in a single gulp.

Jacobs shook his head.

"If you're ever going to hold your own command, Kris, you will have to learn that drinking is more than just forcing alcohol down your gullet."

Jacobs tilted a third of his whiskey past his lips and swirled it around his tongue while inhaling the scent from his glass, then let the smooth amber liquid slide down his throat.

Tunold slammed his glass down. "In two hours I have to help you explain to the rest of the officers why we're going to hit space at eleven percent capacity and how this does not mean that the *Beamrunner* sank us. You should be glad I'm not slugging your whiskey straight from the bottle."

"I suppose you have an alternate solution."

"We have fifty berths still booked, right? So we bump them all up to first class as a thank-you, then we take on extra cargo and store it in the efficiency cabins. The expense of the increased weight will be offset by the reduced food and entertainment costs. We end up close to the same profit as carrying a full load, after we secure the additional permits Mars will demand."

"*Close* to the same profit. This charter flight offers us substantially more, and Starchaser Spacelines needs that money."

"My way is honest, John. We might have to tighten our belts, but we can get by without shady deals with mystery men."

"Whatever business bin Zuka's boss is running isn't our concern. Our deal is legitimate."

"One flight won't save us. If we go the cargo route we gain time to rebuild public trust."

"Leave public relations to Zoltan. For that matter, if one businessman can afford our rate for a charter flight, I'll bet you a year's pay that Zoltan can find others willing to do the same. This could be a whole new line for us."

"You're not betting a year's pay, you're betting your whole business."

"I'm betting my life." Jacobs finished his whiskey and set down his glass. "Everything I have is tied up in this business. I don't have enough years left in me for a slow recovery."

"I hate to suggest this, but maybe you should sell."

"I can still do my job, thank you." Jacobs sat back. "Besides, any offer I'd find right now would be an insult. I've earned a good retirement, damn it, and I mean to have it."

They sat in silence for a time, and then Tunold poured them each another glass. "I'm going to go over their paperwork like I'm checking the hull for cracks. Call in a few favors over at customs too."

"Push through the forms for those permits while you're there. In case we need them. I'll make sure we have enough security to handle any funny ideas our passengers might have." He raised his glass. "We'll get through this."

"Yes we will." Tunold lifted his own glass.

They drank.

DONAL ENTERED THE BILLIARD ROOM AND IMMEDIATELY THOUGHT IT should have been called the library. True, the billiard table dominated the room with the elegance of its workmanship and the stark contrast of its pocketless green felt surface against its white and yellow cue balls and red object ball. Still, floor-to-ceiling shelves lined the walls, leaving space only for the full bar, complete with bartender. Books crowded every shelf, from newer refillables to older, fragile tomes that had only ever held one set of words.

"Drink, sir?" said the bartender.

"Not ... now," said Donal as he looked over titles. A small section was dedicated to poetry, but most of the shelves held novels, from classics to science fiction to mystery to romance.

Donal heard a click, and turned to see Li Hua beside the rack of cues near the bar.

Where did she come from?

The liaison had traded her business suit for a shirt and slacks combination that featured long sleeves, tapered legs, and a neckline just low enough to entice. She smiled over her shoulder at Donal while selecting a cue. "I'm surprised you were able to set that messenger bag down. I was starting to think you'd bonded it to your hand with alchemy."

"Nah. Though I have heard about a technique for enchanting a bag to always return to you."

"I could have used that in college. I was forever losing my purse." She chalked her cue. "Does the enchantment work?"

"I've only heard rumors, but I tried to figure it out during my sophomore year. The sympathetic connection is easy enough to arrange, but the actual movement...."

"A native motive force would be difficult to maintain," Li Hua said, as she saw where Donal was leading, "and the only other obvious way would involve a compulsion for short-term movement that could latch onto whoever happened to be traveling the right direction."

Their eyes met and they both laughed.

"Yeah, I dropped the idea there," said Donal. "I figured I might come back to it after I got my doctorate."

"Doctorate? How did you end up here, so far from academia?"

"Some black marks keep the grant money away. Like misappropriation of reagents."

"Ouch. What did you do?"

"Stole some supplies to reinforce a homeless shelter during storm season. I walked past that place every day, watching it decay. I had to do something." Donal shook his head. "But it turns out that doing a good thing the wrong way pisses off the money people. I got acceptances, but no funding."

Li Hua smiled in sympathy. She gestured to the billiard table. "Do you play?"

"Where are the pockets?"

"I'll take that as a no." She set her cue back on the rack. "Perhaps we should forgo the billiards and talk over wine?"

Maybe Donal's imprisonment worries had been paranoia. Li Hua was treating him like an honored guest. She probably housed him three floors underground to make sure Donal lived to deliver the package. After all, people had tried to kill him once or twice today already.

Could he relax enough to enjoy an evening in the company of a pretty woman?

"A syrah would be lovely if you have any; if not a pinot noir would be a good alternative."

"That's right, you're a California boy. I think we can find you a syrah." Li Hua turned to the bartender. "Phil, a bottle of Morgan '75 and two glasses to the library, if you would." A good choice, if everything Donal had heard about the vintage proved true. The bartender left the room, and Li Hua turned to Donal and said, "The library is through here."

She pressed on a bookend shaped like a door. With a loud click, an entire section of shelves swung into the room: a concealed door. Donal chuckled as he saw the solution to the mystery of her entrance.

Li Hua led him down a broad, well-lit passage to a larger room at the other end, and Donal understood why the billiard room was named for its game table. The library had to be fifteen meters square. Books covered every wall and filled freestanding bookshelves in narrow but even rows. Diffuse, sourceless lighting kept the plentiful shelves from casting intimidating shadows.

Donal gasped. There must have been hundreds of original bindings. He had never seen so many. Even his college library used refillables. This collection must have been priceless. Donal could smell its age and wisdom.

One corner of the room had a sitting area with a dark green couch flanked by nut brown recliners. In front of the couch stood a low, cherry wood coffee table that had been carved to tell a story of some sort. Donal thought the carvings looked Eastern, but he did not recognize the tale. More books filled shelves on the walls above the furniture.

"Whose house is this?"

"Mr. Mancuso's." Li Hua sat on the couch and gazed fondly at the collection. "A good safe house needs a lot of entertainment."

"So the safe house sees a lot of use then?"

"No more than anyone else's, I'd imagine."

Donal hesitated. Should he sit with her on the couch or take one of the recliners? Was Li Hua a hostess entertaining a guest or a woman flirting with a man?

Someone tried to kill me and I want to hit on my bodyguard? The woman who complained that the people trying to kill us were inept?

Donal sat on a recliner, but chose the one nearest her. Li Hua's eyebrows ascended the barest margin.

"How did you know I'm from California?" he asked. "And that I'm a Journeyman, not an Initiate? You never took the time to check me for magic."

"We've been studying you since the homeless shelter incident. Mr. Mancuso is old friends with the Dean of Alchemy at U.C. Santa Cruz. Did you think it was coincidence that you were offered this assignment?"

Donal's breath caught.

Li Hua laughed: not a dire, menacing laugh, but sincere amusement.

"If you could see your face." She laughed again, and Donal once more felt her cheer infect him, crack his face in a lopsided smile. "I'm sorry. After the day we've had I thought you could use some humor. It's standard procedure to review the profile of any courier handling sensitive papers."

Donal shrugged. "I admit I'm more magician than courier."

"You say that, but you run around without a familiar."

"Your familiar didn't help you spot the package at the spaceport, even though you knew I had it."

"True, but that doesn't explain why you hamstring yourself magically."

"I spent a semester of independent study exploring the Enochian work of John Dee."

Li Hua stared at him. "What did you do, manage to destroy a

familiar? You know, by law I can require you to use no magic while a guest in this house."

"You don't have to do that. I didn't destroy a familiar."

Li Hua quirked a smile and an eyebrow. Was she teasing him?

"So what does Dee have to do with it then?"

"I took the elemental-focused approach to his work. The partial- and cross-elemental ideas fascinate me, and I suspect that his use of the Spirit element might work with recent discoveries about the spirits native to space. I wondered about the potential of binding a partial- or cross-elemental as a familiar. So I've held off in the short term."

Li Hua leaned back and sucked in her lips as she considered this. Donal tried not to think about how appealing she made the pose. He had not gotten to discuss thaumaturgy with an attractive woman in months. Her brow furrowed in skepticism. "I don't think it would work. There's an ancestral component to the familiar conjuration."

"I think that results from the structure of the usual steps. If I reconstructed the process using a derivative of the 'calls' that Dee and Kelly devised, I might be able to take the conjuration and binding in a new direction."

"But to try to develop a deep connection with something so alien." Li Hua shivered, and Donal wondered if she knew how fetching the movement looked. "You know, a part of you goes into the binding process. It's a symbiotic relationship."

"I have taken the classes," Donal teased.

The topic drew them closer, as Donal described the potentially groundbreaking aspects of his theory. Soon they sat on the edge of the recliner and sofa. Li Hua seemed to follow most of Donal's logic, though he could tell she had never explored Dee's work to the same extent that he had. Still, maybe there was more to this woman than a tactician and bodyguard. And she did have pretty eyes, soft brown with a hint of caramel.

"Impressive," she said when he finished his explanation, and the respect in her tone sounded sincere. Donal was sure he had just risen in her esteem. "If you pull this off, you'll carve out a place in the history books." She placed a hand on his arm. "I will warn you though, that you are doing dangerous work out here, and without a familiar you're exposed. Naked."

Was that a smile in her eyes or an invitation?

"Speaking of which," Li Hua continued, sitting back on the couch, "I suppose you'd like to know about the people trying to kill us."

<hr>

MACHADO, SHIP'S MAGE FOR THE *HORIZON CUSP*, ROLLED HIS EYES. IT was bad enough that he had to attend these officers' meetings, even though they almost never touched on anything that affected his work. This meeting was worse because Captain Jacobs had summoned his ship's officers to this cramped room instead of their regular gathering place - the crew mess hall. Apparently the upcoming voyage merited a private briefing.

Machado hated the formal meeting room. Bare walls without even a porthole to provide convenient distraction. The wooden table was huge and heavy, and barely left him enough room to lean back in his chair without hitting his head on the wall. He had long suspected that the *Horizon Cusp's* designer forgot to include an officer's meeting room, and that a supply closet had been converted just prior to commission.

Worst of all, Fredrickson.

Machado understood that Fredrickson, the ship's alchemist, was probably as bored as he was. A small passenger complement meant that, if anything, her job would be easier. She probably worked through some alchemical puzzle in her head to stave off meeting tedium. He just wished she would do it quietly, instead of drumming her potion-stained fingers in an irregular staccato that never failed to irritate him. Machado had to pay enough attention to notice if the captain needed his opinion, which made him vulnerable to Fredrickson's lack of rhythm.

Machado, a Magister with a Master's degree in Thaumaturgy, was trying to compose an article on his zephyrpad about the development of a long range detection network in space that would bind a series of lacunas, space elementals, to metal cubes all forged from the same ore. The lacunas would act as beacons and provide current, accurate information about the region of space around them. At least, they would if the bindings worked with the cubes' associations the way Machado suspected they would.

His theory would make a great article for *Astromancer*, the trade magazine for magicians who worked the space lanes. His network might one day revolutionize space travel.

If Fredrickson would knock off her damned racket.

"Questions?" asked the captain.

Machado had none. The *Horizon Cusp* would hit space again despite recent developments, and that was good enough for him. Forty passengers or four hundred, his job did not change: keep the magic running and under control. From the incessant finger drumming, Fredrickson must not have had any questions either. Machado could guess the other officers' reactions to this strange charter without looking up. Tunold, the executive officer, would watch the others with his big, square jaw thrust forward in support of the captain. Machado pitied Tunold for his swift metabolism: a skinny man with a big chin. The ex oh would never carry the weight of authority that Machado's fullness gave him.

That abrupt popping sound over the drumming fingers would be Goldberg, chief of security and head of the ship's watch, cracking his neck the way he did before a fight. Goldberg would have questions. Goldberg always had questions. Doctor Ramirez, ship's physician, probably blinked his owlish eyes rapidly, imagining logistical issues if all the bodyguards started attacking one another. The doctor was nothing if not prepared. Professionally, anyway. Personally he could not hold onto a wife, though *Oxalá* knew he kept trying. Jang, the chief engineer, probably grinned and hunted for an excuse to use the charter flight for some experiment.

Machado settled back to his writing. He had the article outlined, now he needed to balance the formulae and he could start putting the words together. Machado began by considering the powers to balance.

Jang slapped her hands on the table. Machado sighed and glanced up to see her lean forward in a movement than might have been impressive if she had been fifteen to twenty centimeters taller, ten kilos heavier, or both.

"I want to disconnect the main drive for this trip, and let the Deception Drive try it solo."

"Denied," said Captain Jacobs. "Next question?"

"This is the time to do it, Captain. It handled the last flight as predicted, and this voyage will prove it's time to dump the old HK Drive. We'll be carrying a lighter load—"

"Mr. Machado."

"Sir?"

"My standing agreement regarding the Deception Drive includes five more voyages before it attempts a solo. Is there any reason to cut that trial process short?"

Jang tried to respond, but the captain cut her off with a look.

"No, sir," said Machado. "The Deception Drive is the future of space travel, but right now the engine still has enough kinks in its interactions with other systems to merit further research. I've detailed them in my latest report." He shook his head. "I wouldn't sign off on it."

"Mash..." began Jang, and Machado could imagine the coming torrent of threats and invective. Her opening salvo would assault his weight, his manhood and his parentage. Then she would get mean, assuming that Machado let her vent. He could understand her frustration: Jang would never be better than an Initiate. Her dedication and will made her respectable - she had several certifications and was well qualified to hold her position - but she lacked the vision necessary to go beyond the Associate's degree level at Thaumaturgy. She could grasp theory well enough to apply it, but she could not innovate: always a technician, never an artist.

But Machado would not brook her insults, especially when they pulled him away from his writing. If she finished that sentence, he would give her a day of pain for every word.

"Five more trips," said the captain, loud enough to shut the engineer's mouth. "Request denied. Next question?"

Machado went back to his article. He could hear Jang tap her fists against the table in annoyance - the sound made an odd counterpoint to the arrhythmic drumming fingers.

"Captain," said Goldberg, "instead of tripling my team to thirty for this run, can I make it twenty-seven plus a mage?"

"What?" Machado slammed shut his zephyrpad and glared at the chief of security. "Captain, I object." Goldberg tried to say something, but Machado spoke over him, "I don't interfere in your security, Saul, stay the hell out of my magic."

"Stand down, Mr. Machado," said the captain, standing up. "Ms. Jang, wipe that grin off your face. Mr. Goldberg, I assume you have a good reason for not following protocol here?"

"Excuse me, sir, but I am following protocol. This is a security matter that affects my budget, and I am clearing it with you."

"Captain," said Machado, "all thaumaturgic decisions have to be cleared through me."

"Mr. Machado, I said 'stand down.'" Captain Jacobs swept the table with his eyes, and what he saw must have satisfied him because he sat down. "Why do you need a magician, Mr. Goldberg?"

"For this charter flight we will have two opposing interests coming aboard, each with at least one spellcaster backing its moves. I want a 'caster on our side who has nothing else to do but keep an eye on them. Captain, an Initiate will do, if he has the right specialty."

"Mr. Machado?"

"My contract specifies that, as ship's mage, I am to be consulted before any other crew magician is hired, whether on a temporary or permanent basis. I was consulted before Ms. Jang was hired and I should have been consulted here."

"Dr. Ramirez, Ms. Fredrickson," said the captain, "do either of you have any questions?"

Machado might have thrown his zephyrpad in frustration, but he refused to risk his article. Ramirez and Fredrickson both shook their heads.

"Goldberg, Machado, stay where you are. Everyone else, dismissed. Go start your preparations. We leave in three days."

The others filed out. Most looked eager to get out of there, but Tunold lingered as though he might stay. A look from the captain sent him out as well.

"Gentlemen, I expect my officers to behave like officers. I do not like power plays," he glared at Goldberg then turned to Machado and concluded, "and I do not like tantrums. You two hash this out between yourselves when we're done here, and I expect this to be the last I hear of it."

Captain Jacobs leaned forward and said, "Now, Mr. Machado, I want your assessment of the chief's idea."

Machado reached for the calm that every magician needed and let it flood his system. He did not forgive Goldberg in the process, but he gained the clarity to consider an idea that angered him.

"It's a smart move." Machado rubbed his chin. "A good Initiate will notice things your other watchmen won't. However, if, for any reason, we have to work together, the Initiate answers to me, and," Machado leaned forward and tapped his large chest with one finger, "I reserve the right to commandeer the Initiate's services, in the event that a magical emergency threatens the ship."

"Agreed," said the captain. "Threats to the ship come first, and rank is not in question." He wrote something in that anachronism he called a notebook. "All right then, twenty-seven plus an Initiate. Any other questions?" They shook their heads, and he continued, "Then you are dismissed."

The captain left, and Machado tried to take notes about his article, what he could remember from where he left off, but Goldberg stepped close and said, "I should have run it past you, shouldn't I."

"Yes." The essential power balance, that was where he left off. He needed to narrow down the terms first.

"Mash," Goldberg started, but Machado cut him off.

"Saul," Machado said without taking his eyes from his work, "if you don't let me finish my article..."

"Right." Goldberg put up his hands. "Would *caxaça* help?"

"Always." Next, he listed the associations that would be necessary for the spells to work, and the associations that could not be avoided.

"I'll pick you up a bottle when we get to Earth."

"Thanks, Saul." Machado looked up. "Need any help with the résumés?"

"Nah. I have it all under control."

Goldberg left and Machado focused on his formulae so he could move on to composing the text.

***

Donal shifted so that he sat deep and upright in the recliner.

"Aetheric Dynamics, right?" he said.

Phil the bartender arrived with a decanter of wine, two glasses and the cork. Donal saw no coasters. He hoped the fancy table was warded against stains and liquids.

Phil offered the cork, and Donal saw that it was firm and free of corruption. Phil poured two glasses and Donal held his at an angle for contrast against the white background of the towel on Phil's arm. Donal did not know Morgan wines well enough to judge the slight fade of its color, but it looked about right for a syrah. He sniffed as he swirled his glass and the scent delighted him. A touch of blackcurrant. Professor N'Kembe once told him that only the finest wines traveled well off-world, and as far as Donal could tell, this Morgan vintage had retained all of its reputed subtlety.

"To Mr. Mancuso's swift return," said Li Hua. Phil set the tray on the table and left as they raised their glasses. Donal moved his toward his lips, then hesitated. Less than an hour ago he had worried about drugs and poisons. His hostess' camaraderie seemed sincere, but what if his worries were not paranoia? He smelled the syrah's bouquet once more until Li Hua took a sip.

She drank her wine without fear. Donal tried his, and was happy to learn that the Morgan tasted as good as it smelled. He tried to think of a brilliant observation about the wine, something that might impress his hostess and cover his hesitation to drink, but Li Hua spoke first.

"Aetheric Dynamics competes with us over every aspect of carterite mining, refinement and shipping. On Earth we all have to play nice together. Here on Mars, though, the government doesn't have the infrastructure to enforce good behavior, so our competition can get ... a little out of hand."

There was that smile again. Why would she smile about that?

Maybe she's just proud of her work. Now play nice with the pretty woman who saved your life.

"Thus, safe houses," said Donal.

"We don't stop there. Right now there are two other couriers in two other safe houses who think they have the real documents."

"Having the same conversation?"

"Not likely. Pete and David aren't much for small talk, and they could never have followed your Enochian theories." She leaned toward Donal along the arm of the plush couch and smiled again. "And they have terrible taste in wine."

Was that a compliment? Was she flirting? Donal smiled and toasted the Morgan vintners. But if 4M hired three couriers to make one delivery, then...

"Who has the real package?"

"Who is being guarded by the Regional Director of Corporate Security and not one of her assistants? Which reminds me: you said that I didn't check out your magic when we met, but I did. I just did it without drawing your attention."

Suddenly the events of the day fit together in Donal's head. He understood why this Aetheric Dynamics was willing to kill, why his room was three floors underground, and why Li Hua would explain so much: Donal carried something critical to major corporations, who considered Mars some kind of lethal playground. A bodyguard might keep Donal safe, but a Regional Director of Corporate Security would make sure that Mr. Mancuso collected his package, not matter how it might ... inconvenience a courier.

"Obviously I can't tell you what you're carrying," Li Hua continued, "but it represents a major step forward for us." She smiled into the distance, between triumph and predation, and said, "If we pull this off 4M will be the only name that matters."

She drank to that, but Donal did not join her.

3

A knock woke Donal. He glanced at his watch. Eight o'clock local time. The knock could not have been for him. Donal had set his intention to awaken at nine, so he still had time to sleep. He began to settle back into his comfortable tangle of sheets and spells.

The knock persisted until Donal came fully awake. He stumbled to the bathroom for a brown silk robe, which he held closed when he opened the hallway door a crack. On the other side was a strange man with strong, clean-cut features, who wore a white jacket and shirt with black pants: an actual servant's uniform. The Romanov Hotel indeed.

"Your suitcase, Mr. Cuthbert." True enough, the suitcase he held up looked like Donal's: patchwork plaid, but distinctive in its reds and blues. "Shall I bring it in?"

"No, thank you. I'll get it."

The servant took that as a dismissal, set down the suitcase, and left.

Donal swung the bag onto the bed then locked the door behind him. He drew a deliberate breath to slow his thoughts, then passed his hands along the zipper while mumbling the right words. He felt a warmth grow once under his fingers, but that was to be expected.

When the first faded and a second warmth followed, Donal caught his breath and focused harder. He prolonged the pass, in case of a third, but the warmth did not return.

Twice. Donal sat back and resumed breathing. Customs would only have searched his bag once. So who went through it a second time?

Donal put the suitcase on the floor and walked a circle around it once, clockwise. He dragged his finger behind him in the air until the circle closed and severed any active magical connections between what lay within it and what lay without.

Nothing happened. Donal waited, but the stillness persisted. No traps triggered. He grabbed his tuning fork from the nightstand and stepped inside the circle, which did not break at his entrance. A magician's magic always knows the magician.

Using the circle to restrict the reach of his own spells, Donal whispered an incantation and tapped his tuning fork against the suitcase. Sweet harmonies filled his ears, and every one of them a part of his own magical signature. No spells had been left behind by others.

Donal sighed relief, rolled his shoulders, and dismissed the circle with a wave of his hand. He opened the suitcase and confirmed his suspicions. It had been searched. At least nothing had been taken or added. This time. He needed to take more precautions.

Donal picked a spot on the underside of the dresser, focused his will on that spot, knelt close enough to hover his hands scant millimeters below it. He gathered all of his attention on the deep mahogany of the dresser's structure, the lighter ash wood of the trim, the silver touches of the handles, then spiraled down to the one centimeter square he had chosen near the right, rear leg. Donal cast a false trail, a further spell of hiding, to protect the calfskin bundle concealed against the nightstand behind him.

Another spell on the room itself? Donal sighed. No, that would be going too far. He was still a guest.

Donal stretched, shook out his hands, and returned to his suitcase. He closed and sealed it tight with the right gesture, left it in the middle of the floor, and went into the bathroom to take his morning shower. If he was a guest, he would enjoy a good breakfast once he was clean, and if he was a prisoner, he might at least find out why they searched his luggage.

The administrative offices of the New Leningrad branch of the Mars Customs Department perched near the docks like a bird of prey, not so high that it interfered with the tower, but enough to make sure nothing slipped past its waiting talons.

Kristoff Tunold mounted the dozens of stairs, passed through a quick security check of his identification and purpose, and soon stood outside a door that had Jerry's name on it. Was his old friend an executive now? Tunold entered without knocking. Jerry sat at a red sandstone desk and manipulated a phantasmal display of warehouses and crates, circling some as he went. Tunold stepped straight up to the desk.

"What kind of negotiations have to take place at space?"

"Hello to you too, Kris," said Jerry without looking up. "Marcy and the kids are fine, thanks for asking."

"Glad to hear it, but I have to be back at the ship in twenty minutes and I need an expert's opinion."

Jerry stopped arranging crates. He waved the display away and looked up at his impatient friend. "Twice a year I get to see you and this is, what, a quick interrogation and run?"

Tunold started to speak, but saw enduring steel in his friend's gray eyes and heaved a sigh from his waist to his fingertips. He dropped into a chair and Jerry smirked in satisfaction.

"Don't get smug on me," said Tunold. "I'm only sitting because the glare from your pate was blinding me. At this angle it's tolerable."

"You wish you looked this sexy." Jerry shook his saggy frame in his chair. "And don't stress the time crunch. I have an appointment soon anyway. How's space treating you?"

"You didn't hear about the *Beamrunner*?"

"Crap, that was one of yours?" Jerry waved his hands between them as though to ward off an attack. "Hey, I have no say in any investigation that may or may not be happening, and I couldn't discuss such a thing if it were."

"Get this. Jacobs has us doing charter work. Two big shot companies want a ten-day flight for 'business negotiations.' It's got to be a cover, right?"

"Maybe not." Jerry shrugged. "If your clients have interests on Mars and Earth, maybe—"

"Bullshit. They're pulling something. Got to be. Ten days for a seven day flight? Just their people and no one else? What else could it be?"

"Kris, your world is very small: the borders of your ship. Me, I see everyone and everything that lands on or leaves Mars. Who are the companies chartering you?"

"4M and Transterran Properties."

Jerry whistled. "Then we're definitely talking about the big leagues here. Corporations like those have offices everywhere and more considerations than guys like you and I can imagine. Did they bring their own security?"

"Plenty."

"Then it sounds to me like you have two high chiefs coming together for some major deal." Jerry shrugged. "Situation like that, executives get paranoid enough to do something like charter way too much ship for way too much time."

Tunold shifted in his chair as he considered this.

"I don't buy it. It's not cost effective."

"Maybe it is, for a certain level of security. Tell you what. How about I talk to a few people and make sure their documents and bags get a very thorough check."

"That would be a huge favor."

"Yes it would."

Tunold gave his friend a questioning glance and saw raised eyebrows and an expectant blink.

"All right," Tunold acceded. "I'll bring you a pound of fresh crab legs on our next run."

"One pound for this much scrutiny?"

"Fine. Two, you pirate. But don't expect a Christmas present this year."

"Deal. Now clear out of here. There's a Red Sun muckety-muck due any minute, and *she* had the courtesy to make an appointment."

Tunold stayed seated.

"I also need this form filed." He tossed the completed document onto the desk. "Just in case we need to haul more cargo. You see—"

"Damn it, Kris!" Jerry jiggled as he bounced out of his chair and tried to pry his friend out of his seat. "I'm not kidding. Rowan MacPherson is not a woman you keep waiting."

"Oh, it's a woman? Maybe we make it one pound of crab legs and I don't mention this meeting to Marcy."

"I wish this meeting were blackmail material. Now please..."

There was a knock. Tunold sprang to his feet and beat Jerry to the door. He opened it, bowed to the beautiful red-haired woman and said, "Sorry. Our meeting ran late. Entirely my fault."

Tunold didn't wait for an answer. He slipped past her and started back for the ship.

***

BREAKFAST WAS SERVED IN THE SUN ROOM ON THE RECREATION FLOOR, only one level below ground. Donal expected a room with skylights or a magical means of admitting natural light, but was unprepared for the scope of what he found. The walls, floor and ceiling of the sun room had been enchanted to display the view from a spot high above New Leningrad: underfoot Donal saw only a one kilometer drop into the center of the city, with red mountains and plains visible in every direction past the shimmering Barrier, while overhead a clear blue sky stretched until it met the Barrier and turned yellow. Donal got as far as one step into the room before he leapt back, clutching the doorframe for support while his heartbeat pounded in his ears.

"Everyone does that the first time," said Li Hua, and Donal realized that she sat at a small, round table in the center of a star pattern of small, round tables. The tables and chairs had been decorated in blues and whites, so Donal, fixated on the view above and below, had mistaken them for clouds in the sky. She continued, "It took me a week before I could walk across the floor without holding my breath and staring at my destination. Did you sleep well?"

Donal peeled his fingers loose, and chided himself for getting caught up in the illusion. He calmed his breathing and heart rate, and focused on the present.

"Does 4M search its guests' luggage?"

"4M has a lot of divisions, but I'm not aware of one that does that. Will bacon and eggs be all right? I wasn't sure what to tell the chef to have ready." When he hesitated, Li Hua put down her fork and said, "Donal, neither I, nor anyone acting on my orders, have searched your bags, your room, or your person. Now will you join me for breakfast or must I eat alone?" She made her point with a sip of pomegranate juice.

The spells on the room must have been masterwork. Even knowing they were illusions did not diminish their effect. Donal managed his way across the sky, chair to chair, until he sat opposite Li Hua. The food smelled delicious, though he could not quite place the seasoning.

"Thank you," she said. "I'm afraid I was too hungry to wait for you, so you will just have to trust that my food comes from the same dishes as yours." Had she spotted his hesitation over the wine last night? Her little smile returned. "Director of Regional Security. Did you think it was just a title?"

Donal realized he had lost the upper hand in this conversation. If he'd ever had it. He considered how to regain it as he filled his plate from the platter.

"Someone went through my suitcase."

"Anything missing?"

"My clothes aren't that fashionable."

"True." Li Hua looked over Donal's felt shirt and denim pants. "Perhaps a brighter color would help."

"Gee, thanks."

"Of course! The first step is admitting you have a problem. You might consider a light blue to bring out your eyes." She topped off their coffee from the carafe. "I don't think it was Aetheric Dynamics. They would have taken the bag and you would have been told it was lost in transit." She took a long drink of coffee and cupped the mug in her hands. "Customs, most likely. After the explosion they probably ran a second check on incoming and outgoing luggage."

Li Hua called forth her familiar, but spoke to it in English this time. "Go to Pete and David. Find out if their charges' luggage was searched twice." The vaporous dragon spun in on its tail and vanished.

"What about customs?"

"If your bag was the only one targeted, it's a moot question. We need to know if someone knew you had the real package." She sipped her coffee. "Mr. Mancuso has been further delayed, by the way."

A chill crept across Donal's skin like a winter breeze.

"How long?"

"It shouldn't be more than another day." Li Hua certainly looked sincere, but that might have been her soft eyes. "You'll make your flight."

"But what if he's—"

Donal's next words were lost as a cargo ship blazed into the atmosphere and roared past their table toward the spaceport landing zone. Donal stared. No one would program that into an illusion, not at the expense of conversation. The room had to use a direct sensory link to its apparent viewpoint high above the city. Only the lack of wind proved that their breakfast table did not float free in the air. No wonder it felt so effective. Why simulate something when you can display it?

The cargo ship, an eyesore compared to modern designs, resembled a rocket ship out of the pulp stories of a hundred years ago, complete with cones that generated fire out of the back and left a trail considered gauche by current standards. It even needed runway space to land instead of simply coming to a halt. Not at all like the artistic beauty that brought Donal to Mars. The *Horizon Cusp* was shaped like a gryphon with wings spread and full-scale claws and paws for landing gear.

Donal took advantage of the distraction to study the magic of his breakfast companion. He slid his breath into a rhythmic pattern and trusted his peripheral vision. She carried no active spells, but she wore three ensorcelled items: an earring, a necklace, and the brooch that housed Pinyin-Lung. Her general sense was closer to his classmates than to his teachers, so she was probably a Journeyman. Donal dropped the investigation when she spoke again.

"I've been thinking about your Enochian research, and though I haven't gone as deeply into the subject as you have, your ideas sound plausible to me. I think you're making a mistake to go without a familiar though. You limit your magic, a big risk outside of academia." She crinkled her eyes in thought. "There's a ... depth to the familiar bond beyond what they tell you in school. Without one, it's like you're playing billiards with one arm." Donal tried to think of a reply while she finished her coffee, but did not have one before she said, "I have business to tend to while we're in town, so I'm afraid you'll be alone a great deal until Mr. Mancuso arrives, but I will try to at least be here for breakfast and dinner. If you need anything, ask one of the servants. And any one of them can get a message to me."

"So I should just stay here like a good boy?"

"Might be safer for the general public. Aetheric Dynamics blew up a spaceport to get to you. Do you think they won't blow up a museum or store?" She quirked a smile. "Besides, the next courier they send might not know his wine."

Donal felt as though he swallowed a stone the size of his fist. He had been so worried about his own survival that he forgot all about the innocent travelers killed and injured by that explosion. But now he could hear their screams of panic once more.

Li Hua's head came up in a movement he recognized: she had set a magical alert for a certain time. "Speaking of business," she said and stood. She wiped her mouth, and tossed the napkin onto her plate. "I have to run. I hope you don't get too lonely. Check out the library. I don't think we have anything about Dee's Enochian work, but I'd be surprised if Mr. Mancuso didn't have at least one book about the man. Rumor has it that Dee was once an agent for the Queen of England, you know." She began to leave, but paused in the doorway and smiled at him. "Oh, and Donal? If you ever decide to pursue a career in field magic, you'll have to learn to shift your awareness without a crutch. The schools only teach twelve breathing patterns for focus, and using them makes you obvious. See you at dinner."

Donal made a mental note to practice that shift whenever he was alone. But just then he needed the crutch to get the sound of screaming people out of his head.

"No ship at sea is perfect." Captain Nemeth said that back when Jacobs was a young helmsman steering his first line ship: the Decatur, a Forrest Sherman class destroyer. "The time to worry is when all reports are five-by-five. A set of flawless reports means something was missed."

Jacobs looked up from his reports. Everything was five-by-five, but times had changed. A seaworthy old naval vessel could hide a few bumps and bruises. Spaceworthy helioships were all too brittle in comparison.

Jacobs remembered. He remembered when his second helioship, the *Shining Hope*, lost a key spirit in its engine and floated dead in space. He remembered how the ship drifted on its carterite alone with less chance of rescue than a wounded bird landing amid arguing cats. Two days it crept off course as its supplies dwindled....

Benny Sugg leapt onto Jacobs' desk and marched straight onto his paperwork. The white tom, official ship's cat and Jacobs' companion for eight years, knew Jacobs' moods better than he knew them himself.

A lopsided smile forced its way onto Jacobs' face and he chuckled. "Was I dwelling, Benny?" He scratched the cat with both hands. "Or were you just feeling ignored?" Benny purred, sat on the engineering report, and knocked Jacobs' pen off the desk with a sweep of his tail.

"Was that necessary?" asked Jacobs, but Benny only purred in response. Three quick raps at the office door announced Jacobs' yeoman. Not *his* yeoman, Jacobs reminded himself for the hundredth time, not enough budget room for that. The yeoman supported Tunold as well. "Come in, Mr. Kelly."

As usual, Kelly opened the door and leaned in to speak. He never entered unless he had paperwork.

"Port security to see you, Captain." The man's posture was so stiff that he even leaned at a crisp angle. Jacobs mused that if he ever inspected the crew quarters, Kelly's would sparkle.

"Send him in."

"Her, sir."

The port security officer swept past Kelly and into the room as though she commandeered it. This was the same officer Jacobs had met in the spaceport after the explosion: he recognized her by the combination of assertiveness and boredom. She took a seat without hesitation or permission.

Benny Sugg wanted no part of her; he jumped down and sped away, belly low to the deck and fur disgruntled.

"Captain Jacobs, thank you for seeing me," the officer said. "We spoke yesterday about certain businesses of concern to Mars, do you remember?"

"I assure you, Officer..."

"Gardner."

"I assure you, Officer Gardner, that my memory is quite intact."

"Excellent, then would you mind telling me why you neglected to mention that ten of your inbound passengers worked for Red Sun?"

"Why should I care what they do for a living? I'm a helioship captain, not a social secretary."

"Well, then I'm sure you're familiar with this year's addenda to the Mars Port Codes, such as addendum three, section four dee."

"'All incoming ships are required to report to port security the presence of any passengers named on the Mars watch lists.'" Jacobs assumed her silent stare of reply was intended to intimidate him. He let her enjoy it for a moment before he continued. "None of my passengers were specifically named on the watch lists, so no report was necessary." Jacobs leaned down and retrieved his pen from the floor beside his chair, then looked back the young officer. "If that ordinance was intended to include company names then it's unenforceable anyway. Earth doesn't require passengers to report their professions when they travel." He set down his pen. "I submitted my passenger list and cargo manifest, of course."

"So you claim you didn't know they worked for Red Sun?"

"Why would I?"

"They were on your ship for a week."

"So were three hundred forty others."

"One of them was the North American Regional President, and he never sat at your dinner table?"

"Was he the one who couldn't hold his rum or the one who wouldn't shut up about baseball?"

"Captain Jacobs." Gardner leaned forward with her stylus poised, no doubt ready to inscribe his doom on her memoboard. "Starchaser Spacelines is in trouble, isn't it. If you don't want to cooperate with Mars, Mars may not be able to cooperate with you."

Rage seethed through Jacobs' gut. His fists clenched until the knuckles popped and begged for the feel of her arrogant jaw. *Stand down, old man. If you touch her you don't just risk your job.* His nostrils flared through a long, slow breath. With more than sixty years of command behind him, Jacobs showed Gardner what an intimidating stare should look like. She paled and leaned back in her chair, eyes wide. When Jacobs spoke again, his voice was quiet and terrible.

"I have survived far worse than this. And before you make a threat, you better be damned sure your superiors will back you. I have no legal obligation to know the professions of my passengers, nor to report that information to you. I have done everything required of me by both Mars and New Leningrad, and this *courtesy* visit is over. Dismissed."

Jacobs picked up Machado's report on the Deception Drive but anger blurred the magician's jargon. Gardner merely sat, no doubt listing inwardly from his broadside, and taking on water. That was a limitation Jacobs found with space travel: no colorful sayings. The crew of a breached ship at high space did not survive long enough to invent them.

Jacobs grimaced and read the words of his ship's mage for the third time: "The harmonics register low-level discordance among spirits of the third and fifth orders of maintenance, but the effects should be overcome by the coherency quotient. Address the issue in port."

Officer Gardner finally recovered enough to speak. "Thank you for your time, Captain Jacobs, and please contact our office if you think of anything that would help. Mars appreciates your cooperation, and the boost to tourism that Starchaser Spacelines has brought us." Jacobs nodded, and Gardner slipped out of his office and shut the door quietly behind her.

Jacobs poured himself a shot of whiskey and tossed it back. He gazed at the images on his wall of all the ships he had served on over the years until he had to press his palms against his tired eyes to hide a trace of moisture even from himself. He sat and stared until he felt ready to return to Machado's report.

When he did that last line jumped out at him: discordance in the orders of maintenance. Jacobs would have to speak to Jang about this, once he figured out what it meant. He drummed his fingers. Perhaps helioships were not so brittle after all. This discordance issue might be the *Horizon Cusp's* version of a bump or bruise. Jacobs found the thought oddly comforting.

Billiards is a pointless game.

Donal watched the cue ball meander around the table, refusing to cooperate with his cue. Pool at least let you sink the balls and change the playing field with every shot. But in billiards, you sent your cue ball spinning just to strike two other balls. Why bother? Even if you do it, you only have to do it again.

Pointless.

Donal caught the signs in himself: misery, rooted in a problem he hid from. Unlike his college days, when he might have suffered guilt for the minor infraction of avoiding academic or social responsibilities, Donal could hear the screams of spaceport tourists just beyond the verge of his thoughts, tourists who suffered and died because of him. Donal needed to act soon, before his mind showed him the panicked crush of bodies as travelers scrambled for their lives.

He knew he should not blame himself. Donal had not hurt anyone, and Aetheric Dynamics would have done the same thing to try to kill any courier in his position. They were after the papers, not Donal. It was business, not personal. Recriminations would not help Donal or the victims.

Still the images hovered on the edge of his mind.

Donal recalled the words of Professor N'Kembe. "Above all, a magician must have clarity. Strong emotions are part of life, but you must not let them consume you. This is why we study meditation. A magician who cannot focus his thoughts is a danger to himself and others."

The first rule of magic: fear devours.

Donal looked about. He was alone. Phil the bartender would not start his shift until evening. Donal hung up his cue and sat on the floor in the first pose of meditation. The passage of time did not matter. Where he sat and why he sat there did not matter. The package he needed to deliver did not matter. Even grad school did not matter. Only this moment mattered. Each breath came slow, smooth, and deep. Little by little, Donal's tight muscles unclenched, his turbulent stomach settled. One breath at a time, Donal calmed.

Ready at last, Donal confronted his experience in the spaceport: his fear at the explosion, his confusion as Li Hua led him to safety, and his guilt that he had done nothing to help. Moment by moment, Donal accepted the event, the terror that surrounded him, the horror of other travelers, and bit by bit incorporated it all into himself.

Donal did not yet know what lesson to take from the experience, but now he would not become lost within the memory. Now he could face it. Now it could not devour him. And perhaps he would be ready, should there be a next time.

Donal's efforts carried him through lunchtime, so he settled for a roast beef sandwich from the kitchen and sought entertainment in the library. It turned out that about one book in five was a refillable. That made this collection of originals the largest Donal had ever seen.

Still, extensive as the library might be, its themes were plain: economics, history, political theory, and tactics and strategy. Nothing that would help his research. Donal found the book about John Dee that Li Hua had mentioned, but it focused entirely on Dee's work with cyphers and his spying for the crown, about which the author seemed certain.

Donal tried the histories, but even they had a political theory undercurrent, rather than a deeper, analytical examination of their causes and effects, which Donal would have found much more interesting.

Donal paged through one called <u>Causes of War</u>. It purported to analyze World War I, but did not discuss the actions and decisions surrounding the outbreak of war. Instead it explored elements such as the evolution of relations between Germany and Austria-Hungary, the diplomatic difficulties of the Ottoman Empire, and the "hidden political agenda behind the timing of United States involvement."

Donal had enjoyed as many History electives as he could fit into his schedule in Santa Cruz, but these were angles he had never heard of. The whole library seemed like a corpus of graduates' theses.

That thought earned a snort. Other disciplines had it easy. They just had to argue a thesis well. A master's or doctoral candidate in magic had to demonstrate an original effect to the satisfaction of his future peers. No pressure or anything, just prove that your theory was sound while you sweated and stressed, not even allowed the help of an assistant or familiar. As though any magician who had a familiar might lose access to it.

A familiar. Donal paused his book browsing. Could he have helped people at the spaceport if he had had a familiar? Might a familiar have warned him to avoid that route? Li Hua had asked about his familiar as though it might have made a difference to their escape. What about the innocent bystanders who had no spells of their own?

The Enochian spirits could wait. Donal needed a familiar.

He hustled back to his room. What kind of familiar would serve him best? Ravens and wolves had been popular among the students in Santa Cruz, but were not quite right for Donal. He wanted a familiar that would make his family proud, something with ties to their roots in the Celtic Isles. Something like ... a *cú sidhe*! Perfect! The fae hounds were said to be strong, loyal, quick and clever. Donal would summon a *cú sidhe*.

No sooner had Donal slammed the door to his room behind him than he dropped into the third seated pose of meditation. Li Hua had been right about the telltales of formal thaumaturgy, but this was not the time to try things her way.

Nor was Donal ready to cast the spell. He needed a focus first, a material base that would house his familiar. Donal hopped to his feet and tore through his luggage, but he could not find an appropriate object. He settled for a gift from an old girlfriend: a pendant of a faun, dancing and playing the pipe. Not a good match, but better than an orphaned shirt button. At least the faun was made of silver.

Donal sat again on the floor, his legs folded under him. He needed no other trappings, components or reagents from the outside world. The conjuration of a familiar required a magician to work entirely within himself. Donal closed his eyes and extended his will to create a circle about him. More than a boundary, this circle revolved and both gathered and built power within it. Martian power instead of the terran power Donal was used to, which might add an odd resonance to the spell, but if Donal maintained sufficient clarity of purpose, the resonance should not taint the work.

Within the circle, Donal pulsed to the beat of his signature harmonic. He began the first chant of power: slow, deep and composed of open vowel sounds. He eased the chant from the minimum base repetitions of three to the perfect foundation of five. Donal then began the second chant, fast and staccato. "Like claves overlaying a Latin rhythm," his first college roommate had described it.

The third chant of power challenged Donal with its contrast, because its syncopated rhythm jarred against the honeyed tones of its harmonics. Donal sweated and shook through this stage as he fought for focus through the demands of holding so much magic. He held steady and directed the chant to agitate the mix of power and raise it to a fevered pitch.

Only enduring spells required such intensity, but enduring spells mattered the most.

With the power shaped and ready, Donal must next wield it to carry his call to the spirit who would become his familiar. Donal had time for one deep breath, then he began the first verse of the conjuration. The first verse of all spells to conjure familiars was the same, and opened the way into the fabric of the universe itself. Dangerous without enough power to hold the opening, deadly without the concentration to shape the desire. Donal had both.

The remaining verses of the conjuration varied from magician to magician, by necessity. Donal had to imagine his desired familiar in thorough detail, as only he could conceive it, and sing the spirit to life with words only they two would share. Donal began to form the image in his mind: a deerhound one meter tall, with fur of emerald green and eyes that blazed with courage.

The fae hound melted into being as the Donal sang it, nose to tail, tooth to claw, for him, by him, of him, but not him. When Donal's chant built to its crescendo, the *cú sidhe* solidified, barely fitting within the circle.

"What shall I call you?" Donal rasped.

"My name is Fionn."

"Fionn, this base shall hold your essence."

"A faun?"

"Best ... I had." Exhaustion began to dim the edges of Donal's vision, but he had to complete the ceremony or waste all his effort. The *cú sidhe* shrugged with a tilt of its head and dissolved into green light that focused on the pendant before fading.

Donal had never possessed the patience for proper alchemy, but no thaumaturgy undergraduate completed his training without learning the simple steps to bind a familiar. He wiped the tiny statue against his brow for the sweat of effort. He yanked out nose hairs until he had tears for consecration. He broke a scab on his elbow, remainder from a handball game on his flight to Mars, for the blood he and Fionn would share.

Donal's final words were no chant of power, but they sealed the binding: "My tears, my blood, my sweat, your life."

The spell complete, Donal slumped onto the floor, smiled, and let the circle dissipate.

4

Jacobs had barely knocked on Goldberg's office door when the chief called, "Come in, Captain."

Jacobs opened the door and wondered if Goldberg's file cabinets had exploded. Paperwork cramped and overflowed every surface, not just his desk, but tables, chairs, and even large sections of the limited floor space had been crowded by what might have been interpreted as "piles." Jacobs made his cautious way along the single open path to the desk, where Goldberg hunched over three papers as though they were boots he had to shine for inspection.

"My God, Saul, you've just given me a stronger argument for switching to the ship's phantasmal reporting system than anything Mash has ever said."

"Don't tell him that. His nibs is still sore about the meeting." He looked up. "Tell me something. How would you judge a magician's credentials?"

"Ask him to fly, and if he..."

"Yeah, yeah. I'm serious. I've narrowed it down to three guys here who all have the kind of background in security I'm looking for: five years of field work since getting their Initiate creds, including at least some real action." He put up both hands to forestall Jacobs' reply. "Already interviewed them. Arrogant, like most 'casters, but they seem to have their heads screwed on straight. I'm almost ready to put all three applications in the galley next to Benny Sugg's food dish and see which one he steps on first."

"Nah, that's how you hire a boatswain or a yeoman." They shared a laugh. "Ask Mash what he thinks."

"I was hoping you wouldn't say that." The chief sighed.

Jacobs sat in the sole clear chair.

"Remind him who got him off the hook back in Kennedy." Kennedy was a popular lunar vacation spot noted for its lax law enforcement where Machado had enjoyed his *caxaça* a little too much one night. He was a good mage, but needed a tight rein on his rum. "He could have lost his license."

"That might do it. I thought that nightclub owner was going to slice him into strips and dry him for jerky." Goldberg chuckled with a tired wheeze. "Can't blame him. He was a man who should not appear in public naked." The chief paused as he noticed that Jacobs was seated. "So what can I do for you, Captain?"

"I only came down for a status check, Mr. Goldberg, but what I see does not reassure me." Jacobs slowly surveyed the rough sea of paper surrounding him. "Where do you stand on your preparations for the charter?"

"I've already hired the seventeen extra men. I just need to finalize my choice of a 'caster this afternoon."

"Have you and Mr. Tunold discussed where the passengers will be berthed?"

"Sir?"

"We will carry only forty people - not counting the courier - most likely twenty each from two interests, both of whom feel the need for their own security." Jacobs saw the chief's eyes widen in understanding. Normally passenger accommodations would not concern him, but for this trip....

"One second." Goldberg dug out his book of layouts, which contained cross-sections of the ship arranged according to different priorities and indexed for ease of reference. Every officer had one, in case of emergency, but here Jacobs saw a copy in heavy use. Goldberg's book of layouts had a coffee ring on the front cover, and Jacobs saw food stains on the pages his chief flipped. "Here! Berth one group on Promenade One, port side, and the other on Promenade Two, starboard side. They'll walk the same distance to the meeting rooms and main recreation areas, but two floors and the breadth of the ship separate them. They'll be far enough apart to not bump into each other, but not so far apart that we look nervous."

"Good. Take it a step further and give the P1 passengers fore cabins and the P2 passengers aft."

"Aye, sir. With your permission I would also like to seal off decks seven through sixteen on both sides, excepting routes necessary for the crew. We can tell our guests that we're performing routing maintenance on the empty cabins."

"Permission granted. I'll even have Tunold order the maintenance. But leave an access point open on P7. We need to put that courier somewhere out of the way."

"Trouble?" Goldberg rolled his neck and shoulders, probably an unconscious gesture.

"Shouldn't be, at least not from him, but there's no reason to risk it." Jacobs looked over the layout. "Where are you going to put your 'caster?"

Goldberg flipped a few pages and thumped a finger onto a map.

"Right here."

"The masseuse quarters?"

"It's perfect." He snatched up a piece of paper, seemingly at random. It was Tunold's crew manifest for the coming voyage. "We only need to carry one or two massage therapists with so few passengers. That leaves three berths empty, on the main recreation deck near all the meeting rooms."

Jacobs looked at all those piles of paper again. Perhaps they were not so random.

"Good plan, Chief." Jacobs stood and stretched his neck. "Let me know if you need anything."

"A quick way to pick this 'caster without asking Mash?"

"I told you to straighten that out yourselves. Neither one of you wants me to make it official. And let me know when you're done. I need to talk to Machado about a few things myself. If I'm not on the bridge I'll be down in engineering."

"Talking to Jang?" Goldberg snorted. "Good luck to us both, then, Cap."

DONAL CLIMBED OUT OF THE LAP POOL, INVIGORATED BY A MORNING swim. A glass of iced tea waited for him on a small tripod table beside a lounge chair for when he finished beneath the drier - a clever fillip of elemental magic that shunted water off of his body and into a grating beneath, where it would be purified and returned to the pool.

Next to the tea glass sat a book from the house library, a theoretical work about the political potential of religious magic based on hypotheses about the thirteenth century Roman Catholic Church. Donal considered the hypotheses unlikely, but acceded that if modern theories were correct about the prominence of magic before the Industrial Revolution, then how it was applied became a valid point of study.

Donal stretched out on the lounge chair and picked up his book. He sipped his tea and saw Fionn slip into the room through the closed door. Donal smiled. He had a resource that would not have shown up in his courier profile, a resource that even Li Hua did not know he had.

Donal had been tempted to impress her with Fionn, showing off not only Donal's talent, but his wisdom in taking her advice. But Mr. Mancuso had not arrived by dinner last night, nor breakfast this morning, and caution won out. Donal might yet have to escape his plush prison.

He may have impressed Li Hua nonetheless. Donal would swear that she could tell something had changed about him, that he had gained an air of mystery that made him more interesting. She had lingered over both meals since Donal had bound his familiar.

"We are not guarded. That much is certain." The ghostly deerhound spoke with an accent somewhere between Scottish and Irish. "They patrol the border, but do not watch us. They defend against something that seeks us, something unfocused, not blind, but wishing to look all places at once."

"That must be Aetheric Dynamics." Donal sipped his tea. "So you think they'd let us walk out of here?"

"I do not know that. They may be confident that either we would not attempt to leave, or that they could stop us if we tried."

"No wards hemming us in?"

"Nothing active, but I did not take time to investigate every latent spell."

"Triggered wards? Yeah, they'd be more effective because I couldn't study them to find a weak point, but maintaining those things would cost...." Donal sighed. "Right. Triggered wards. Anything else to report?"

"I could not reach the hidden place."

"The sealed floor?" The *cú sidhe* nodded at a slight slant. Donal considered for another sip, then said, "Probably Mr. Mancuso's personal residence." Another sip. "By any chance did you see a good escape route, one that would not take us past latent spells?"

"Three potentials, but they would require more study. Shall I go now?"

"No, I want to limit your exposure. Right now they don't know about you. Let's keep it that way."

"I could find a clear path and study the guard routines without drawing attention."

"Next time. Thank you, Fionn."

His familiar tilted its head, as though it considered speaking, then nodded again and shifted into the pendant. Donal had two days before his ship left, two days to study the house layout and guard rotations through a familiar no one knew he had. With one spell, Donal had shifted himself from trapped courier to preparing magician. If Mr. Mancuso arrived to claim his package, fine, but if not, then Donal would carry it back to Earth.

A servant came in. Kolchak, if Donal remembered correctly. "More tea, sir?" asked the man who might be Kolchak.

"No, thank you. I think I have everything I need."

5

When Jacobs smelled herbs, incense, and alchemy, he knew he was close to the engine room. In his youth, he would have expected grease, gas, and the tang of metal. Now engineering smelled like the med bay, and both places called to Jacobs' mind a little tea room he knew back in Los Angeles, where a young officer on leave could charm a date in convivial privacy.

Jacobs wondered why they had such similar smells, given the disparity of their purposes and contents. He knew it was not the scent of alchemy, because Fredrickson's lab smelled like a pile of leaves burning in a bayou. The only thing engineering and med bay had in common was that both had at least one bunk, and engineering's was unofficial. Jang thought her cot was hidden in her office closet, but no one could keep secrets from a good executive officer, and a good ex oh kept the captain informed.

The main engine room, which housed the HK drive, was an octagonal chamber five meters across. Binding enchantments had been inscribed into the seams and joins of the walls alongside about thirty ongoing spells tied to other arcane symbols. Inside the chamber, four columns of varicolored light shifted and shimmered but were held in check by four circles distinct enough in size and complexity that even Jacobs could tell them apart. Not that he knew what those differences meant.

Jacobs did know that side rooms held redundant systems, spirits kept dormant and constrained by spells one step shy of completion: an elaborate network of magic that formed a system of travel almost one hundred percent reliable.

Jacobs stared, but did not enter the room. *Will I feel nostalgia for this when it's been replaced?*

Continuing on, Jacobs took a side passage past the supply closet to Jang's office. He found a paper wheel affixed to the door. In big black letters was written, "The Chief is," followed by eight options: in, asleep, pissed off, HK Drive, Deception Drive, around, in a meeting, out. A small arrow pointed to her current location: the Deception Drive.

Down a cramped hall then, past rooms dedicated to other systems, such as communications, navigation, and detection, to the end of the hall and the Deception Drive.

A small, square room housed the new engine, only three meters across. The walls held similar symbols and bindings to the HK Drive, but instead of four huge columns of light, the main part of the Deception Drive comprised a single magic circle that contained a song.

Jacobs knew that inside that magic circle a bound spirit manifested in this world through sound, and God knew that Machado and Jang explained the technical side of it a half-dozen times at least, but Jacobs could think of it only as a song. Sometimes three notes, sometimes seven, and once even thirteen if Jacobs' count had been right, the tune danced according to melodies and structures he could not quite follow. It could be beautiful, and it could make his teeth ache.

Once, on the last voyage, Jacobs had seen eyes inside that circle. Three other crewmen had been present, but no one else admitted seeing the twin spots of indigo, compressed as if in thought.

No eyes this time, and five notes sang a resemblance to a barbershop number. Jang repeated a short, legato chant and moved about the room, twirling a chain in a circular pattern to wave incense from a censer the size of a deck of cards. Jacobs waited. She might suffer from excess enthusiasm, but she held an Associate's Degree in Thaumaturgy, five certifications in sky and heliosphere transportation, and she had ten years' as a spacer, five aboard the *Horizon Cusp.*

The final notes of her spell harmonized with the song. Jacobs wondered if that mattered. Jang closed the lid on her censer and slid it into a pocket in her potion-stained coveralls. She came out of the room, said something that sounded like Latin, and snapped her fingers to seal the wards.

"What can I do for you, Captain?"

"How's she running?"

"True as carterite, sir. The power and control are steady, and fewer spells means fewer weak spots. I'll bet you a trip's pay that we don't need the main drive to get home."

"And the interactions with other systems?"

"No problems, sir. This baby ties straight into the hull, so atmosphere, comfort and the other systems aren't involved. Again, fewer weak points."

"Mr. Machado has expressed concerns about harmonic dissonance between the Deception Drive's bindings and those of our detection and communications systems."

"Dammit, Mash," Jang growled with a fierceness that belied her short, slender frame. "Sir, I swear, the chances of those harmonics causing a problem are almost nil. It's a hypothetical worst-case scenario."

"What would happen?"

"Mash didn't tell you in exacting detail?"

"I'm asking you, Chief."

Jang looked at him, gritted her teeth, and drew her posture straight. She tapped her knuckles together as she spoke, as though distracting herself from physical pain.

"Aye, sir. The two systems of binding are discordant enough that if their harmonics produce the wrong resonance at the same time, that resonance might act as a bridge, making a temporary hole in one of their bindings. But the secondary bindings don't have this problem, Captain. Even if one of the spirits slips loose, it won't run free."

"But we'd lose at least one of those systems?"

"Only until the spirit's re-bound."

"However long that takes, we could be blind, deaf and dumb, drifting on carterite." Jang started to object, but Jacobs shook his head. "Even if it happened in an empty part of space, we would still lose our course, which would cost us more than repair time. But suppose it happened near port, shortly after take-off or, heaven forbid, before landing?" The captain held the engineer's gaze to drive his point home. "Dead. All of us, and anybody we hit. We couldn't even send a distress call."

"Sir, the circumstances—"

"Could this be what happened to the *Beamrunner*?"

"Sir, we can't know that until—"

"That's right." Jacobs shook his head. "Chief, everyone is watching us on this trip: investigators, future clients, even the press. Zoltan did three interviews this morning alone. We cannot afford to have anything go wrong."

"Sir, I swear—"

"Even away from port, suppose something went wrong with the attempt to re-bind the spirits. What would happen?"

The skin of Jang's knuckles turned white.

"If Machado and I combined somehow failed?" She closed her eyes and blew out a breath. When her eyes opened again, some of the tension had left her face. "We'd eventually have a collision or simply be lost at space until we ran out of supplies."

"Exactly. Everything you, Machado, and every other 'caster have ever told me about spirits comes down to one point: maintenance is one hell of a lot easier than binding."

"Sir, don't let the *Beamrunner* blind you. No engine will ever be perfect. The Deception Drive has given us fifteen solid trips. She's ready."

"I said twenty and you agreed, Chief. Five more trips. Then we can try a few without the main drive. In the meantime, I suggest you work with Mr. Machado to find a way around that harmonics problem."

Jang grimaced. She seemed to like Machado well enough, but they held a tension between them, and Jacobs could never decide if it were professional or personal. "Oh, and Ms. Jang? I've been talking with the budget boys, and if you and Mr. Machado can clear up that last issue in the Deception Drive, the two of you will get to outfit the main drive's old bay as a research lab."

Jang's eyes grew slowly wide until she blurted out, "Yes, sir!"

"For that to happen, Ms. Jang, Starchaser Spacelines must stay in business. And for that to happen we need..."

"A perfect flight. Yes, sir. I'll get us to Earth safely if I have to carry this ship on my back."

"I know you will, Chief."

Jacobs could hear her whistle something as he walked away. He smiled.

6

Donal spent the afternoon reading, then took another dip in the pool before it was time to clean up for dinner. He had seen no sign of Mr. Mancuso, and Donal's flight was due to leave the next afternoon. He was combing his hair, following his shower, when Fionn came back from a perimeter check.

"The guards rotate every four hours, and retain a respectable level of attention throughout their watch. They seem well prepared for invasion."

"Could we slip past them, if we need to?"

"I think I have found a useful route. It appears free from latent spells, and has a key point you could get past with a single distraction. It will require stealth and timing, but once past that point—"

There was a knock at the door.

Donal gestured for the *cú sidhe* to vanish from normal sight and opened the door. Kolchak again. "Sir, I have just received word from Ms. Tai Shi. She regrets to inform you that she will be late for dinner and that you should begin without her. Shall I tell the chef that you still intend to eat at the designated time?"

"Yes, thank you."

Kolchak left, and Donal closed the door. Fionn cocked his head to one side.

"We should leave now."

"What?"

"The routine has changed. What must you carry?"

"She's just running late."

"Something will happen tonight."

"Fionn, stop." Donal threw his comb down on the bureau. "I have to give Mr. Mancuso one more day. That was the deal."

"Today we know the patterns, and they do not expect resistance. Tomorrow will be too late."

Donal sat on the bed and leaned forward, elbows on his knees. "You told me we're not guarded."

"You told me we are not free to go. The mind guards better than a cell."

Donal considered that.

"But what's waiting for us out there? You've been to the perimeter. Have you seen any signs of the hunter?"

"I know only that something seeks you."

Donal stood up and finished dressing.

"You must travel light," said Fionn. "We must burn whatever you leave, so they cannot track you."

"We're not leaving. Not before tomorrow."

"Then we might not leave at all."

Donal cleaned the hair from his comb, rolled the strands in a ball and incinerated them with a word. The comb he tossed on the bureau. He turned back to Fionn and said, "This job may be more dangerous than I expected, but I agreed to it. I'll see it through."

The *cú sidhe* whuffed and slipped back into its pendant. Donal strolled into the sun room and walked casually to a center table - a feat he had practiced for three hours that day, and now no one was here to witness his moment of triumph.

Delicious steak eased the ache of that disappointment, pink enough in the center to drip a hint of blood with every cut, and seasoned with sharp, strong flavors that took turns in his mouth. The vegetables looked like a type of orange celery, but had the consistency of yams and a taste reminiscent of beets, perhaps a local product. The bread tasted like fresh San Francisco sourdough, too much like what Donal had known in the Bay Area for it to have been locally made. Yet another show of wealth, but he saw no reason not to enjoy it. The bread certainly tasted good.

He had gotten perhaps halfway through his meal when the dining room door burst open and in stormed a whip-like man with black hair, a thin mustache and a very expensive suit. Five people trailed him like the tail of a kite: a man and woman in suits, each of whom carried a memoboard, two men in casual business attire, and Li Hua, who brought up the rear in a charcoal grey skirt suit.

"Bastards! The lot of them," said the man who had to be Mr. Mancuso. "Well, we'll just see how well they negotiate in a week or so, eh? Who is this?" He stopped in front of Donal and pointed a finger as though he directed a firing squad. "Who sits here eating my steak? And where is *my* steak? I haven't had a damned bite since noon."

"This is Donal Cuthbert," said Li Hua, hustling forward. "The courier."

"Good. Excellent. No, don't get up. Eat your dinner. Kept you waiting long enough. Least I can do is let you finish your meal before we get down to business."

Servants filed into the room and arranged food for everyone. The strangers in suits began to organize the seating, but Mr. Mancuso interrupted them. "No, no, no. Tai Shi and I will eat with our guest. I'm his damned host, about time I acted like it. And who brought him water? My guests don't drink water unless they want water. Get Cuthbert here some proper wine. You do drink wine, don't you, boy?"

"Yes, sir."

"Thought so. Never met a mage who didn't. You are a mage, aren't you? You've got that look."

The man spoke so fast that even though Donal kept up he felt three sentences behind. "What look is that, sir?"

"Like you're looking at the same things the rest of us are and seeing something different. Half the time I don't know what the hell

Tai Shi here is looking at, but she gets damned good results. Grab a seat, Tai Shi, and none of this female 'light eating' crap. That goes for you too, Stevens. We've all got a long day ahead of us tomorrow and we're going to need fortification."

Li Hua sat in the indicated chair, and when she met Donal's eye she looked exhausted but still had a smile for him. Everyone else sat where they were told: the two suits at the next table, positioned to flank Mr. Mancuso, and the two others spaced equally two tables away, angled so they could watch the doors.

"How do you like my little hideaway here, Cuthbert? I hear you've been enjoying the pool and the library, but you're still spending a lot of time in your room. Not having trouble adjusting to Mars, are you?"

"No, sir, I—"

"Good. I can't stand a man with a weak constitution. My last business assistant needed a day to adjust every time we landed someplace. Earth, Mars, Luna, didn't matter. Puking his guts out for a full damned day. Don't have time for it. Didn't last a month. Stevens, how long have you been with me now?"

"Fourteen months, twenty-three days, sir," said the woman in the suit, a blonde who managed to snap the words out without making them harsh or rushed. Donal did not even have time to notice if she were pretty before Mr. Mancuso pushed the conversation along.

"Precision, my boy. The hallmark of a good assistant. Reminds me. Davis, we're going to be on Earth for at least a month if we pull this off. Make sure I entertain my three most important clients. You know the ones."

"Yes, sir," said the suited man in a baritone that Donal envied. "You also promised to attend a dance at the Farnborough estate if you were in the country, and the current schedule should have us there."

"Damn. Add it to my calendar." Mr. Mancuso pointed to Donal's, Li Hua's and his own wineglasses, and a steward filled them. "Ever get involved in politics, Cuthbert?"

"No, sir, apart from voting."

"Smart boy. Elected officials are nothing but useless bastards filling their own bank accounts with money they don't earn. Business is a breeze, my boy, but politics will kill me." He swirled his wine and sniffed it, then took a drink. Donal followed suit, and decided that it made the Morgan vintage from the other night taste like grape juice in comparison. Mr. Mancuso set down his glass. "You're a sharp lad. How do you like courier work?"

"I'd rather be in grad school."

"Learning what?"

Donal felt the weight of Mr. Mancuso's full attention, the scrutiny of a demon testing a binding circle. Was it as dangerous? Li Hua leaned forward as well.

"I have a talent for conjuration, and I want to go into research. I have this idea for a project surrounding the Enochian tablets of Dr. John Dee—"

"Tai Shi, translate for me, would you? You speak mage."

"The Enochian Tablets of Dr. Dee form a system of elemental magic so deep and intricate that it could revolutionize modern thaumaturgy, if anyone cracks it."

"Think he can do it?"

"He has talent, he's adaptable, and I've heard potential in his theories." She nodded. "Yes, I think he might."

Donal smiled and started to speak, but Mr. Mancuso overrode him.

"Good. High aspirations, but maybe realistic. A good sign." He glanced down at Donal's empty plate as servants brought food to the late arrivals. "Done eating? Good. Go get the papers and we can finish our business while you finish your wine."

Donal shook himself as he made it out of the room. So that was what it felt like at the center of a tornado. He shook himself again. He retrieved the package, tested its seal one last time, took a deep breath to set himself, and went back into the sun room.

As Donal sat back down, Mr. Mancuso said, "How long have you been staying here, Cuthbert?"

"This is my third night, sir."

"And he walks across this room like he's been living here six months. You're a sharp kid. I like you. I'll keep an eye on your career.

Maybe we can do business one day, when you finish school." Mr. Mancuso finished his glass of wine and gestured for a refill. "Stevens, my I.D."

Ms. Stevens handed over his passport, and Mr. Mancuso held it up and said the formal words: "I solemnly swear that I am Donatello Michaelangelo Mancuso, intended recipient of your package."

Donal pulled from his pocket a piece of enchanted silver shaped like the three letters of the IIX logo. He tapped it against the passport and saw the recognition signs glow in response. Confirmation.

"Mr. Mancuso, here is your package."

"Thank you very much." Mr. Mancuso broke the seal and read through the five pages within. Contracts and legal records, the last bastions of paper not yet subsumed by spellwork. A feral smile lit Mr. Mancuso's face. "Perfect. Absolutely perfect." He snapped a pen out of his jacket pocket like a quick-draw artist and signed the last page, next to two other signatures. "It's official. I will be negotiating for all three of us." He held up his wine. "To the future!"

Everyone drank. Even Donal would drink to that.

7

DONAL SCUFFLED BACK TO HIS ROOM. FOR DAYS HE HAD BEEN UNABLE TO decide if he were an important guest or a valuable prisoner, but he was just a courier. No sooner had Ms. Stevens copied the signed papers through her memopad than Mr. Mancuso dismissed him. "Thank you, Cuthbert. Now go prepare them for return delivery."

Donal tossed the papers onto his bed. He did not bother to ward them. No one would tamper with them. Not here. The papers were safe behind deep layers of security.

No need to escape now. 4M would want Donal on his flight so the papers could reach Earth as soon as possible. Even Aetheric Dynamics would back off. They would know that Mr. Mancuso had returned, presume he had signed his papers, and conclude that they had copies of the completed documents. Killing Donal would stop nothing now. At best, it might slow down whatever those papers accomplished, but not by much.

Unspent adrenaline twitched through Donal, but he saw no easy outlet for it. He paced his room listlessly, then gave up and went for one more swim.

Later that night, Donal packed and laid out his travel clothes on the bureau. Fionn broke the hours-long silence.

"We will be well quit of this place," said the *cú sidhe.* "Far better to return to lands where none seek your death."

"No one sought my death here. They didn't even know who I was. Killing me would have been incidental to getting the papers."

"You would have been no less a corpse."

Donal blinked.

"You warded that wisp, but not your person. When prudence would have had you escape, you stayed to do your duty." Fionn's emerald eyes met Donal's. "Perhaps you are not yet renowned for your magic, but you have acted as a man of honor." Fionn lifted his ears with his head at an angle. "I would say that was more valuable."

Donal thought about that as he lay in bed, and he wondered if Li Hua would agree.

DONAL BREAKFASTED ALONE THE FOLLOWING MORNING WHILE SERVANTS buzzed about. He saw no sign of the house's other occupants. Perhaps that was just was well. He was ready to go home. When his runner arrived, Donal scribbled a brief goodbye note for Li Hua and left without a backward glance.

The runner waiting in the garage for Donal had four legs instead of six. *Probably 4M's idea of an economy model.* At the reins sat the same scarred man. Donal climbed onto the rear bench seat and realized that the runner's top could open. The giant lizard body had a large hole carved in its back, but wings had folded in to form a sealed roof. Donal asked twice to watch them unfold, but the driver ignored him the first time and grunted refusal the second.

Donal turned his attention to the horizon where majestic mountains towered, their reds and tans exotic in the morning sunlight. He smiled, then closed his eyes and sighed at the sun's warmth on his face. A dozen deep lungsful of unprocessed air later, Donal opened his eyes and gazed upon the domes and twisting towers of New Leningrad. They seemed not simple houses and offices now, but groves of secrets, full of lives and ideas as alien to Donal as this planet was distant from Earth.

He longed to share this moment with Fionn. He touched the silver faun pendant, but before he began the call, the driver swore at a passing runner. Donal covered his face with his hands. He was in a 4M vehicle, driven by a 4M employee. The job was not yet over. True, there was no longer a reason to kill Donal, but could Donal count on Aetheric Dynamics to know that?

The domes and towers now looked sinister. Any of them might house conspiracies, very human people who would bomb a space-port over the papers in a courier's bag.

Donal thought of playing spy games with Bran when they were boys running wild in the woods behind their parents' house / carpentry business. Even then, Bran was the star and Donal the side-kick. Now they were adults, and Bran starred in a great exploration while Donal got upstaged by pieces of paper.

Donal's eyes squeezed tight while with two fingers he rubbed his forehead. For all his spells, he felt powerless: millions of kilometers from home, enmeshed in a fight he did not understand over stakes he did not know. At any moment, some unseen hand might destroy him, sweep him off the board with the other pawns. Anonymous.

And Donal would make that hand's job all the easier if he did not pull himself back to the present.

Deep breaths, yes, even use the pattern this time ... deep breaths, slow ... try to fill your whole body with air.... Air pushes the tension out of your muscles, the worry out of your thoughts, the fear out of your eyes....

I am calm. I am clear. I am a magician.

Donal opened his eyes. The arched entrance of the New Leningrad Spaceport came into view: a great, wide double-helix of carterite and copper, twenty meters tall and sixty across. In the exact center of the apex hung the Martian standard, with "Barsoom" written on one side, the original name of the first colony, and "Mars" on the other. A banner below the standard read, "Keep Mars Free - Buy Local." Donal had read that this arch was enchanted to serve as the first Martian commercial transport beacon, and still functioned as an emergency backup. He might have studied the spells of the beacon, tested the resonance and harmonies of the carterite and explored its interaction with its copper twin - if only he had not been trapped underground for three days.

But Donal could study the arch on another trip. His time in the safe house had given him Fionn, whose depths as a resource Donal had only begun to plumb. Like Professor Mubarek had told him: "once you have a familiar, you wonder how you got along without one."

The public transit station bustled with activity outside the space-port. Hundreds of people rushed about, catching or leaving elegant, twenty-meter carts that rolled through New Leningrad under the guidance of magicians from a central tower. Life went on as though the explosion had never happened.

Donal filed into the crowded port and consulted a floating map for directions to the local IIX office: fourth segment of the outer ring, a few hundred meters from where he stood. Originally the company had been Intraplanetary Express. When they began handling off-world deliveries, they changed it to Interplanetary Express, but lost all their domestic customers. The marketing team settled on IIX because no one would bother saying Inter and Intraplanetary Express.

Donal still marveled that the speaker had admitted this during orientation.

He gripped his messenger bag and wove through the crowds. The businesses along the outer ring did not interest Donal, just the same assortment of cheap restaurants, rental lockers, and impulse-purchase stores he might find in any port.

Donal almost walked past the IIX office. He had expected some-thing large and secure, like the one he worked out of in the port of San Francisco. Instead what he found was little more than a kiosk with a back room, like any of the small shops Donal had passed along the outer ring. He checked in with a Martian teenager behind the front counter and asked to speak with the local supervisor.

The supervisor was an older man with a serious face. He had no special news or instructions for Donal, but thanked him for his fine work, gave him his return ticket, and told him where to meet his ship. IIX had already been informed about the attempt on Donal's life, and the supervisor confirmed that Donal would receive combat pay for the whole delivery, including the return trip. At that rate Donal could fund his graduate studies within another six months. If he survived.

Donal made the supervisor certify in writing that the combat rate was in effect for the entire trip. "Bureaucracies run on paperwork," his mother always said. "Never settle for an oral contract; make them put it in print." This had been a family credo since Donal's great uncle was cheated in a duel back in 1981. Great Uncle Rory McCleary had verbally agreed to a duel to first blood over ownership of a prize horse. Uncle Rory wounded his opponent's sword arm, scoring first blood, but when he lowered his sword his opponent stabbed him in the shoulder. Rory's second must have taken a bribe, because he swore to police that the opponent had scored first, confirming Rory's loss. Since the duel contract had been oral, not written, no licensed judge had been required, and the false testimony of a second sufficed.

The McCleary family had refused oral contracts ever since, and after Colleen McCleary married Robert Cuthbert, she passed the tradition to her sons Bran and Donal.

I'll have to visit Mom and Dad when I get home, thought Donal as a customs agent performed a routine scan, touching Donal's bag with a baton enchanted to detect contraband, then opened the bag for a visual search. *See if there's any word from Bran. His expedition must have reached Ganymede by now.*

"You're clear," said the customs agent, a man with sharp eyes and soft, rounded edges, skin tinted red as a native. Something nagged at Donal.

"Sir, I arrived on Mars just before the explosion the other day. Would my bag have been searched a second time by customs?"

"Nah. The early reports showed that the explosives came from Mars. This was some local problem."

Donal paused next to the benches at the edge of customs, where other passengers organized their possessions before entering the port proper. So who did search the bag? And why? Was it this Aetheric Dynamics after all? Were they stupid enough to think he would have left an official package in his suitcase? Did they have some other agenda? Was he still in danger? Donal scanned the crowd, but saw no one skulk or brandish a weapon.

He left the customs area and entered the main part of the port. He wondered if he could safely stop for lunch before he boarded the ship.

"Donal Cuthbert?"

Donal turned to see a woman about his own age, a redhead with skin as smooth as the Devil's voice and a business suit cut to emphasize what it covered. He held his messenger bag a little tighter.

"Yes?"

"My name is Rowan MacPherson and I would like to make you a business proposition. May I buy you a cup of coffee?"

Her smile was bright and charming. Donal's mother would have applauded if he brought home a woman like Rowan MacPherson, a beauty descended from the Celtic Isles. What were his chances of running into such a woman in a Martian spaceport, much less one who knew his name?

"No."

"I promise this won't take more than five minutes of your time."

"Why bother? I think you just told me everything I need to know." Donal glanced about, in case she was a distraction, but spotted no threats. "Let me guess. You work corporate security for Aetheric Dynamics."

"Mr. Cuthbert, there are facts you don't have." An urgent tremor threaded through her words. "Please. Five minutes. Even if we reach no agreement, you should hear the other side of the story. 4M is more dangerous than you realize."

"Forget it. Try not to kill any innocents on your way home."

Donal stepped around her, but Rowan MacPherson had a parting shot.

"No one is neutral in this fight, Mr. Cuthbert. Choose your side carefully."

JACOBS STOOD ON A WALKWAY ABOVE THE BOARDING AREA THAT ZOLTAN referred to as the "reception hall." Jacobs called it the gangplank, and the rest of his crew had adopted the term. He had to admit, though, that Zoltan had made the area look good to passengers: comfortable chairs and benches decorated in a gryphon's nest theme with gold and silver chasing, in a large room designed to look and feel like a mountain cavern, complete with a blue sky view along the aft wall where the shuttle would enter. In a few minutes, the hippogriff-shaped shuttle would arrive and land among what appeared to be its brethren's unhatched eggs. Perfect aboard a passenger liner that was shaped like a giant gryphon in flight.

Jacobs checked his watch, though he knew the shuttle would land on time. Five hundred things to do before the *Horizon Cusp* hit space and its commanding officer had to waste time up here to personally welcome every "guest" aboard his ship. Jacobs sighed a momentary longing for his Navy days, when a captain could ignore passengers during boarding because only VIPs merited his attention. Zoltan, however, insisted on all captains giving this formal greeting and would not hear of delegating the task to an ex oh. To make matters worse, the other captains enjoyed it. They were younger men, and took as much pleasure in the fact of command as in the work.

The hippogriff shuttle flew in and landed at eleven hundred hours sharp. Both groups of passengers filed out. Jacobs spotted bin Zuka and nodded to acknowledge his gesture of recognition. Bin Zuka spoke with a man who wore a keffiyeh with a modest business suit and moved like a leader of men. That had to be al Rashid, head of Transterran Properties and bin Zuka's boss. The other group surrounded an oily man in an expensive suit, who spoke as though he had to issue a thousand orders in his next hundred steps. That would be Mancuso, al Rashid's counterpart from 4M.

Each group comprised twenty people, fifteen of whom all but screamed security - muscled men and women in color-coordinated pants and collared shirts bearing company logos. The clothes might have let two or three of them move unnoticed through a crowd, but clustered together the uniform effect branded them bodyguards. No visible weapons at least, which should help Goldberg and his new Initiate with the initial check-in. Jacobs knew from the passenger manifest that each group had two 'casters, a Journeyman and an Initiate, but could not pick them out by sight. But then, Jacobs had not pegged bin Zuka as a Journeyman, and he had met the man. Still, Goldberg's Initiate would be able to spot them. Jacobs noted to ask during the next report. Best to discover these things ahead of time.

One passenger remained unaccounted for. Jacobs turned to the purser, a new man who joined them just before the flight to Mars. Joffries? Yes, that was right. "Mr. Joffries, has there been any sign of the courier?"

"Aye, sir. Mr. Cuthbert checked in an hour ago. I showed him to his room and explained the situation with the cruise, as ordered."

"Good man. This is everyone then?"

"Aye, sir," Joffries said, consulting his memoboard, "assuming the names match."

Jacobs turned to his yeoman.

"Mr. Kelly, send word to Mr. Tunold that our passengers have arrived. Tell Ms. Jang to fire up the drives. All stations are to begin final preparations for launch on schedule."

"Aye, sir." Kelly carried out his orders double-time, as always.

Jacobs cleared his throat and spoke in his loudest, most resonant tone, or at least the version that lacked the imperative of command.

"Ladies and gentlemen, welcome aboard the *Horizon Cusp*. I am Captain John Jacobs, commander of this vessel and your host for our ten-day trip to Earth. As we leave Mars we will swing out between the twin moons, which will afford you a beautiful view that you will not likely enjoy on any other trip. Starchaser Spacelines is committed to bringing our passengers the best possible travel experience.

"Because part of that experience involves keeping you safe, I'm afraid I must ask you all to submit to one final weapons check performed by our security team, as stipulated in your travel agreement. I assure you that this is strictly a formality. Our insurance company requires this check as a concession for allowing you to bring your own security teams on this voyage.

"I speak for my entire crew when I say we look forward to serving you. We hope you will enjoy your flight to Earth, and that you will choose Starchaser Spacelines for all your future interplanetary travel needs."

Jacobs started for his office before any of the passengers could call him down for a personal introduction. He hoped he had time to wash the taste of that speech out of his mouth before takeoff.

8

Jacobs stared at the great red planet around him through a bubble of magic. Behind him he could hear the sounds of his bridge crew performing pre-flight systems checks and discussing what they did during the break between flights, but before him he could see the spaceport as clearly as he could have from the ground. Jacobs touched one finger to the smooth, transparent ceramic bulkhead in front of him. He knew it was a half-meter thick. He knew that layers of spells made the ceramics stronger than steel and would keep him safe when his helioship left the Martian atmosphere. He had commanded the *Horizon Cusp* for ten good years, and he knew he could rely on its magic as well as its crew.

But sometimes when Jacobs stood on the bridge he felt as if he stood in a soap bubble. He could see in a three hundred sixty degree arc around him as well as above him. Only looking down could he see the body of his ship, a great gleaming gryphon some two hundred fifty meters long. The bridge was a soap bubble dome on top of its back, between the outstretched wings.

Adding to the eerie sensation, the ship preparing for flight made less sound than falling snow. The rise of magic had carried human life to other planets, but magic's stillness had supplanted the visceral pleasures of Jacobs' youth. No gears to grind, no electricity to hum, no grease to smell, no turbines to roar vibrations throughout the ship - when the bridge crew fell silent, the only sound Jacobs heard was the hush of his own breathing.

But he could waste no more time pacing the dome. He turned back from the perimeter walkway with its view of the port and the city to head for the stairs that led up to his duty station. The work stations on the bridge - helm, communications, scanners, damage control, and the executive officer's station - were arranged in a ring in the center, with the captain's station on a raised platform above them.

Sound still dominated Jacobs' thoughts. The electro-mechanical, seagoing battleships and carriers of his Navy days had been alive, and a captain could hear his ship purr with health or complain of ailments. The engineers and technicians might as well have been doctors and nurses. But the last of those groaning, grinding steel ships had died sixty years ago. A few of their corpses now served as dock-bound museums, tributes to a defunct way of life. These quiet new ships with their fancy shapes and ceramic hulls were mage-powered, and moved by a process of "correlations" and "decans."

Jacobs glanced at his ship status display, a miniature illusory representation of the *Horizon Cusp*. Near the gryphon's beak was the official launch countdown, provided by the port magicians. One minute to go.

In flight all the information fed to his station came from lacunas, spirits native to space. Lacunas also powered the engines. An old ship would develop its own spirit through quirks and personality. The new ships had spirits thrust into them. Unnatural. That was what bothered Jacobs more than silence, near exposure to space, or strange coordinate systems. Magic was unnatural.

Jacobs shook his head. He had no time to indulge in an old man's ruminations. If he had grown up with magic, like his crew had, he would probably consider it natural too. What mattered now was that he had a ship to command and a good crew to do the job. Some things never changed.

"Helm, report," he said.

"Five by five, Captain," said Burke. "Ready for launch on schedule. Traffic's light today."

Jacobs spun back to his ship status display. None of the subsections flashed with urgency. All maintenance complete, the ship looked ready to fly. Jacobs wondered how the final pre-flight reports of the *Beamrunner* looked. He touched the engine room, and the display focused in on that section, with the latest numbers just above it. Nothing updated from the last flight's official report, so he opened communications with a twist of his finger.

"Engineering, report."

"All systems standing by, Captain," said the image of Chief Engineer Jang's head. Pride shaped her features. "The Deception Drive is ready to engage as soon as the local boys release us."

"And the HK Drive?" Jacobs scowled when Jang hesitated. "Ms. Jang, I expect that HK Drive ready to go on a moment's notice, just in case. If it isn't, you'll spend a week as my personal punching bag. Bridge out."

Jacobs picked up his pen and notebook to log a reminder that he wanted Machado to check on the HK Drive.

But no seat belts needed fastening for takeoff, and no hatches needed battening, not since commercial docking regulation 1033(b)2 required passenger liners to provide regular ports of call with pieces of the ceramics used in their ships' construction. The port's magicians handled all landings and takeoffs, guaranteeing smooth safety. Jacobs had gotten to watch the procedure when it was first introduced as a mandatory practice: a roomful of hotshot young magicians playing with toy ships. They had a large table laid out as a scale model of the spaceport, with miniature versions of each ship. When a ship was cleared to lift off, one of the mages would guide it out by hand, using its tiny model and sympathetic magic to clear the atmosphere. Landings followed the same procedure, in reverse.

Jacobs hated it. If anything went wrong the ship might wreck, the passengers and crew might suffer injuries or death, but the magician responsible sat safely in the port. Once upon a time, local pilots who

knew a harbor's hazards would board a ship to bring it in and out of
dock, but at least those pilots shared the risks.

Jacobs stood and returned to the perimeter walkway. He would
pace until the *Horizon Cusp* hit space.

"NOT EXACTLY A 4M SAFE HOUSE, IS IT?" DONAL'S STATEROOM WAS
larger than the one he had on his last flight, but it did not come
close to the luxury suite he had enjoyed on Mars. It looked half the
size and the amenities did not compare. The twin bed felt stiff and
creaky as a plank of wood. The writing desk built into the opposite
wall looked like a table, with three drawers added as an
afterthought. The dresser felt like pressboard with a veneer of finer
trim, and the beige carpet might have been designed for use on
scratching posts. Two cheap reproductions of space scenes adorned
the walls, though the one depicting a red nebula was pretty
enough. Neither of them bore any spells. The stateroom did have a
small round table with two chairs by the porthole, which was a
plus. But calling the bathroom cramped would not do it justice.
Donal could touch all four bathroom walls when he stood at the
sink.

But then again, it might have appeared worse to Donal than it
really was, after the opulence he had enjoyed on Mars.

Fionn snorted and looked at him.

"All right." Donal raised his hands in a quick surrender. "You have
a point. It's still bigger than my apartment, and the bed's at least as
good as the one I had growing up. Plus the view out of the porthole is
magnificent." Donal had expected a twenty-centimeter porthole, like
the last one he had, but the one above his table was easily a meter
across. "But you have to admit, the place on Mars was pretty posh."

"Here we are not confined and under threat. Find your comfort in
that." Fionn twitched his ears. "Ship personnel will guard the documents well in their safe?"

"I met the ship's mage on the voyage to Mars. He's a Magister. My wards should be so good." Donal smiled. "Maybe when I get my doctorate..."

"I could check on them."

"Later. Right now I need you to vanish. I'm going to stretch my legs a bit, and I want you watching my back until we know how much freedom we have."

"Remember that I cannot hide myself from the eyes of mages."

"Yeah, if they're looking for you."

The emerald deerhound sat and regarded its master.

"Or watching for familiars." Donal sighed. "So if I stay here and send you they'll see you but they won't know you're mine. If I go but leave you in the pendant, no one watches my back." He sat and thought. The *cú sidhe* waited. "Hell with it. That purser said three times that I don't have to stay in my room. I'm going for a walk." Fionn returned to the pendant around Donal's neck.

Outside his room, the ship felt deserted. Donal did not see, hear, nor smell any signs that the other staterooms on his floor were occupied. It was as though he were under quarantine. Donal found the nearest water tube and slid the lever to call the bubble. Moments later the steel cage arrived. Enchanted against water and propelled by undines, the cage rode up and down the tube in a bubble of air that refreshed at each landing.

"Main deck, please," he said to the undines.

In school, Donal had had peers who insisted that a magician must command spirits. But whether he summoned elementals, fae, or genii loci, Donal had always gotten his best results when he addressed spirits with respect. But then, Donal believed that everyone responded better to good manners.

He thanked the undines when he reached the main deck, and stepped into what looked like an ancient Greek village. Illusions turned the high ceiling into a clear blue sky, with only a hint of clouds. Donal remembered that it would darken as evening came on, but that stars and a full moon would provide ample light. The shops and boutiques, bars and restaurants, game rooms and exercise areas were all arranged in rows of standalone buildings that completed the image. Their structures looked to have been built from cut marble, fitted without mortar, and polished to a shine. The air carried a hint of dust and sea smells, more illusions, but any authentic odors were sanitized away.

An ancient Greek ghost town. When Donal had last stood on this deck, he had been engulfed in a sea of excited tourists and drunken revelers, accented with children screaming for joy, or their parents, or their friends, or whatever else they screamed about. Now the game rooms stood dim with disuse, the dance floors empty, the bars and restaurants lonely, and the benches at the secondary observation hull vacant. The high ceiling echoed only the past. Donal had the whole place to himself.

After Mars he would have liked some company.

Donal strolled down a row dedicated to entertainment. Should he watch a shadow play, an illusory portrayal of some recent thriller or comedy? Perhaps he should go for a swim or get a massage. Down a side street he spotted four bored men outside an open door. Donal had assumed that the unlabeled block of buildings were restricted to employees, yet none of these men wore the attire of the ship's watch. They did appear to wear uniforms, though, with their matching polo shirts and cargo pants. Were they guarding the big meeting that required special security? The one Donal was forbidden to approach?

He walked toward the men. The guards stood straighter and two moved to meet him. Donal smiled.

"Hi, guys. Since we're neighbors and all, I thought I should come introduce myself."

"This is a private meeting," said the one with the crew cut. "You can introduce yourself later."

"I don't mind, my name is—"

"Later," said the other. "Don't make us ask twice."

Thugs. Bullies whose muscles moved faster than their minds. But perhaps Donal was unfair. They might get in trouble for letting someone linger near the precious meeting, especially if they could not detect the use of magic.

"No problem." Donal smiled again. "Nice to meet you gentlemen.

We'll talk another time." He had learned what he wanted anyway - he could hear voices from within but no distinct words, see shapes around the bodyguards' bulk, but no faces. Whoever met there used privacy magic. Even their own guards would not know what businessmen said.

Showy paranoia. Why not just close the door, or meet in a private room? Well, let them have their public privacy. If everyone's here, there won't be a line for a massage. He started toward the spa, but got no further than three steps when he heard one of the guards say something that stopped his feet.

"Should we report this to Ms. Tai Shi?"

Ms. Tai Shi? Did he mean Li Hua? What would she be doing here?

Donal cut short his exploration and hustled back to his room. He needed to talk to Fionn.

JACOBS WAS DUE AT DINNER IN TWENTY MINUTES. DINNERS WERE command performances, sideshows like the events made out of boarding and disembarking. Come see the captain! Ask your inane questions and watch him pretend he has not heard them a thousand times!

Jacobs poured three glasses of whiskey, placed two on his desk near the guest chairs, and sipped from the third. He sat and swiveled around to look over the titles on his shelves. Two sets of his own handwritten logs, a dozen refillables about space travel, almost as many originals and refillables about modern air navigation and travel, and nearly two score originals about navigation and seamanship in the old ways. When Jacobs died, he might leave those to a museum. Perhaps that was why Jacobs hated the command performances. He felt like a museum display himself.

At last the knock he awaited came. "Come in, gentlemen."

Goldberg and Tunold entered, offered quick, simple greetings and went straight to their chairs and whiskey. No doubt they were eager to get to dinner. They had probably skipped lunch again. Doctor Ramirez would lecture them for neglecting proper nutrition in space, but they put their work first, same as Jacobs. At least they got to eat with the crew.

"I won't keep you long. I just want a sense of these people before I have to eat with them. You first, Ex Oh."

"We may have been worried over nothing, Cap. Some of their guards are tense, but the leaders are calm. Steady. I didn't spend much time with them, but they seemed in good spirits, eager to come to an arrangement."

"And their paperwork?"

"Spaceworthy. I called in a couple of favors to get it double-checked, and everything came up legitimate. They are who they say they are, and customs had no trouble clearing them."

"Good. Thank you, Ex Oh. Chief?"

"Gotta disagree with you, Ex Oh. We were right to hire extra security, and I hope we have enough."

Tunold shifted in his seat, but Jacobs spoke first.

"Go on, Chief."

"The ex oh spent most of his time with the leaders. I spent most of mine with the guards because of the final weapons check. I love that idea, by the way. Any chance we can make it part of our regular procedures? No?" Goldberg snapped his fingers. "Anyway, that tension the ex oh mentioned isn't coming from all the guards, just some of them." Goldberg drummed his fingers on Jacobs' desk, not a simple trill but a series of rapid movements that resembled playing a piano. Some sort of mnemonic, perhaps. "And it's not nerves. They have the look of seasoned troops who know they have a fight coming. I think their bosses told them to be ready when the word comes."

"Why only some of them?"

"Fifteen troops each," said Tunold. "Probably six-man teams, two squad leaders, and a commander."

"Exactly," said Goldberg. "They'll have the word, but maybe not pass it to the rest, to keep anyone from spooking and jumping early."

The drumming fingers stopped. "There's going to be a fight, captain. Only question is when."

"Jibes with what I saw, Captain. Nice catch, Chief."

"All right, we need to prepare then, just in case." Jacobs leaned forward and pointed at Goldberg. "Tell Mr. Machado I want wards up around engineering, med bay, the bridge, and all command posts. And you better hand out the Pacifiers."

"Already done, Captain, and I'll find Machado before dinner."

"Good man. Mr. Tunold, re-assign all service shifts. I know this will play hell with the crew schedule for the next couple of days, but I want the most experienced personnel possible on duty during those meetings."

"Aye, sir. And I'll find excuses to check up on them personally."

"Excellent. We need to reach port intact, boys, so let's keep the nice passengers from killing each other." Jacobs stood. "Now we better go eat."

Donal slammed his stateroom door and summoned his familiar. The *cú sidhe* lay on the floor between his master and the door, head resting on crossed emerald paws while Donal paced and told of how he had learned of Li Hua's presence.

"What does it mean?"

"It means we are in danger, and you were right to put those documents in the safe."

Donal stared at the ghostly deerhound. He felt his eyes widen as he understood. "They didn't need me to deliver their papers." Donal resumed pacing. "They could have brought them themselves. So why have me do it?"

"The task must carry danger. I suggest you ward the room and not leave it without me."

"I may need you as a surprise."

"Secrets do not help the dead."

"But Li Hua—"

"Did not tell you she would travel on this ship." Fionn cocked his head. "But by choice or by order?"

Donal dropped backwards onto the bed and stared at the ceiling. He heard his familiar stand and pad toward him, felt the deerhound's head lie next to him on the mattress.

"Why does this trouble you so?"

Donal rolled his head and met his familiar's eye. *That's a good question. Why does Li Hua's secrecy bother me so much?*

"Keep your focus."

Donal looked deeper into those emerald eyes. Fionn was right, but was that fae wisdom or some part of Donal keeping himself in check?

Don't get caught up in another distraction. Donal drew a breath, then stood and set about casting his wards.

9

At least dinner did not require any speeches. Jacobs took his seat at the head of the center table in the main dining room of Ambrosia, the largest, fanciest restaurant the *Horizon Cusp* had to offer. Through craftsmanship and enchantment, diners experienced eating atop Mount Olympus at the onset of twilight, with spectacular views of the sea in one direction and Grecian countryside in others. Even the ceiling showed the sky above Greece. The moon shone overhead, and stars twinkled in constellations that varied with the time of year. Currently Jacobs could see a three-quarter moon passing near the belt of Orion the Hunter. Ambrosia specialized in Mediterranean fare, but carried a selection of specialties from other parts of Earth, and occasionally Martian and Lunar delicacies.

For most trips, six of the eleven other chairs at the captain's table could be reserved for a fee, while the captain filled the remaining five by personal invitation. Jacobs preferred to assign that task to Kelly. For this voyage, the seats had been arranged in the contract. Mancuso and his crew sat on Jacobs' left side, likely in order of rank: Mancuso first, then two women and two men beyond them. On Jacobs' right sat al Rashid's group, starting with al Rashid himself, then bin Zuka and three other men. The captain mused for a moment at the tirade his ship's alchemist would have thrown over the gender imbalance in al Rashid's party. At least they had shown enough respect to dress for dinner. All the guests wore dark suits or evening dresses.

Jacobs saw the courier seated across the room, past tables full of guards in their work clothes. The boy sat alone where Olympus' peak sloped sharply downward, which meant he was next to the wall. Jacobs shook his head. No one should have to eat alone at Ambrosia. At the foot of the captain's table was an empty seat. Perhaps ... no. No reason to draw more attention to the poor lad. At least alone he could eat in peace.

Jacobs decided to consult Goldberg later about letting the courier dine with the ship's watch for the rest of the trip. Not tonight though. On this first night of the voyage the chief arrayed his entire force at tables behind the captain. Ostensibly the watchmen had come to eat, but glances from Mancuso and al Rashid made clear that they understood the message: if they could not maintain control, Goldberg would.

PERHAPS *I* SHOULD DINE SOMEWHERE ELSE TOMORROW NIGHT, THOUGHT Donal. If the other restaurants were open. They might not be, since Ambrosia had more than enough space for everyone. Donal counted almost twenty empty seats in this room, and the brochure said Ambrosia had two other dining rooms.

Not that another restaurant could have been as spectacular. The statuary Greek gods were rendered so well that Donal expected music from Apollo's lyre. Illusions provided a breathtaking view. From the peak of Mount Olympus, Donal could see ships at sail on gentle seas, ancient Greek towns at ease by firelight far below, and even shepherds tending their flocks on distant hillsides. A tiny red speck among the faint stars above marked the position of the *Horizon Cusp*, relative to Earth. Further enchantments gave the wait staff the appearance of satyrs and nymphs, albeit dressed to convey elegance rather than lasciviousness. Ambrosia would have been a perfect place to bring a date, and Donal was joined only by an empty chair.

There sat Li Hua, right next to Mr. Mancuso. Her black evening dress covered her from ankle to wrist to throat, letting its contours tell its story. Perhaps Donal should have dressed up for dinner, but then, she had company and he did not, even if her meal was a business dinner.

Don't stare! The guards gave Donal suspicious glances, as though they expected him to try to assassinate one of the oh-so-important people at the center table.

Maybe he should eat room service for the rest of the trip. He might even persuade the kitchen to deliver to the Observation Deck. A good view of the stars while he ate -- Donal could do worse.

Wait, was that quick smile from Li Hua meant for Donal?

AT THE HEAD OF THE CENTER TABLE, JACOBS TRIED TO LOOK INTERESTED in the prattling of Mancuso.

"I love the feel of being in space," said the 4M business magnate.

"*At* space," said Jacobs. "If you were *in* space, you would be drifting outside the ship." *If that's what you want, Starchaser Spacelines would be happy to accommodate you.*

"It's the crowning achievement of mankind," Mancuso continued, "to break our reliance on the planet of our birth and go to space, surviving by our wits and power alone. What greater testimony to humanity can there be? Am I right, Hassan?"

"It is glorious, but would you not miss the feel of firm ground under your feet? The approximations we construct in rooms like this one are wondrous, but can they replace the smell of dirt and grass and sand? Filling your lungs with natural air and drinking deeply of water from a stream?"

"Small price to pay, and we can always visit it. Life in the vac is our destiny."

The "vac." The media invented that word, and tourists thought it made them sound like spacers. It derived from the Pre-Rise days, when scientists insisted that space was a vacuum. As far as Jacobs knew, no one could say for certain what space consisted of. He had heard Machado use the word "aether," but he might have been joking. Mash had a strange sense of humor, even for a mage. He even once wrote a personnel report in Pig Latin.

Whatever space consisted of, Jacobs noticed that no one volunteered to step outside the ship without a safe suit.

"What do you think, Captain?" Al Rashid asked his question with quiet intensity, as though his interest were sincere, not part of some hypothetical discussion. "You spend most of your days at space. Do you miss the feel of dirt under your feet? The taste of pure air on your tongue?"

"I was a seaman before I was a spaceman. The land has never called to me. 'All I ask is a tall ship and a star to steer her by.'"

"That's what I'm talking about, Hassan. Space. Complete control, don't you think?"

"Space has no history, Donatello. No ties, but no connections. A man too long at space loses his sense of his fellows from Earth. Meaning no offense, Captain. To sail the spacelanes is a very different way of life."

"No, you're right. I don't know what you landlubbers are talking about half the time." People laughed, so Jacobs smiled and pretended he had been joking.

FRESH LOBSTER IN SPACE: DONAL COULD NOT BELIEVE IT WHEN HE SAW it on the menu, included as though an afterthought in the section titled "Fare from Foreign Lands." This seemed even more miraculous than Earth magic on Mars. The spells needed to preserve a taste like lobster required a delicate touch. The meal on his plate had to have come from Earth, but it tasted better than the day's-catch lobster Donal had enjoyed once at a conference in Monterey, which meant alchemy had preserved it for twelve days at a minimum. Ambrosia went to a great deal of trouble and expense for its menu.

Donal offered a prayer of thanks to the Dagda that he had not had to pay for his own ticket or his meals. But then, IIX would never have sprung for Ambrosia on a regular trip, much less Donal's larger cabin. The meals must have been courtesy of Mr. Mancuso or his counterpart.

Donal glanced at the center table and noticed that a swarthy man across from Li Hua paid her far too much attention, with smiles and easy conversation. *Focus, Donal. Why should you care who the lethal woman flirts with?*

Donal could almost hear Fionn echo the call to focus, reminding Donal that he should take this dinner as an opportunity to assess possible threats. He considered calling Fionn, but from the stern expressions of the nearest guards, any spell he cast might draw an attack.

Any spell, perhaps, but not necessarily any magic...

Donal refused to tip his activity through patterned breathing, and shifted his awareness while drawing only his customary half-deep breaths. In scant moments he achieved a state that had taken minutes only days before. He smiled his pride into the distance and wondered what else he could practice at odd moments.

Donal saw little magic on the diners. Li Hua and the swarthy man were magicians, as were two of the guards and one of the ship's watch. Those last three were specialists though, and felt like Initiates. They lacked the strength to have done graduate-level work. Donal could tell a mage with an Associate's degree from one who held a Bachelor's if he could spot the telltales. An Initiate carried power that looked focused but narrow, compared to a Journeyman, whose Bachelor's degree provided a broader education in Thaumaturgy. Personal training could elevate a magician beyond his formal education, so Donal would only know the magicians' capabilities for certain if he made a deep assessment and examined each of their signatures, but a public dinner was hardly the time and place.

Besides, he considered a deep investigation rude unless he had a pressing need.

Li Hua and Swarthy each wore two or three enchanted toys about their persons, and every member of the ship's watch had a club that carried spells. The clubs were probably Pacifiers, which could put a man down without even hitting him. A near miss would do the job.

A magician in the ship's watch looked up at Donal, and he turned his attention back to his excellent lobster. *Just eating my dinner, not checking out your magic.*

TWO BOTTLES OF WINE WITH DINNER, AND NOW MANCUSO ORDERED A *digestif*. Did he always drink like this, or was it a statement? Jacobs noticed that al Rashid's party drank no alcohol, and of Mancuso's assistants only the blonde woman, Stevens, drank beyond her second glass of wine. Jacobs himself stopped after one glass, enough to be social but no more. Not while eating with the passengers.

"Captain," asked al Rashid, "you have commanded many vessels, have you not?"

"I have captained five ships at sea, ten in the air, and ten at space. I have served on almost three times as many."

"But where," broke in Mancuso, "can you go from being a captain?" Al Rashid's mouth tightened into a line. Jacobs picked up his water glass. Mancuso continued, "Once you've hit the top, the whole ship is yours, don't you need another ship? Be a captain of captains? An admiral?"

"In the navy, yes, but in private industry you go into business for yourself."

"Exactly!" Mancuso started thumping his index finger on the table. "You. Must. Expand. Sail the seas until you can sail over them! Sail the skies until you can sail over them! Then you go to space! The whole damned universe, Hassan. That's what I'm—"

Al Rashid spoke over Mancuso for the first time that evening, in a clipped tone that suggested he was equally accustomed to authority.

"My question, Captain, is this. You have captained many designs of ship - what is the best location for the bridge? Where is the most effective center for command?"

Mancuso started to scoff, but Jacobs replied before he could interrupt. A passenger had finally asked a question worth answering. Perhaps he should mention it in his log.

"The bridge can be fore, aft or amidships, so long as it is well enough designed and connected to receive the information it needs to issue commands throughout the ship. I prefer a central location; less distance for orders to travel by foot, if the internal comm system should fail. That's why the *Horizon Cusp's* bridge is amidships. The most important factor, though, is that the bridge cannot be set close to engineering."

"Why is that?" asked al Rashid while Mancuso paid unsteady attention.

"Because if another ship destroys the bridge, engineering must remain intact to function as a secondary bridge."

"Now there's a happy thought, Hassan. If our bridge gets destroyed, we'll still have engineering. If we survive to get there."

"The analogy is flawed, Donatello, because a ship can have only one captain."

Conversation along the table faded with its echo and the two businessmen regarded one another, al Rashid with a cool glare and Mancuso with a more level gaze than Jacobs thought the man could have managed just then.

Jacobs lifted his napkin, signaling Goldberg to be ready. Jacobs heard the chief crack his neck, so loud in the silence it reminded him of his youth and the sound of a sloop's mast breaking in a storm.

At last, al Rashid spoke.

"But I believe I am ready to retire for the evening. Captain," he said, though he kept his eyes on Mancuso, "Thank you for the meal, for your company, and for your excellent thoughts on ship design. I bid you all good night."

"Good night, Hassan," said Mancuso, "and don't worry. We can make this work."

Al Rashid and his assistants left together. Their guards provided cover while Mancuso's watched them, and Jacobs could feel Goldberg's attention shift with the movement. Past the guards the courier seemed to linger over his dessert. Or maybe he just enjoyed his chocolate cake more than most passengers.

———

THE LOBSTER WAS DELICIOUS, BUT THE CHOCOLATE CAKE TASTED SO good it must have come from faerie. At that thought, Donal's hand stopped with its fork halfway from plate to mouth. Some reflexes from childhood were faster than rational thought. He narrowed his eyes at the rich, moist dessert. The cake seemed solid enough, and it smelled right...

Donal laughed, and three days of tension poured out of him. His terror at the spaceport explosion, confusion at his getaway, paranoia at feeling hunted and trapped in a safe house - all this and more pushed his laughter near the edge of hysteria. He clamped one hand over his mouth and another around his belly, forkful of cake forgotten on the plate as he struggled to conceal the eruption, but nearby guards whipped around, their hands reaching for absent weapons. One look at Donal shaking with laughter turned them back to their employers' table, where conversation seemed to have hit a lull. Donal hoped he had not caused it.

Deep, steady breaths now, not for magic but for control. How many stories had his grandmothers told him about faerie and the *daoine sidhe*? Hundreds, at least. Donal could probably recite half of them from memory. But why would he think of them now? Perhaps it was because he sat alone among opposing armies that discussed either war or peace or both. Donal felt so out of place among such tension that he might as well have wandered into faerie.

Still, his meal at Ambrosia might have had magic involved in its preparation, but it was not faerie food. He knew he had not crossed into faerie anyway. Every story Donal had ever been told about mortals venturing into the Fae realm had involved travel through a mist. The *Horizon Cusp* might have been at space, but it had passed through no mist.

Donal was not in faerie. There was no glamour in his food. His cake was safe to eat.

Back in control, Donal saw that one group had left, and that Mr. Mancuso's group made its way to the door. He could not see Li Hua, nor the captain, and even the ship's watch had left their tables. Donal would have to finish his meal alone.

He turned his attention back to the cake, but a voice interrupted him when that forkful of cake was again halfway to his mouth.

"Excuse me, Donal Cuthbert." Pinyin-Lung, the smoky, sinuous spirit dragon that served as Li Hua's familiar, floated in the air before Donal. "Tai Shi Li Hua requests the honor of a conversation, if you would be so kind as to meet her on the Observation Deck in one hour."

"I'll be there."

"Thank you," said the dragon with a dip of its head. "I will inform Tai Shi Li Hua." It slipped away through the air and faded from sight as it left. Donal took the opportunity to practice and shifted his awareness to watch it whip back and forth like a water snake as it flew out of the room.

Donal smiled and finished his cake.

10

THE LARGE, OVERSTUFFED CHAIR ONCE SAT IN THE HOUSE OF JACOBS' grandfather. It had been reupholstered five times, held a place of honor in four residences, and finally found a permanent home on its third starship. No seat could be more comfortable for a bit of light reading at the end of a long day. Even a captain needed a place of his own to be off-duty for just a few minutes.

Jacobs sat, closed his eyes, and unclenched muscles clear down to his toes. He savored the quiet, then reached for his novel.

Someone knocked on the door.

Jacobs considered ignoring it, although he could not pretend to be asleep or elsewhere. He knew his reading lamp, a brass, oil-burning antique, would give him away. He had checked once, and its light could be seen from at least three paces down the hall.

The knock persisted. Tight, possibly urgent.

The captain sighed and set down his book. "Come," he called.

Goldberg hauled himself into the room and managed to approximate standing at attention. Jacobs felt fierce pride burn through his chest that a man a third his age looked as tired as he himself felt. At eighty-five, Jacobs was not yet too old to command.

"Saul, you look like you've been pulling double shifts on the Flying Dutchman."

"Sorry to bother you, sir," said the chief, noticing where his captain sat. "But what I saw at dinner tonight looked like two gang leaders on the verge of throwing down. I'd like permission to have Cromartie ward the crew quarters, starting with yours and Kris'."

"Have your Initiate ward whatever you like, Chief, but for this trip only, and don't let him put up anything that will interfere with crew business. Anything else?"

"No, sir."

Goldberg let loose a yawn that must have started from his heels. Jacobs fought not to get caught in its tide, but yielded an answer. No reading tonight.

"Then get some rest, Saul."

THE OBSERVATION DECK WAS DOWN IN THE GRYPHON'S BELLY, A PLACE where the hull had been rendered transparent from the inside to offer an unimpeded view to all sides and below. Gunmetal gray walkways led to small, opaque rooms of relief for those unnerved by apparent exposure to space.

Donal stood far to the stern, fascinated by the view. He once thought of space as a vast blackness peppered with intermittent points of starlight, but out here away from the influence of a single planet, he could see sweeping panoramas of blues, reds, greens - places some great painter had tested a blend before applying it with precision to a planet. So many shapes and colors, and each or any might be a key reference point for navigation or perhaps a point of power to draw on for certain types of magic. Donal had heard that a thaumaturgy center in Livermore researched the spells and sources of space, as did the National Center for Stellar Research and Travel.

"I read once," said a soft voice behind him, "that if you make a wish into one of those red spiral nebulas, you can turn unrequited love into the possibility of happiness."

Donal turned to find Li Hua standing less than a full meter from him, still lovely in her evening dress. How could she have snuck up on him in those heels?

She stepped up beside him without a sound, still staring at the view.

"Whenever I travel to Earth I spend as much time down here as I can. The constantly shifting beauty is mesmerizing, and I always make a wish on behalf of a stranger's unrequited love. Just in case."

"I never made it down here on my way to Mars. I thought the observation wall on the Main Deck was impressive. I had no idea." Donal shook his head in amazement. "Do you go to Earth often?"

"Every couple of months. Mr. Mancuso usually has some big meeting to attend, and I take the opportunity to check in with the home office." She smiled. "That's in San Francisco, by the way."

"What a coincidence. IIX operates out of San Francisco."

"Practically neighbors."

They turned to face one another, and Donal forgot about the view. Li Hua stood so close that he could smell her subtle jasmine perfume, feel her warmth. Donal felt his blood rush through his veins. He yearned to close the gap.

Donal, you saw her kill people. What are you thinking?

"I got your note." She smiled. "It was sweet."

For the life of him, Donal could not remember what he had written.

"I did want to see you before you left," she continued, "but Mr. Mancuso had us tied up in early meetings. I hadn't even known I was coming on this trip."

Donal longed to touch her, to stoke her smooth, reddish cheek, to smile into her sincere eyes. She had asked to meet him, invited him down here. Perhaps her flirting on Mars had been more than business. Perhaps she had been impressed by his knowledge of wine and Enochian magic. But still....

"Why did you kill those people?"

Li Hua drew back a step. "What people?"

"On Mars, when we were being chased. What you did to that runner."

"Oh," she said as comprehension smoothed her features. She put a gentle hand on Donal's shoulder. "You've never killed, and I respect that. But the cost of doing business on Mars is sometimes paid in blood." She shook her head. "If the competition thinks you're weak, they push, and you have to fight harder just to keep what's yours already." She smiled. "Remember, it *was* self-defense."

"Does that make it right?"

"Excuse me?" said Li Hua. "Would you rather I'd let them kill us?"

"I just wish there had been another way."

"It's easy to wonder that later, but in the moment you do what's necessary to survive."

"Even if it means killing?"

Li Hua blew out a breath, her stance more rigid. "Even when it means that they die so we get to live. Sometimes it's what the job requires."

"Why do this at all then? There are other ways to make money."

Her mouth drew tight, her nostrils flared. She said quietly, "Not all of us aspire to research, Donal. I like action. I like excitement. This job offers me both and keeps me challenged, physically and magically."

"But the killing—"

"I never said I like to kill. I don't murder. But if someone tries to kill me I'll damn well stop them by any means necessary."

"I hate to interrupt," said a voice from Donal's left.

Donal and Li Hua turned together and saw a woman dressed in the uniform of the ship's watch, who grimaced in discomfort and held her hands out in apology.

"Your Mr. Mancuso is calling all his advisors together and sending his guards out to find them." She focused on Li Hua. "Since you were sitting at his table, I figured that meant you, and maybe you didn't want his guards to walk in and see..." she trailed off. She shrugged again and left.

"I don't see why she hurried off," said Li Hua. "There was obviously nothing to interrupt."

She turned to walk away, but Donal said, "Li Hua, wait. I didn't mean for this to become an ethics debate."

She kept walking and said, without looking back, "Neither did I."

"Can we try again?"

She pulled the lever to call the bubble. "I'm not sure there's a point."

She stepped into the cage, and the bubble took her away.

Donal stared, then called forth Fionn.

"I smell jasmine," said Fionn, tilting its emerald head at its master.

"Li Hua was here."

"I also smell frustration."

"The conversation did not go well."

The spirit deerhound twitched its ears forward and back. The two of them stood silent for some time and watched the stars pass.

11

THE NEXT DAY JACOBS SAT IN HIS CAPTAIN'S CHAIR AND REVIEWED THE latest status updates for the *Horizon Cusp* by touching various parts of its miniature gryphon display. He imagined commanding a ship was similar to conducting an orchestra: he set the rhythm, paid close attention, and issued corrections to bring the best performances out of the different sections. When they came together just right, like now, he got to enjoy the harmony. Jacobs' peers had almost all retired, and though he considered it annually he had yet to find something he loved to do more than oversee ship operations.

He smiled. Twelve hundred hours and all was well. Time for a treat.

Jacobs touched the engineering section and turned his finger to open communications. "Bridge to Engineering."

Moments later, Jang's puzzled face melted into view above the display.

"Engineering, aye."

"Report."

"Five by five, Captain."

Jacobs waited for Jang to go on, but she did not. Her eyes shifted. Her cheek twitched.

"Chief, whatever that project is, I expect it to be in your full report."

"How did you ... I mean, aye, Captain."

"I also wanted to have a word with you about the Deception Drive's performance this trip."

Jang's jaw clenched tight enough that Jacobs could almost hear her teeth grind, but she squeezed her eyes shut and slowly opened them. Her jaw unclenched.

"Aye, sir?"

"I expect you to keep one ear trained on the Deception Drive's song at all times, because we will not be reducing speed as originally discussed."

Puzzlement again, her brow drawn together and down, tongue flicking against her teeth, visible thanks to a loosened jaw. Jacobs hoped Jang never took up poker. She would find it an expensive hobby.

"Sir, the charter is no longer a ten-day flight?"

"It's a ten-day flight. But we can't test the drive properly if we give it a soft run, now can we? I've re-routed the trip to account for the extra days. I expect you to hold a good speed and keep us on schedule."

Jang's mouth clamped shut, but her whole aspect sang with powerful joy. Jacobs could see her eyes stare past him as her mind looked ahead to tests and measurements, schedules and maintenance: opportunities she thought she lost when she believed that the *Horizon Cusp* would run at little better than half its cruising speed for the entire trip.

"I imagine I've just made your day a busy one, Chief, so I'll leave you to it. Bridge out."

As Jang's image faded, she snapped an honest-to-God salute. Jacobs smiled. That was a sight he would hold onto for some time. Each member of his crew reacted differently to Jacobs' little surprises, but all the responses were gratifying. Tunold would let out a roar that he insisted was the word "yes," though Jacobs could not distinguish any letters in it. Goldberg would pump his fist and buy the captain a bottle of whiskey. Kelly would actually smile. It was the only time the yeoman smiled, and Jacobs felt certain that each smile measured the exact same dimensions.

Jacobs stepped down the stairs from his chair and began to pace the ringed walkway that surrounded the bridge duty stations. Time for a status check. "Helm, report."

"Steady as she goes, Captain. Last triangulation showed us exactly on course."

"Scanners, report."

"Clear space, Captain. By the charts."

"No signs of another ship?"

"No, sir. Should there be?"

"I'm not expecting company for dinner." Jacobs did not mention that his official flight log listed the extended schedule, but not the change of route. This was an old precaution Jacobs had used since his Navy days whenever some aspect of a voyage made him suspicious, such as multiple reports of curiously well-informed pirates, a squabble in port with a vindictive rival, or a "business" charter that included three times as many security agents as businessmen. Unofficially rerouting his course carried some risk because if anything went wrong, no search team would know where to hunt for them. However, it ensured that no one could plan to intercept them, and sometimes the extra peace of mind was worth the smaller margin of error for the trip. It had occurred to Jacobs that the *Beamrunner* might not have been wrecked by an accident.

Jacobs gave the stars a sardonic smile. Following his old precaution this time was probably an old man's paranoia. The thirty bodyguards might have been a show of force, a negotiating tactic between top professionals. Any tension Jacobs noticed between Mancuso and al Rashid might have been bluster, a psychological game to gain some small advantage. Everything about the trip was probably calculated to impress one of them or the other, no matter how many resources the two wasted in the process.

The captain paused on the walkway, stared out at the colors of space. At least this voyage was good for Starchaser Spacelines. Higher profit when they needed cash flow, and with so few berths in use the remainder could be overhauled and examined in flight, wasting less time in port before the *Horizon Cusp* next took space. Also, a first private contract might lead to others. Mancuso and al Rashid represented only two companies, so surely dozens of others could afford a charter once Zoltan explained the benefits to them. Jacobs had to give his partner credit: the man might have been a miserable failure as a spacer, but he could sell passage to a lacuna.

If everything went well on this flight, the two of them might not just save the business, but expand it. Jacobs imagined adding three or four smaller ships - escort class if the *Horizon Cusp* were a cruiser - to ferry private clients to the Moon, Mars, and even Venus as that colony expanded. Venus might be ready for tourist travel soon. Jacobs could become the first man to captain a commercial passenger vessel to Venus. Jacobs smiled and pumped his fist. That would make a solid finish to a fine career. If he could accomplish that, Captain John Jacobs might finally feel ready to retire, as though he had earned the right to spend the rest of his years lounging and reading. He logged the idea. He would need to start the necessary research and planning as soon as he reached Earth.

But first, he had to get his ship to Earth.

Jacobs returned to his station and braced himself. Now to find out if Mancuso and al Rashid prepared to fight or negotiate. He touched the gryphon's heart, turned his finger, and said, "Security, report."

"Light airs, Captain."

Jacobs popped his ears to clear them. Had he heard that right? The phrase itself was fine - Jacobs had ordered security to use code phrases in official comm reports. Magic could make someone sound like Goldberg, even look like Goldberg, but not give him Goldberg's knowledge. Still, 'light airs' was an old Naval term for a gentle breeze, not worth deigning to call a wind. "Say again?"

"Light airs, sir." Goldberg shook his head as though he did not believe it either. "I've checked with my guys three times and they keep telling me that the wind has not picked up."

Bluster then. God save me from politicians and businessmen. Perhaps

Jacobs would have time on this trip to begin plotting a viable route to Venus.

———

BREAKFAST AND A MORNING DIP IN THE POOL KILLED A FEW HOURS, BUT Donal still had the whole afternoon ahead of him. He did not feel like sitting through a show or playing a game by himself. He could have read, but he had spent days reading. He wanted to talk to Li Hua, but her meeting would keep her busy all day, if she would agree to see him at all.

Wait a moment. While the two businesses met, Donal had most of the ship to himself. He was left to his own devices, with hours to spend howsoever he chose. Excitement bubbled out of him in a laugh: time to experiment. Donal had a theory about the relationship between space and the position of the spirit element in Dee's tablets. If he could develop a strong sense of the magic of space, he could establish personal benchmarks for later reference in his Enochian research and add depth to his whole graduate thesis.

Donal called a bubble for a quick trip down the water shaft to the Observation Deck. He spent half an hour standing in different spots, looking for as complete a view as he could find, with only the barest obstruction from relief zones. He also sought a position where as few spells crossed as possible, to minimize interference. Not that Donal had anything dangerous in mind, but he needed to harmonize with the magic around him. He intended to examine space itself, and protective spells could cloud his view.

Donal called forth Fionn. The *cú sidhe* looked around from Donal's chosen location and said, "What will you be sending? This point is dangerous, if shattered." Its bright green eyes tracked the air about Donal, then it added, "Forgive me for saying so, but if that is your intention, you have not the power to accomplish it."

Donal thought about that.

"Does anyone on this ship?"

"No," said Fionn slowly, tilting its head as it weighed the matter, "I do not believe so. Not from this location."

"All I want to send is my awareness. The Earth has power. Mars has power. But what about space itself? I want a look at it firsthand."

"Shall I tether?"

"I shouldn't need it." Donal felt uncertainty creep along his forearms. "I won't touch anything, just look."

"You have done this before?"

"Not in space."

"Safer to tether. Something may touch you."

Donal agreed, but dread of what might touch him gnawed at his concentration. He imagined vast, ancient spirits lying dormant until the inquisitive proximity of an eager young mind supplied them with dinner. He had to resort to formal breathing patterns to clear his thoughts, shift his awareness, and strengthen his control over the movement of power. All life generated power, and the same flow that pumped Donal's heart and carried his thoughts exceeded his physical needs, filled him to overflowing. Collegiate magical training included methods to trap that overflow and contain it as a ready supply for whenever the need arose. The efficiency of this process grew with time and practice, thus an advanced magician appeared more powerful when viewed from the right state of mind.

That power allowed one to cast spells without an outside source or the aid of a spirit. But such a flow of power did not keep well in an organized structure, so spells stagnated and decayed unless a magician maintained them through spirits, alchemy or repetition. Spells could make a ship like the *Horizon Cusp* fly through space, but bound spirits and alchemy made that flight practical.

This simple acknowledgment of the process of magic served as a sort of prayer for Donal, a way to prepare himself before a risky, if not dangerous act. He uttered a more literal prayer aloud, asking the gods of his ancestors to watch over him during his effort.

No circle for this sort of spell, no containment or exclusion. Such procedures would have been important for a direct spirit contact, or for a summoning or binding ritual. Instead Donal needed harmony.

He sat on the floor in his chosen spot. Fionn guarded him from behind, jaws open and teeth ever so lightly touching the back of its master's neck.

Donal reached within himself for his core, the spark of essential Donal-ness inside him. Once he held it, he stretched above himself into infinity, then below himself the same way, not sensing or projecting, but finding a view of the universe that would place him, for a moment, at the center. Holding that image in mind, Donal repeated the process to his left, then his right, before him, then behind him. In the six basic directions, he touched infinity. He became the center.

Now his awareness. Donal observed the spells that established a zone of safety in the vastness of space: held him to the deck and provided air to his lungs, light to his eyes, sound to his ears, even clean smells to his nose. Donal felt the spells, acknowledged them, calibrated his senses for them, and ignored them. He reached beyond.

Into the void his thoughts went. Space felt not quite warm and not quite empty, as though Donal touched the memory of steam. He reached beyond. The colors had flavor out here. The reds tasted like the disappointment of past opportunities missed. The blues tasted like the unexpected joy of love offered freely in the wasteland. The greens....

Wait. A spirit roamed here: timeless, strong, tremendous. At times in his life Donal had felt insignificant, but next to this great thing Donal knew he was a speck. Better to retreat before it noticed him.

Too late.

Donal felt Fionn yank the tether as a spirit tendril stretched for him. Darkness engulfed Donal.

SHARP, STINGING PAIN WOKE DONAL. HIS CHEEK BURNED WITH THE aftermath of a terrific slap. A pudgy Latino man leaned over him, hand raised and ready. Donal put up his hands. "I'm awake! I'm awake!"

"I can see that, you damned fool." The man looked familiar, but Donal could not place him. The man let loose a stream of invective in words that were not quite Spanish — Portuguese maybe — that ended with, "and what were you playing at?"

"I had this theory about the Enochian spirit element and the spirits of space—"

"I don't want to hear it. I have just spent the last twenty minutes setting back down what you called up, and my duties as ship's mage do not include cleaning up your mess. Now listen to me, my little Journeyman, because I'm only going to say this once. If you try one more experiment, just one, that reaches outside the safety of my spells, I am going to make you wish I only had you arrested and your license revoked. Do I make myself perfectly clear?"

"Yes, Magister."

"At least you remember your manners." The ship's mage shook his head as he walked away and left Donal sprawled on the Observation Deck. "It's all under control," the Magister said to the various guards and watch officers in the background. "Let the damned fool be. I think he learned his lesson."

Donal swayed to a sitting position.

"Magister, what was that thing?"

"Oh, no," came the harsh reply. "Ill-conceived, failed experiments do not yield information. I suggest you crack a book."

12

Jacobs occasionally lamented his thin, weak office door. He savored the image a door thick enough to have meaning, one that could guard a private conversation and keep secrets from a curious pressed ear. Perhaps even conceal the light of an oil lamp. But on a ship such a door would add pointless weight and a potential hazard in an emergency.

And if he had had a thick door, Jacobs would never have heard the timid tap-tap-tap intended to pass for a knock.

He continued reviewing the maintenance reports. Let the courier wait. The delay would generate more anxiety in the boy and emphasize their relative positions. Jacobs could also save time later if he finished the reports now.

He turned the last page as Cuthbert assayed his knock again. From what Jacobs could tell, the cleaning and repair crews were taking too much time with the empty cabins. He would have to have Tunold talk to their chief. Jacobs made a note in his log then looked up at his door. "Come," he said.

The door opened and in came the courier, a slight young man, pale as a high sun, his head hung as though he expected to be thrown overboard for his crime. He also looked ill-used, as though he had been towed through an asteroid field without so much as a safe suit to protect him. Perhaps this would not take long.

Donal trudged into an office as big as his stateroom, with the captain himself seated at a huge wooden desk. Five shelves behind the old man were full of books and charts, not crammed, but organized into sections. Donal could not muster the enthusiasm to look over their titles. He had been summoned to account for his crime, and Captain Jacobs had the stern jaw and pitiless eyes of a hanging judge.

Donal stood before the desk, not daring to sit unless invited. He wished he could sit. He felt as though his familiar had yanked his body through the hull when it saved him from that spirit.

"You wanted to see me, sir?"

This was the sort of moment when Jacobs wished he smoked. His first captain, Captain Nemeth, used his pipe as much for conversational effect as for smoking. This would have been a perfect opportunity to tamp tobacco into a pipe and light it, except that Jacobs could not tolerate the taste or smell of tobacco.

Instead, Jacobs closed his report displays and looked over the courier. The boy's posture shrank with fear, but the lad held his jaw high now, ready to take whatever befell him. Jacobs had to bite his cheek to hold a straight face as he recognized the pose from his own youth. This boy was a magician, not a fighter, but he had guts.

If Jacobs' son Carl had lived, Carl's son might be Cuthbert's age.

Jacobs hardened his eyes to scare away the threat of tears. *Not the time to get sentimental, Old Man. This boy put your ship at risk.* There would be plenty of time to think about Rhonda and Carl before bed, as Jacobs did every night.

"I've already heard Mr. Machado's summary, Mr. Cuthbert. Is there anything you would like to add?"

WHAT THE HELL WAS DONAL SUPPOSED TO SAY TO THAT? HE HAD NOT seen any report. Was he supposed to guess what the ship's mage had said about him? Donal took a deep breath and tried to hold himself upright while the room threatened to spin. He could get through this if he treated it as an exam, as though a professor had asked a deliberately vague question. A direct question could lead to the right answer, but a vague question left a student a panorama of ways to expose his ignorance.

Donal refused to twist and writhe like some half-bound spirit. He rolled his shoulders and ignored the exhausted tremor that tried to take hold of his knees and the nervous trickle of cold sweat that slipped down between his shoulder blades. He drew himself up as straight as he could, and spoke.

"Sir, I meant neither harm nor disrespect to you or the ship's mage by my actions, and I in no way wished to endanger the ship. The greatest tool any magician has is information, and it is in our nature to seek it when we may. I found myself with several hours at my disposal and wished to expand my understanding of how magic operates outside the influence of planets.

"In attempting to increase my knowledge, I did not give proper respect to my ignorance. I applied a legitimate technique and approach with the proper personal safeguards, but without considering the circumstances or the potential danger to others. I did not consider that the enchantments on this ship might include spells of obfuscation to minimize the attention it might garner from spirits native to high space. I did not consider that my actions might draw the unwanted attention of such a spirit, or that it might be powerful enough to threaten your ship.

"I did not consider that my personal safeguards would render me unable to cry a warning or muster a defense of the ship.

"I understand the depth of my folly, and I know what I should have done differently." Donal started to wonder how long the captain would let him talk. The sweat on his spine had been joined by more on his forehead and palms, and still more ringing his collar. "I should have consulted the ship's mage before taking any action that reached beyond the safety of his spells. The ship's mage is the ranking magician on site, both in position and in experience. I should have consulted him before risking his work.

"Also, I should have considered that outside of a planetary range, the ship's mage is the legal authority in all matters concerning thaumaturgy, and I should properly have secured his approval prior to conducting any magical experiments within his demesne."

Donal had to check himself from touching his left shoulder with his right hand at the end of the recitation. That salute should only be offered to a senior magician.

JACOBS SCRUTINIZED THE BOY, BUT COULD SEE NO TRACE OF MOCKERY IN the courier's manner, nor hear any in his tone. Maybe all magicians were longwinded. Lord knew Machado could expound at length about any aspect of his craft, and so could Jang.

The boy sounded sincere, and he said all of the right things. Almost.

"There are two errors in your thinking," Jacobs said, and Cuthbert startled. "First, and most important, Mr. Machado is not the legal authority regarding magic on this ship. I am the legal authority in everything relating to this ship, including magic and alchemy. As ship's mage, Mr. Machado serves as my consultant on all matters relating to thaumaturgy, including legal, but the final word is mine. In your case, I am the one who must decide whether you return to your cabin or to the brig, and whether or not charges should be pressed when we reach Earth."

Cuthbert's eyebrows threatened his hairline.

"On that point," Jacobs continued, "I will reassure you. I have decided to take Mr. Machado's recommendation and not punish you beyond a warning. This is the first time you have shown any sign of making trouble for me or my crew, and since this is your second voyage with us that suggests that you generally behave yourself. Also, this is an unusual trip, and I can understand how having so much of the ship to yourself for so many hours at a time made the possibilities seem limitless.

"But make no mistake." Jacobs rose, leaned forward, hands on his desk, and looked the boy in the eye. "Pull a stunt like that again and you might not live to regret it. Understood?"

"Understood, sir. Thank you, sir."

The boy's voice held steady and he did not look away from Jacobs' gaze. Good signs for Cuthbert's future.

"Good. There's enough tension on this ship already without you adding to it. The IIX contract is good for both of us, and I want us to have a long, trouble-free relationship. Dismissed."

DONAL STARTED FOR THE DOOR, BUT WAS STOPPED SHORT BY realization. He turned back. "Sir, you said there were two errors in my thinking. What was the other one?"

The captain flipped though papers, and did not look at Donal when he spoke. "You said that you were unable to raise an alarm. That's not true. Your familiar contacted Mr. Machado even before his safeguards or the ship's scanners detected anything amiss."

"Oh. Of course. Thank you, sir."

As soon as he had closed the door behind him, Donal leaned against it and fought the urge to bang his head through it. So much for keeping Fionn a secret.

13

The afternoon grew quiet again on the bridge, and Jacobs' thoughts turned once more to hopes for the future. The problem with adding smaller ships for business travel would be their lack of entertainment. Passengers could not keep themselves busy for very long, and reasonable ticket prices would allow only a small budget for illusions, games and the like. That might be sufficient for a short jaunt to the moon, but a seven day trip to Mars? Boredom would set in and trouble would follow.

Like today, one kid in his twenties with a Bachelor's degree got bored and put the whole ship at risk. Jacobs shook his head. At least Machado had been able to handle it.

Magic. When there was a problem with the old ships, you organized teams and attacked it with manpower: bailed water, repaired leaks, pulled against rough seas and weather, fought off threats. A captain could understand a ship's problems and a crew could work together to solve them. These days either you had a good enough mage or you died. Maybe you could organize a couple of magicians in an emergency, but even then they had to have their own pecking order and the rest of the crew could do nothing but hope. When that wasn't enough....

Jacobs noted in his log to make sure his crew had enough work to keep them busy. With the reduced passenger load, support personnel might have too much idle time. A bored crew could present a greater hazard than bored passengers.

Ms. Jefferson, who managed the ship's communications web, and Mr. Grabowski, who manned the scanner displays, interrupted Jacobs' thoughts at the same time.

"Captain, security has triggered a full alert."

"Captain, the scanners have picked up another bogey. Two of them this time!"

"Details, Mr. Grabowski. Ms. Jefferson, get me Goldberg and Machado." Full alert would signal an alarm throughout the ship, ordering passengers back to their cabins. That might not be enough for these groups. Jacobs spun in his seat. "Mr. Tunold, get down to that meeting and make sure those idiots go back to their cabins."

"Aye, sir." Tunold jumped up from his station, pushed out of the bridge through the curved door where the transparent bulkhead met the floor, and loped away down the sloping passage.

"Two bogeys incoming, sir," said Grabowski. "Creatures, not ships. One larger, one smaller, both from port like last time. Huge. Slippery, like eels or worms. One is bigger than we are."

"I have Machado, sir," said Jefferson, who had her hands in what looked like a snarl of spaghetti made from strands of blue light, but each strand was a line of communication. She held a junction pinched between two fingers.

"Good," said Jacobs as the image began to form at his station. "Mash, what the hell is going on down there?"

"Please excuse me, Captain John Jacobs." The image that formed was not the ship's mage, but his familiar: a jaguar the color of rain clouds. Not a good sign: it only spoke for Mash when he needed all his focus. "Ronaldo Machado is unavailable at this time. He asked me to tell you that the zuglodon is back, and that it brought a friend. He has commandeered Initiate Aaron Cromartie from the ship's watch, and they oppose the zuglodons from the Observation Deck."

"Tell him I want updates as soon as I can get them." The captain cut the connection and turned back to his bridge crew. "Goldberg next, Ms. Jefferson. Mr. Grabowski, I'm still waiting for my details."

"Sorry, sir," said Grabowski, who grabbed his displays in a series of movements that would show his mind images and analyses from perspectives outside the ship. "I can't get a solid fix on these things. The larger creature appears to be the same one as last time, but it's coming in more aggressively. It never got this close last time. The other is sort of hiding behind it."

"Keep trying, Mister. I want to know what we're facing. Mr. Burke, take us up to three-quarters speed and prepare to evade."

Jacobs brought up his three-dimensional map of the region within an hour's travel, and calculated where the zuglodons had come from and what course corrections might take the *Horizon Cusp* out of their hunting grounds. If they were hunters.

A deep reverberation rocked the ship. Impact, Jacobs knew from the feel: port side, just forward of amidships.

———

"FEEL BETTER?" FIONN ASKED AS DONAL STRETCHED AND LOOKED around. He had chosen a late room service lunch after his meeting with the captain, but the nap had caught him unprepared. Donal did not consider naps a constructive use of time.

"I guess so." Donal stretched again. He had lost the ache in most of his muscles, but his arms tingled at the thought of tucking himself back into his pillow. "Did I miss anything?"

"Twice someone probed at the door to determine that you remained within. The probe carried no malice, and did not attempt to breech the wards, so I allowed it to proceed unchallenged. Is this as you would have wished?"

"Yeah." Donal rubbed his face awake. He yawned to a standing position. "Probably just the ship's mage making sure I don't do anything else stupid. How long did I sleep?"

"Not long enough." The spirit deerhound crinkled its eyes as it examined its master. "I suggest another hour or two, and stronger protective measures before you attempt such a spell again."

"Again? I think once was enough."

"Did you learn what you sought?"

Donal sat down on the bed. Had he learned anything from that experiment? Something he might have missed among his narrow escape, lambasting from the ship's mage, hunger, and exhaustion? Donal calmed his mind and sought his memory. He remembered the tastes of those colors, each a potential source of power, as well as the feel of the great thing that tried to eat him ... Donal dove for his desk, ripped open the top drawer and grabbed his zephyrpad. He closed the drawer with his shoulder as he leaned back against the desk, sitting on the floor with the zephyrpad supported by his close-drawn knees. Donal closed his eyes and mumbled as he noted every detail, every sensation and every relationship he had observed, in sentences, sketches, and a shorthand system he developed in high school for thaumaturgic formulae.

When he finished, Donal sighed in contentment. His head still ached, but he was now fully awake. He held his zephyrpad aloft in triumph. Donal now had experiences and notes that would provide a better baseline for comparison against his future Enochian research than anything a school library could offer. He looked at Fionn. "Yes, I think I did get what I needed."

"Then the experiment succeeded, despite insufficient preparation." The *cú sidhe* nodded, then regarded Donal with a tilted head and ears slightly back. "I still recommend returning to bed."

"I can't go back to sleep." Donal rubbed his forehead, but could not quite ease the throb in his skull. "I should move around some. I'm cold."

"Sleep is better. but if you must stay awake then you should form a plan of action. You have not yet—"

"Full alert," said a voice from the Starchaser Spacelines logo on the wall above the desk, a star trailed by a stylized arrow. "Security has issued a full alert. All passengers and off-duty personnel are instructed to return to their cabins in a safe, orderly fashion. We appreciate your cooperation."

The *cú sidhe's* head snapped to attention, ears perked. "It returns, master, with help."

Someone knocked on the door, three measured raps.

"That was fast," said Donal. "I mean, I've heard of a ship recruiting magicians to deal with a threat, but I expected a little more warning."

Donal rushed to answer, calling Fionn back into the silver faun en route. He yanked open the door and saw a man and woman dressed as guards, not ship's watch. The man spoke first.

"Mr. Cuthbert, we don't want to hurt you, but we will if we have to. Please hand over the package you're carrying."

They raised gleaming sticks, like white billy clubs: Pacifiers.

Donal wished he had gone back to sleep.

The whole stateroom shook.

MACHADO SHOOK WITH RAGE AS THE BUBBLE CARRIED HIM DOWN. Twenty-five straight voyages as ship's mage without a major incident, ten on the Mars run alone, and now two in one day. If Machado lived through this, he might have to spend days in port recasting half of the *Horizon Cusp's* protective spells before it could see space again. If that idiot Cuthbert were responsible...

"The Observation Deck is empty, master," said Machado's ghostly *onça, Saravá,* as it came up through the floor. "And I could find no hint of the Journeyman's magic."

"Trouble trouble trouble." Machado narrowed his eyes. "Find Cromartie and have him join me, then get word to the captain. I'm on it."

His familiar vanished as the bubble unsealed. Nothing but the Observation Deck met Machado's extended perceptions until he looked beyond the wards. The zuglodon had returned, and a second had come with it. This should not have happened. Zuglodons were hunters, and could track a prey for some distance, but after the distractions Machado used following the last attack, plus the little bits of pain he had applied to sour its taste for pursuit, the zuglodon should not have hunted them down, much less recruited help. The *Horizon Cusp* should have had no more appeal to it than an asteroid.

Someone must have called the tentacled beast back. Nothing else made sense.

The large one struck the *Horizon Cusp's* wards with its body and the ship shook with the resonance. The wards held, but they were commercial wards, not military grade. Machado had pushed the legal limits as far as he could, and perhaps a little further, but his wards would not withstand many such strikes before they began to unravel. When they fell, Machado would be too busy holding together life support spells to defend the ship. Not that the crew would need life support long if he did not stop these creatures.

Finding out who called them would have to wait.

TUNOLD SLID DOWN THE ACCESS LADDERS BETWEEN FLOORS, POPPED out onto the Main deck, and charged toward the big meeting. A man who ran for exercise, for fun, and for meditation, Tunold could keep his pace for half an hour before he noticed the effort.

The security alert blared at him every ten meters, repeating after too short a delay in Tunold's opinion. He would complain to Goldberg and the captain later.

Tunold slowed as the meeting room came into view. A single crowd of people swelled outward through the double door before splitting into opposing factions, a well-organized migration. Then one guard swung a right cross and knocked down another. Tunold spat a curse in the language of his forefathers and stepped up his pace.

The fight spread through the gathering like a crew on shore leave through a port town. Punches, kicks, elbows and knees struck out, inviting response. They got it, dissolving the scene into an open brawl. Tunold could hear men shouting for order. He was one of them. Ship's watch thundered onto the scene and moved in with Pacifiers.

Tunold continued to demand order at the top of his lungs and waded into the fray with wiry strength. He ripped a hole between combatants wherever he could and threw several brawlers to the ground. One guard spun him around with an unexpected punch, but Tunold used the momentum to turn back and put the perpetrator down with a two-fisted hammer blow to the solar plexus.

The ship rocked, a violent, sudden tremor that shocked a pause in the skirmish. A voice filled the gap. "We need a doctor! Mr. al Rashid is down!"

"Helm, hard to starboard. Bring us up ten degrees and be ready to punch it on my order."

"Captain," said Jefferson, "I have the chief."

Jacobs whirled on Goldberg's face. "Chief, what the hell is happening down there? If it's that courier again I'll cut him into strips and feed him to my cat!"

"Unknown, Captain. I hit the alert as soon as I got word from Machado. I've got a team tracking Cuthbert down now and I'm on my way to reinforce my squad at the meeting."

"Good. I want updates as soon as you can give them to me. Bridge out." He passed his hand through Goldberg's image and broke the connection. With a twist of his finger, he opened a channel to engineering and started talking. "Ms. Jang, what's the best speed you can give me for one hour?"

"Twenty-five," she said as her harried image formed, "maybe thirty percent above the rated max. But I'll need a few minutes to prepare."

"Get her ready."

"Aye, sir!"

Another impact shook the ship.

Donal spat a Gaelic word and a snarling Fionn leapt out of its pendant and straight through the eyes of the would-be assailant. The deerhound's spirit fangs did no damage, but the man's reflexes tumbled him backward in surprise. His companion turned and swung her Pacifier in his defense. Electric blue enchantment limned the weapon and its arc. The Pacifier whiffed through the *cú sidhe's* insubstantial body and slammed into her companion's forehead, flaring brighter on contact.

The club's rubbery core mitigated the blow, but its spells drained all the man's aggression. He collapsed against the bulkhead, confused and disoriented. His own Pacifier dropped forgotten to the deck.

Donal seized the momentary advantage by reaching with his will and grabbing the point of contact between the second guard and her weapon. He extended that connection to reach the spells on the Pacifier, a simple application of thaumaturgic theory: create a link, a bridge between a target, the woman, and a spell, the Pacifier's aggression drain. The effect was the same as if she had been struck by her own weapon.

She plunked down on the floor, dazed and unclear how she got there.

Donal clucked his tongue. Who told these people to use commercial Pacifiers against a magician? Pacifiers were designed for crowd control. They could disable four or five people with every swing and not do any serious harm. But their spells were unsophisticated. The military grade version had safeguards, but the commercial model was easy prey for any competent Journeyman.

Fionn ruffled its emerald fur as it examined the downed guards. "Will they recover soon?"

"No." Donal locked his door behind him and left the attackers where they fell. "They need rest and a good meal before they'll be ready to go another round."

"You must hide. Others will come for you while the ship is under threat. We must find you a safe place."

"No, now we find the ship's mage. He may need our help."

As Donal ran for the bubble, a second impact shook the ship.

MACHADO HATED TEMPORARY CIRCLES. HE HATED THEM WHEN HE WAS A high school prodigy and they limited the spells he could cast beyond his grade. He hated them as an undergraduate, the way they never held power properly, never pleased his teachers just so. He hated them in graduate school, where the best facilities at CalThaum San Luis Obispo were reserved for doctoral candidates, not master's candidates. And he especially hated them in his professional life. Machado had designed his own laboratory aboard the *Horizon Cusp* to have connections to every part of the ship so he would never have to feel those restrictions again.

Unfortunately, Machado had neglected to plan around the need to repel attacks from a pair of aggressive zuglodons, overgrown space elementals with delusions of grandeur. Instead of working from the comfort of his lab, he had to improvise down here on the Observation Deck where he could see the creatures and deal with them directly.

A Magister working important spells through the limited capacities of a temporary circle. If Machado survived this attack, he would have a permanent magic circle inscribed on the floor of the Observation Deck. He would not suffer such an indignity again.

But first he had to survive.

Machado glanced over at Cromartie, who worked in a temporary circle of his own. For someone with just an Initiate's license, the kid was not bad. He had enough confidence to give his gestures and incantations style, like performance art. Magic was a touchy craft, and underconfidence could weaken a spell as surely as a lack of focus. Machado had needed several more years of professional practice to develop as much panache as Cromartie had already, but then, Machado stood s good thirty centimeters shorter and lacked the younger magician's deep, resonant voice.

Unfortunately, this situation demanded more than style.

Cromartie was a good Initiate, but an Associate's degree was a long way from a Master's, and thaumaturgy made no allowances for effort. Machado had tasked him to reinforce the wards and create small, illusory distractions. Cromartie's reinforcement work provided serviceable support, but his deceptions lacked depth.

"Focus on the wards," said Machado. "If they go down the rest won't matter anyway." He did not wait for a reply, but assembled a spell that might turn the zuglodons against each other. They seemed to sense through a series of long, off-grey tentacles that projected out of their enormous, serpentine heads, but from no other part of their bulbous bodies. Machado had come up with a spell that he hoped would use those senses against them, with a hallucinatory component to make the long, whip-like tail of the larger zuglodon appear to be a tasty spirit escaping the ship, and a gentle compulsion to nudge the smaller one into action. He spread the spell wide enough to touch as many tendrils as might notice an "escaped spirit."

Machado forced patience into his words and gestures. Rushing through a spell like this would leave errors, places the deception could not take hold, slips of power that might jar a wary sense organ. He crafted the working with a gentle rhythm, built it until he felt the parts slide into a cohesive whole, then released it into the fight.

The large zuglodon rocked the ship with a second slam of its body while the small zuglodon arched its tendrils inquisitively.

TUNOLD SHOVED HIS WAY THROUGH THE BRAWL AND STEPPED OVER pacified combatants to reach a tight circle of al Rashid's men. He grabbed one by the collar and said, "You. Get Doctor Ramirez. Follow the signs. Now."

The man's feet were moving even before he turned back to get confirmation from his own superior. Imenand bin Zuka nodded assent and the man took off at a run.

"It is too late for that, Mr. Tunold. Hassan al Rashid, the Light of Alexandria, has passed from this world. May a thousand houris sing him into heaven." Bin Zuka pondered into the distance. "Or may his sins balance against the weight of a feather on the scales of Anubis. In all the years I knew him, we never discussed religion."

"I see." Tunold kept his voice neutral and glanced to see how the guards reacted: nothing. If they found their leader's response odd, they were too well-trained to show any sign.

"Do not misunderstand me. I am not unaffected by Hassan's passing. He was a good friend and a good employer. I shall mourn him. But now is not the time for mourning." He raised his voice. "Bring forth the murderer."

Two of al Rashid's, or perhaps they were now bin Zuka's guards who lugged forward a beaten, half-conscious man clad in the same outfit that they wore.

"One of yours..." began Tunold, but bin Zuka interrupted him.

"Yes. One of my own men shoved a knife in the throat of my friend, and twisted." Bin Zuka spoke without a twitch or quiver, but Tunold finally heard some heat in the man's voice. "When your watch has finished quelling this brawl, I would be pleased to remand him to your custody."

If al Rashid is dead, what about Mancuso?

Tunold turned to see the ship's watch and their Pacifiers sweep across the brawl in a tight wedge formation with Goldberg at the vertex. He saw no sign of Mancuso.

"Goldberg!" Tunold bellowed.

The chief of security left his lieutenant in charge and jogged over, limping.

"Al Rashid's dead," said Tunold. "Bin Zuka has the killer under control. Take over here. I need to find out if anything's—"

The ship rocked with a second impact on the wards. Tunold held his footing amid a crowd of staggers and continued to update the chief. "If anything's happened to Mancuso." He shook his head. "I knew this charter was a bad idea."

THE *HORIZON CUSP* ROCKED WITH A SECOND IMPACT. IN HIS SHIP display, Jacobs saw the gryphon's body flash orange.

"Damage control, how is she holding up?"

"Hull integrity still intact, but the wards are getting battered pretty hard. I don't think they'll hold through two or three more of those strikes."

"And her insides?"

"The thaumaturgic systems should hang on as long as the wards do, but it's a good thing the port side staterooms on P6, 8 and 10 are unoccupied."

"There's a small blessing then. Mr. Grabowski, please tell me you have more details."

"Not much sir. One of the bogeys is about three hundred meters long, and the other maybe a third that, but they've formed some kind of whirling link, so I can't be sure."

"Whirling?"

"Yes, sir. They've grabbed each other's tails. They could be winding up for a larger strike."

"That doesn't sound right." Jacobs came over and looked for himself. He grabbed a pair of the display links, hand grips below each illusory quick-view summary - and the crisp sight of the two zuglodons snapped into his mind's eye, giant, ugly transparent gray snakes with bulges in the middle and tentacles at the front end. Manipulating the links, Jacobs swept his viewpoint out and along the side of the *Horizon Cusp* for a more complete look, but he could not get far enough from the ship to circle the zuglodons. From what he could tell, Grabowski was right -- each clung to the tail of the other by its feelers and together they spun in a circle. Could they have turned on each other? Either way, they were too busy to assault the wards.

"Machado," he said to no one in particular. "He's found a way to buy us time." Jacobs returned control of the station to Grabowski and stepped up to Jefferson. "Jang," he said, and she nodded a moment later as the engineer's impatient face appeared above the communications station. "Ms. Jang, is the Deception Drive ready?"

"Not yet, Captain. Two more minutes."

"We don't have two minutes."

"Then buy me two minutes, damn it, or the strain will collapse the bindings!"

Jacobs blinked in surprise. Five years Jang had served under him, and not once had she defied him.

"All right, Chief. I'll just ask the giant space monsters to wait."

"Sir," said Jefferson. "Message coming in from security. Mr. al Rashid is dead."

DONAL WAS WAITING FOR THE BUBBLE WHEN PINYIN-LUNG COALESCED through the floor to pause in the air before him. Fionn stepped between them before the spirit dragon spoke. "Greetings, Donal Cuthbert. My mistress fears for your life. She has asked me to guide you to a protected place until hostilities have ceased."

"What's going on?"

"I am afraid that is beyond the scope of my orders. I can tell you only that Tai Shi Li Hua wishes me to see you to a place of safety."

Fionn bared its teeth, emerald fur hackling at its shoulders.

"It would serve no purpose to attack me," said Pinyin-Lung. "I cannot compel you, and I cannot disobey my mistress."

"Give Li Hua my thanks, but tell her that no place on this ship is safe. I'm going to help the ship's mage."

The spirit dragon bowed half of its body and slipped away as the bubble arrived. Donal and his familiar boarded.

"You should not have told her were to find you," said Fionn. "We cannot trust her."

"Oh, come on. I know she's mad at me, but she doesn't want to hurt me."

"Did you not notice? The guards that attacked us wore the 4M security colors. Their orders must have come from her."

MACHADO SWORE AS CROMARTIE COLLAPSED ON THE DECK, DEPLETED and probably unconscious. Out of the fight. Still, he had lasted longer than Machado expected. This sort of fight was too much to ask of an Initiate. Advanced training in magic taught more than spells. It taught efficiency, how to achieve maximum effect with minimum effort. It taught the ability to focus in multiple directions. It prepared the body and mind to channel intense levels of sustained power.

In other words, it taught all the basic abilities one needed to fight off a zuglodon or two.

Machado offered a quick prayer of thanks to *Iemanja* that Cromartie had held out long enough to see the smaller zuglodon driven off. He had held the wards together while Machado played the zuglodons against each other until the large one forced the little one to flee or be devoured. But the large one remained, angry and hungry.

Now Machado had to maintain the wards and still convince the thing to leave. Destroying it was out of the question. Even had he been prepared and rested, Machado would have had to expend most of his considerable resources to slay it, and even then he might have failed. But now, at the end of a day's work that had included one battle already, complicated further by dealing with its junior partner this time, Machado feared that he might not have the strength left for survival.

A thread of that fear spiderwebbed a crack in his power. He caught the slip almost immediately, but it cost him the remains of the illusion that the zuglodon chased. Back on target, the creature swept out in a soaring arc and bore down along an attack vector. Machado dropped his offensive spells to focus on the wards. He could see the zuglodon's forehead tentacles sparking. They had not done that before. Machado paled. It did not intend to ram this time. The thing was going to grab the wards and shred them.

He doubled the speed of his chanting, but held the same beat. He adjusted his gestures in synchronicity and poured as much power into the wards as he could manage. A final act of defiance. Even if the wards held through the onslaught, Machado would wind up useless on the deck from the strain.

Down the thing came, gaining speed. Its tentacles spread wide, dripping with fell purpose...

And turning?

The creature banked hard to starboard, carrying it aft. It missed the ship entirely. Machado adjusted his focus from the defensive spells and saw someone else's magic deceive the zuglodon, trick it into thinking the ship had reversed direction to escape. It whirled its forehead tendrils after its hallucinatory prey, but the illusion tantalized just out of reach.

Machado could see the spell well enough to recognize a signature he had learned earlier in the day. He turned to his right and saw the source of that signature: Donal Cuthbert stood in a hasty circle and cast as fast as he could while his deerhound familiar worked in tandem. Before Machado could speak, the young mage collapsed like Cromartie had. That was no surprise. Cuthbert had abused his system earlier in the day, stretched his magical resources further than he would have understood at his level of education.

Machado pursed his lips and nodded in impressed approval. To pull off a spell that potent, complex and fast under the circumstances showed real talent.

Machado was checking on the status of the zuglodon when the ship lurched up and to starboard.

———

Tunold halted in the passage and considered the four guards outside Mancuso's suite. They stood with their feet apart and fists at their sides, knees and elbows bent just enough to keep their weight on their toes. They did not crowd together, but spread out to form a wall, which suited the impassable look in their eyes.

The Horizon Cusp *is under attack. Passengers are dying. And four punks in "uniforms" are ready to defend their boss from the ship's executive officer.*

Tunold strode up to them using what he thought of as his "officer's walk:" clipped, stiff strides, chin leading and face set with an expression that promised suffering. He knew he did not quite move the way he imagined, but tried to ignore that Captain Jacobs had dubbed it "the angry bear's gambol."

As Tunold reached the wall of guards he held up his master key and said, "I have to talk to Mr. Mancuso. Now either one of you is going to open that door or I am. I will kill the first man who tries to stop me."

He gave them a moment to decide.

The guards looked at one another, weight now on their heels. Perhaps their current instructions conflicted with a standing order about ship's officers. Tunold felt a twinge of sympathy, but refused to show it. Finally, three of them stepped back. The odd man out opened the door and called in, "Executive Officer Tunold here to see you, sir."

"Well don't keep him waiting in the hall. Send him in, send him in. You four stay out there, though. Tai Shi and I will be fine in here. Are those extra wards set, Tai Shi?"

"Yes, sir," said the Chinese Martian woman as Tunold entered the suite. He was always impressed at the spaciousness of some of the guest accommodations on this ship. This suite had to be the size of Jacobs' quarters and his combined, with furnishings that outshone the place Tunold had stayed on the ill-fated honeymoon of his ill-considered marriage: the room had been beautiful, but the fights were ugly.

Mancuso reclined in a chair broad enough to have passed for a love seat. He wore a chocolate brown robe with matching slippers and held a snifter of brandy in one hand and a book in the other. Behind the lounger, Tai Shi pretended to casual indifference near the porthole. She appeared involved in the color of her wine, but Tunold noted that she had not drunk any of it.

Scattered along the walls like statuary stood more guards, rigid in their attention to Tunold's every step. He ignored them: the enlisted men did not matter. They would follow their officer's lead. Tunold focused on Mancuso.

"I see you aren't troubled by the death of Mr. al Rashid."

"Stick to ships, Tunold. You have no head for business."

"Care to explain that before I—"

"I've been working on this deal for ten years!" Mancuso slammed his recliner upright, book forgotten in his waving hand. Behind him, Tai Shi watched Tunold, predatory in her patience. Mancuso continued, "Ten years I've been pitching ideas, making arrangements, pushing mergers, and bringing together all the right people in all the right places. Ten years, Tunold. The whole thing just went to hell, and I might not be able to fix it. Ten years' work - gone. So if you've come here to grill me about Hassan's death, I respectfully suggest you find something more productive to do with your time. Perhaps there's a deck you could swab."

Tunold slid into an at-ease stance that positioned his hands behind his back so Mancuso would not see his fists clench in anger. It was a trick he had learned as an enlisted man, to conceal his emotions from a superior officer. Tunold did not serve under Mancuso, and did not consider the man his superior in any way, but knew he had to grasp his temper with both hands and pin it to the deck. This was not the military. Letting his tongue loose here, or worse his fists, would not be absolved by a few days in the brig. It would cost his job, and worse, his prospects for another. So Tunold forced his anger down his gullet and felt his knuckles turn white behind his back.

"Actually, I only came here to see that you were safe, check on your security, and find out what you and your people saw." He dug his fingernails tighter into his palms. Turning only his head, he made a show of looking at Mancuso, then at the guards, then back at Mancuso. "Did you see anything that might help an investigation, Mr. Mancuso?"

"Not much. Talks were done for the day. We had actually reached a verbal agreement, but an oral contract is always tentative, short term until the paperwork is drawn up, which would have happened tonight." His voice grew wistful. "We might have had the papers signed by this time tomorrow." He tossed back some brandy. "The ship shook, that security alert went off, and we started back to our cabins. Then one of the guards threw a punch." He glared at the statue men. "Not sure if the puncher was mine or Hassan's. Tai Shi?"

"Ours, I think. Evans."

"Evans ... one of the new men?'

"Yes. First time around high level negotiations. Tension must have gotten to him."

A troubled look passed the woman's eyes as she spoke. Tunold felt sure of it.

"So Evans probably threw the first punch," said Mancuso. "Once one punch flew, others followed and I had to get out of there for my own safety. Tai Shi almost had me in the bubble when someone yelled that Hassan was down." He toasted the dead man with his brandy, then continued, "That's all I know, but if it was one of mine who killed Hassan, he better hope the watch gets him before I do. Anything to add, Tai Shi?"

"No, sir."

Tai Shi whirled to her left and stared at nothing, the way Machado did once in a while. Machado always had new information when that happened.

"Nothing new to add, Ms. Tai Shi?" asked Tunold.

"No." She crinkled her brow. Not good news then. "Do you know who is protecting the courier through this crisis?"

"I'm sure Mr. Goldberg is taking care of him."

She nodded, still distracted, and began muttering to the air. Mages. Tunold turned back to Mancuso.

"By the way, how did you know that Mr. al Rashid was dead? He might have been injured."

"My familiar," said Tai Shi, still staring into space. "Once Mr. Mancuso was safe I sent it to check on Mr. al Rashid. It reported that he was dead of a stab wound to the throat."

"That reminds me, Tunold," said Mancuso, "I'll want to talk to the captain when this crisis is settled."

The ship lurched up and to starboard. Tunold had not felt any impact, but the *Horizon Cusp* did not have enough acceleration for that to have been the engines. What could have caused it?

"I'll tell him," said Tunold, "but right now I better check on the bridge."

"Ready," called Jang, "and with ten seconds to spare."

"Punch it!" said Jacobs.

The ship jumped up ten degrees and hard to starboard as the helmsman shoved the throttle full ahead, faster than the *Horizon Cusp* had ever gone before.

Jacobs called up his three-dimensional charts to mark potential safe zones along their course in case they needed to stop for repairs. As he worked, he said, "Scanners, report."

"The creature started aft just before engineering was ready, sir," said Grabowski. "It's chasing something, but if I read the scans right it's after an illusion."

"Machado's work, I'm sure," said Jacobs. "Go on."

"It hasn't caught on to our escape yet, and we're gaining good space on it."

"Distance."

"Three hundred clicks and gaining." Seconds later, Grabowski added, "four hundred fifty and gaining."

"Good. Damage control, report."

"Minor damage from the creature, but this speed is riding the edge of the hull's rating."

"Keep an eye on it then. Let me know before it becomes a problem." Jacobs would have to have Machado ready to help Jang, just in case. He noted to give his mage a bonus when they reached Earth. "Communications, get me updates from Machado and Goldberg as soon as possible."

"I have Goldberg," said Jefferson almost immediately.

"Chief, what's our status? What's this about al Rashid?"

"He's dead, sir." The chief's image looked grim. "It's a red sky morning."

Jacobs gritted his teeth. That phrase meant that Goldberg thought the situation was too sensitive to discuss over the comm system and wanted to meet in Jacobs' office.

"Understood, Chief, bridge out." He turned back to his bridge crew. "Scanners, anything new on the zuglodon?"

"It came about at one thousand clicks, sir, but so far there's no sign that it can gain on us."

"Good. Helm, stay the new course, best speed. Damage control, I want updates every fifteen minutes at the latest. Scanners, if it starts gaining, I want to know before you do. Communications, I want any updates from Machado linked through to my office. And tell engineering to keep my ship intact. Jang can bleed the speed if she has to, but I want to know the second she does. And find Mr. Tunold. I want to see him in my office five minutes ago."

Jacobs left the bridge to a chorus of assent.

FOR THE SECOND TIME THAT DAY, DONAL REGAINED CONSCIOUSNESS ON the Observation Deck to see the ship's mage leaning over him. No squad of onlookers and watchmen in the background this time, just Fionn, who sat guard near the bubble. Donal took his familiar's position to mean that the ship's mage was not angry this time.

"You all right?" asked Magister Machado. "Don't try to sit up yet. You've been through a lot today."

"Din," said Donal, but his mouth did not work right. He felt as though he tried to speak around a golf ball. "Ah..."

"I know. You didn't call it back. My familiar found no trace of your signature." Donal's eyes must have widened, because the ship's mage chuckled as he checked Donal's pupils and wrists. "Of course I looked for it. You might have been that stupid." He passed his hand in front of Donal's face and Donal felt a little more coherent. Magister Machado nodded. "Try to speak again. You look like you should be able to control your words this time."

Donal took a deep breath before the attempt. "If there's anything I can do to help you catch the one who called it..."

"Thanks, I may take you up on that. You're pretty handy with the illusions." Magister Machado checked Donal's wrists, eyes and fore-head. "Right now you need rest, though. As soon as you can walk you should go back to your cabin and sleep. I'll have the galley send you food." The Magister shook a finger at Donal. "You need to develop a sense of your limits and soon. Otherwise you'll burn yourself out and possibly kill yourself from the strain. Magic is not a game."

"I had to do something."

The ship's mage sighed.

"Look. You read the situation and pulled off an effective spell with no time, no preparation, and no margin for error. It was solid work and I appreciate the hand." He grabbed Donal's jaw and leaned in nose-to nose. "But twice today you overextended yourself. Don't let it become a habit." He let go and straightened up. "You have a lot of potential. Don't piss it away."

Donal contemplated that.

"Is that thing gone?"

"Yes. Your illusion bought us breathing space to escape. The crea-ture might have caught up, but I had time to lay a few traps in our wake because I didn't have to worry about the wards. By the time it finishes with those, we should be well beyond its reach."

Donal staggered to his feet with only a little help from the squat magician. For the first time, Donal noticed the security magician passed out on the deck.

Magister Machado followed Donal's gaze.

"Yes, Cromartie helped a good deal during the fight too. Acquitted himself well, for an Initiate. I'm impressed that you came around first. You strained more than he did today." He shook a thick finger in Donal's face again. "Now be smart for a change: rest."

Donal managed a weak smile and plodded to the bubble, barely keeping himself upright, one hand in the emerald neck fur of his guiding deerhound familiar.

14

When Jacobs reached his office, he found Goldberg waiting. They nodded quick greetings and entered. No sooner had the door closed behind them than Tunold's frame-rattling knock announced him. Once all three were seated, Jacobs began.

"I assume we all agree - it's no coincidence that someone murdered al Rashid during a brawl that broke out while a pair of giant monsters attacked the ship." Both men nodded. Jacobs guarded his face against his opinion and provoked discussion. "So the purpose must have been to kill al Rashid during the distraction."

"Correction," said Goldberg. "At least part of the purpose was to kill al Rashid. Someone may have tried to get Mancuso as well, and failed."

"Or," said Tunold, "someone might have tried to murder bin Zuka and failed. On the Transterran Properties documentation, only al Rashid and bin Zuka have executive titles. Killing al Rashid and Mancuso would have taken down leaders on both sides, but killing al Rashid and bin Zuka would have left one side with no leaders at all."

Jacobs pulled a notepad close and picked up a pen. "So the question is the goal. What purpose did the attack serve?" He tapped his pen on the pad. "What do we know about al Rashid's murderer?"

"One of his own guards," said Goldberg. "A new hire."

"There's a coincidence," said Tunold. "Mancuso said that Evans, the bodyguard who threw the first punch, was a new hire."

"You suspect a conspiracy?" said Jacobs. The three men grew quiet as they considered the implications.

Goldberg shook his head. "More likely a coincidence." He cracked his neck. "That the assassin was a new hire makes sense if it's a hit, but the punch could have been thrown by a green soldier who snapped under pressure."

"We can't rule it out," said Jacobs. "Assume a conspiracy until investigation proves otherwise." He tapped his pen. "A conspiracy needs a leader. Al Rashid is dead, and bin Zuka is giving the orders for them now, the man who had been handling security, which means he may have hired the killer. What do you think? His move?"

"Too early to say." Goldberg shrugged. "We'll have to question him formally."

"What about Mancuso as a suspect?"

"Depends," said Tunold. "He claims they had an oral contract ready for ink. If that's true then why kill al Rashid? Mancuso might have to start the negotiations over with someone else. If he's lying about the agreement—"

"Damn their intrigues. We're spacers, not cops. I'm turning this whole mess over to port security the minute we land." Jacobs sighed. Whoever was behind this had placed the *Horizon Cusp* in jeopardy to arrange one murder, so they might do it again to go after a second target. Keeping Jacobs' ship safe meant rooting out the problem. "So we need to interview bin Zuka about both the murder and the contract. That's your job, Chief."

On the corner of his desk, Jacobs' comm pad glowed red: Jefferson had a message or call for him. He slapped it with one hand, and her face appeared above the pad as the red glow faded.

"I have Mr. Machado for you, sir."

"Link him through," said Jacobs, and her face melted into that of his ship's mage. Even now, with so many worries crying for his attention, the sight disquieted Jacobs. "What do you have for me, Mash?"

"A kiss for getting our butts out of there, Captain, and commendations for the courier and Goldberg's Initiate. They both went above and beyond on this one."

"The courier? I was ready to feed him to Benny Sugg for bringing that damned thing back."

Across the room, the ship's cat lay sprawled along the back of the couch. At the mention of his name he lifted his head, eyes still closed, and sniffed the air. A moment later he was asleep again.

"Wasn't Cuthbert, Captain," said Machado, "but it was his spell that let us get away. Impressive work, for a Journeyman."

"So we are clear?"

"Aye, sir. The zuglodon's probably lost interest already, but if you can hold this speed for another half hour I'll guarantee that it's gone."

"Good. As soon as you're done, I'll need you to check on engineering. Ms. Jang is pushing the Deception Drive for this speed, and damage control reports the hull might object."

"On it, sir. Machado out."

"Captain," said Tunold as soon as Mash's face vanished, "Mr. Mancuso asked me to tell you that he wants a word when you have a chance."

"That's what the day was missing, a private conference with a passenger. All right, I'll see what His Highness wants."

Jacobs stretched as he stood and tossed his pen onto the notebook, which was blank but for two dozen dots of ink.

"Mr. Tunold, take the bridge. Mr. Goldberg, finish cleaning up that brawl before you start your interviews. I want every thug involved thrown in the brig until we have some answers. And double the watch rotations until we get this straightened out." Jacobs shook his head. "Let's try to make it home with only one body on the deck."

DONAL LEANED AGAINST THE BACK OF THE BUBBLE'S CAGE. HE NODDED at the edge of sleep and lost track of what Fionn tried to tell him. Something about how he should have an escort. The deerhound's ceaseless warnings and corrections blended into noise when all Donal wanted to do was collapse.

He waved one hand and dismissed his familiar back into its pendant. Rapturous silence. Donal almost fell asleep, but the bubble stopped and the cage opened. He had reached his floor.

He stepped out and saw two guards outside his door, both dressed in the 4M colors. Had Donal been more awake, perhaps more rested, he could have slipped back into the bubble and been gone before they knew he was there. Instead he half-tripped over his own feet and lurched to a halt against the bulkhead. He heard the guards shout greetings or orders, but lost their meaning under the staccato sound of his pulse. He tried to call Fionn, wished he had not dismissed his familiar, but the attempt to focus careened pain from his temples to the back of his neck and shaved the edges of his vision into darkness.

The guards ran toward him. The tak-tak-tak of their boots on the ceramic deck syncopated against Donal's thumping heart and added a drumbeat to the ringing in his ears. Donal shoved himself off the bulkhead, his body angled to fall back into the bubble and escape, but he watched his salvation slip away to answer another call. He smacked against the ward that held the tube's water in check and slid down to the cold deck.

Donal looked up to see two men reach for him as blackness overtook him.

JACOBS DRUMMED HIS FINGERS ON HIS DESK. MANCUSO WAS LATE, probably a small revenge for Jacobs' insistence that they meet in the captain's office.

Finally the man arrived, accompanied by his right hand woman and two assistants. Mancuso sat in one of the visitor's chairs. His companions stood behind him, Tai Shi in the center and the secretaries on either side. Jacobs amused himself with the mental image of them breaking into a barbershop number. Only age and experience kept a smile from his lips.

"Mr. Mancuso, let me begin by assuring you that the murderer is in custody, and we are taking steps to further ensure your safety for the remainder of our voyage to Earth."

Mancuso gestured at the display on one wall. "Have you really served on all those ships, Captain?"

Jacobs sighed at the change of subject.

"Every one and commanded about half. But about your safety, there are additional steps we can take. I can move you to new quarters without announcing their location, which should minimize your exposure. From there Mr. Goldberg can either have ship's watch protect you or arrange an outer ring of watch security and leave personal protection to your own guards and Ms. Tai Shi. I would even be willing to approve stronger wards of your own casting, provided they are observed and approved by my ship's mage."

"Yes, yes, that would be fine." Mancuso dismissed the topic with a wave of his hand. "That creature that attacked the ship. Have you ever fought one before?"

Are you a businessman or a schoolboy? Aloud, Jacobs said, "Creatures like the zuglodon are a rare hazard of the space lanes. Usually, if they venture near a ship, there are ways to divert them before they do any damage. We should have smooth space the rest of the way to Earth."

"Have you ever had to fight off pirates, Captain?"

Schoolboy then. Jacobs trotted out his pat, dinner-conversation answer. "Piracy is rare in space, and what there is focuses on cargo ships, where the potential return is more likely to outweigh the risk. Pirates tend to ignore passenger vessels like the *Horizon Cusp*."

"I understand that it's rare, but that does not answer my question." Mancuso actually steepled his fingers. Jacobs could not recall the last time he saw someone do that. Did he think it looked impressive?

Jacobs forced himself to think about the future of Starchaser Spacelines. He needed to keep this landlubber happy. Jacobs could survive one more inane conversation.

"I have fought pirates on the seas and in the skies, but have only faced them twice at high space. Both times my ship was faster."

"Good enough," said Mancuso with a nod. "Captain, you're an experienced spacer and a good man in a crisis. Whatever Starchaser Spacelines is paying you, I can double it."

Jacobs felt his eyebrows make a halfhearted attempt to rise. The man had nerve. On the other hand, at least the strange questions now made more sense to Jacobs. Mancuso thought this was a job interview.

Did Jacobs need a job? First voyage after the *Beamrunner* incident, and only three days out of port there had already been two zuglodon attacks and a murder. Even catching the criminals might not be enough. This cruise might scuttle Starchaser Spacelines instead of saving it. Perhaps Jacobs should consider the offer....

No. He and Zoltan built this business up from one little moon shuttle. If this voyage sank the business, Jacobs would go down with the ship.

"Mr. Mancuso, I am a partner in Starchaser Spacelines. If your purpose here is to offer me employment, then I believe we're finished. I have a ship to run."

Mancuso stared for a moment, then nodded.

"Of course, Captain, of course. I'll leave you to it." He stood and strode toward the door with his lackeys falling into step behind him. He issued orders with every step. "Stevens, find out more about Starchaser Spacelines. Who the partners are, how much it makes, a full report. Davis, get me background about the partners: schooling, connections, that sort of thing...."

Jacobs watched the secretaries take notes until the door closed behind the group. He snapped his pen in half. Benny Sugg slipped into the room from one of his many hiding spots and jumped onto the desk to demand attention. The captain scowled, then sighed, then finally managed a half-smile. He scratched the white tom behind the ears. "We're still a week out of port, Benny. Maybe someone will kill him too."

Benny purred.

Donal knew he was awake because his mouth tasted terrible, as though he had tried to get rid of the flavor of cough syrup by wiping down his tongue with a bar rag at closing time. At least his ears had stopped ringing, but his head clamored and his limbs were cramped and sore. Almost like he was tied to a chair....

Donal's eyes snapped open, only to be closed again by bright light. In that fleeting glimpse, he saw ropes that bound him to a stateroom chair, and paintings that were different from the ones on his walls. Donal had worried about being a prisoner on Mars. Now he really was one.

"We know you're awake."

Donal did not recognize the woman's voice. He eased his eyes open a little at a time until he could see the stateroom and five seated people: three men, two women. Two of the men and one woman wore 4M colors, while the others wore those of Transterran Properties. None of them smiled.

"Your pendant is safe," the woman in the 4M uniform continued, and Donal realized he could not feel it around his neck. "It's in a drawer for now, cut off from you by a circle." She pointed at the floor by his feet and Donal saw that he was enclosed in a textbook magic circle. "We'll give it back to you after you've heard us out."

Donal tried to expand his awareness, but his headache would not allow it. He shifted his breathing, but the woman said, "Please don't attempt to break the circle. You've had a hard day as it is. Don't make us hurt you."

Donal slumped forward, paying attention only to what he felt: he had so many sore, stiff, and cramped muscles that he knew he could not fight his way out. His headache threatened to burst out of his skull as though it intended to run off and seek its fortune, so he doubted he could think his way out. Donal looked at the spokeswoman. He *had* seen her before. She was one of the magicians he had noticed at dinner. Recognition made him nod. Just a bare movement, but she took it as acquiescence.

"First of all," she said, "thank you for giving us the idea of the creature attack. It was a far more effective distraction than what we originally had planned, and the risk to the ship was still minimal."

Donal snorted.

"You must understand, Mr. Cuthbert, that we are not the real danger here. We don't want to hurt anyone on this ship except for Mancuso and al Rashid." She made a fist and pounded the next words into her left hand. "They. Must. Die." She stood and paced. "They represent not only the single biggest threat to Mars since the Corporate War, but the greatest threat to Earth since the fall of technology."

Not the real danger? Donal strained against the ropes, then blinked at her. A ripple of discomfort spread through the room. She stopped pacing.

"Yes, we're all sorry that it was necessary to tie you up, but you dispatched two of us last time. We had to make sure you stayed still long enough to hear our side of the story." Donal held his silence, so she continued. Her eyes and tone grew more urgent. "Mr. Cuthbert, Donatello Mancuso and Hassan al Rashid have spent the last several years positioning themselves to form a sort of interplanetary shadow government. They have forged alliances with companies who control business interests on Earth, Luna, Mars, and are making headway into the new settlements on Venus. But there's more.

"Each of those various companies has strong political ties, from groups of lobbyists on their payrolls to elected representatives who rely on their campaign contributions. Alone, those companies wield vast economic and political influence. Combined under the leadership of a single banner, they would solidify their power base and expand their resources until they held absolute authority over all of humanity."

Donal cleared his throat. "I understand," he said, "that one can avoid their influence through the use of a simple spell. It doesn't even require alchemy to maintain it, just a focus. I think thin, pliable sheet metal is traditional, shaped into a hat."

She sat down in her chair.

"We're not crazy, Mr. Cuthbert. Those men did not come here to make an ordinary business deal. That's why they chartered a helioship, and why they conducted negotiations outside the scrutiny of any planetary jurisdiction." She sighed and seemed to shrink a few centimeters. "And it's not like I could have them arrested for treason or conspiracy to commit treason. They aren't actually overthrowing any governments. They are establishing themselves as a higher authority that existing governments would have to answer to." She shook her head. "Individual governments are so wrapped up in their own self-importance that none of their investigators would even know how to recognize what these conspirators are doing."

"But you can see it, of course."

"Yes, we can." She gave Donal a level look, and he had to admit that she did not look insane. A bit intense, perhaps, but then she did have him tied him to a chair. "We at Red Sun have paid close attention to 4M for business purposes, and our Finance and Records department noticed that they were meeting with companies that would have violated Martian antitrust laws, had they been looking at mergers or buyouts. But nothing official has been filed. What they are doing goes beyond corporate law. It's closer to forging a treaty, as though they are independent sovereign nations joining forces." She waved one hand, exasperated, before settling on an image. "It's like they're kings, agreeing to establish an emperor."

Donal had to stifle a yawn, and not only because he was tired. Treaty was just another word for a contract, and alliances were just mergers. She could dramatize the situation however she wanted, but 4M and Transterran Properties were just corporations doing what corporations did. Donal's package might even have been evidence that they would file their paperwork sooner or later. These Red Sun agents were no freedom fighters. Donal was tied to a chair for corporate espionage reasons, nothing more.

His kidnappers might be fanatics, but Donal doubted that they wanted to hurt him, at least not while he might prove useful. That meant he had to wait them out. If he could pretend interest long enough, they might let him go.

"Where do I fit in?"

"If you would let us examine the package you are delivering, we could prove what we're telling you."

"That won't help you stop them. They have true copies. Best you could do is slow them down." Donal paled at a sudden thought. A thread of sweat trickled down his face. They knew. They knew what he was carrying. They knew about the copies. They were not trying to prevent some treaty. They wanted the signatures.

It was a standard procedure to thaumaturgically strip away magical influences in legal documents to reduce the risk of some spell clashing with the wards used by the Recorder's Office. That made those signatures perfect links to their targets: scrubbed clean and wide open. Part of the contract process would keep the companies involved from using them against each other, but a third party would not have that restriction. The signatories were vulnerable until the documents reached the Recorder's Office.

Wait, am I delivering the package to a Recorder's Office? Donal could not remember. He had given the destination only a cursory glance because it would not matter until he reached Earth. He could only remember that it was going to San Francisco.

Wherever the package was headed, right now it was protected by the courier's pouch, which warded the contents and would destroy the documents if anyone unauthorized broke the seal. The spells were Hierophant-cast. Only another Hierophant, a Doctor of Thaumaturgy, could disarm them, and even then the process would take days. Donal was no Hierophant, but as the courier he was authorized....

"I see you understand, Donal. May I call you Donal?" He did not reply. The spokeswoman continued, "Our attempt on Hassan al Rashid succeeded, but Donatello Mancuso's personal magician foiled our strike on him."

Donal bit his tongue to keep from saying Li Hua's name. He winced at the pain, and the spokeswoman misunderstood.

"We aren't proud about committing murder. But we do what we must for the sake of all humanity." She folded her hands and implored Donal. "Please, give us the contract. Let us end Mancuso's life with the minimum of risk to everyone else."

"What happens if I refuse?"

"To you? Nothing." She knelt to put Donal at eye level. "We are not threatening you or holding you hostage, however it may look right now. We are explaining the truth of our situation in the hope that you will help us, the same way Rowan MacPherson approached you in the spaceport on Mars. No one is neutral in this fight, Donal. You must choose a side."

That was where Donal had heard a pitch like this before. He had almost forgotten about her. But he thought she represented Aetheric Dynamics. He had said as much, and she had not corrected him. How big was this conspiracy? Donal felt his body chill with more sweat as another thought made it past his headache.

"You were the ones who searched my luggage."

"Did you know you can pull a similarity link to a person without actually taking a possession? I read an article about it a few weeks ago. It was supposed to help us track you, but 4M must have gotten you behind strong wards before we could use it. That, or underground..."

"I must have missed that issue." Donal swallowed. "And the explosion? The day I landed on Mars? All those people killed?"

"Only six died." She at least had enough grace to avoid Donal's eyes. "The others were only injured. We regret the need that made us do that, but if we had stopped you there, the rest of this would not have been necessary. Some of the corporations Mancuso and al Rashid had gathered were unsure about their agreement, and stopping you then might have turned them away."

Might? Six people killed and more injured, all on a *might?* Donal felt nausea swell in his stomach, threaten his throat. He drew shallow breaths until he could be sure he would not vomit.

"Donal, you must understand that we take only the steps we *must* take. These men must be stopped, by any means necessary."

The pain in Donal's head would not ease. He could not concentrate. These people expected an answer to their lunacy. As though there could have been any justification for their deplorable actions. He had to buy time.

"How long do I have to think about this?"

"Until the end of the trip. We ask only that you do not tell anyone about us or where to find us, even you speak to the captain to retrieve the package from the ship's safe. That would force our hand and matters would get very ugly. We don't want to kill everyone aboard this ship, but we can and we will. We hope it won't be necessary."

Donal did not want to trust their idea of 'necessary.' He looked at his various captors in turn. None of them seemed shocked or surprised at the thought of dying for the cause. What could he say that would persuade them to let him go?

Phrasing was critical here. As a magician, Donal had to be very careful with his promises. They did not bind him magically, but a magician had to maintain confidence in the power of his word to affect the truth. Lying, asserting something he knew to be false, could undermine that confidence. Fortunately, his specialization in the magic of deception had shown him a gray area for almost-truths.

"All right," said Donal, "I promise I'll give it the serious consideration that it merits."

Someone came up behind him and cut the ropes. That meant there were people in the room he had not seen. Donal looked over his shoulder and saw one of the "guards" he had pacified earlier. The man still wobbled, unsteady on his feet. Two others stood behind him, one of them the woman Donal had pacified. The spokeswoman retrieved Fionn's pendant from a dresser drawer, dismissed her magic circle, and handed the silver faun back to Donal. As he took it from her hand, he felt a whisper of magic. He looked properly at the spokeswoman now, with no magic circle between them, and realized that her features had been disguised with illusions. Not her clothes, just her person, although that meant that the spokesperson behind the illusion might have been of either gender. Donal slipped the necklace over his head and took comfort in its slight weight under his shirt.

Donal walked unhindered through the door - not looking back

even when he passed through their wards - and sighed as it closed behind him. Donal had not promised to keep his silence, but before he went to any authority, he had to see Li Hua. If she foiled their attempt on Mr. Mancuso, she was not one of them and had nothing to do with the Pacifier attack on Donal. Maybe she would tell him what 4M hoped for out of this deal.

Maybe he already knew her answer. The words of the toast she made on Mars returned to him: "4M will be the only name that matters."

15

JACOBS PORED OVER CHARTS IN THE AIR ABOVE HIS STATION ON THE bridge. He moved a tiny duplicate of the *Horizon Cusp* along a route and studied the effect on travel time, difficulty, and supplies. Even Jacobs had to admit that the illusory three-dimensional charts gave him a stronger sense of his ship's travel than their old paper equivalent. In half an hour of study, he could learn more about alternate routes than he could previously have learned in half a day.

Jacobs could have even permitted the system to project images directly into his mind so that he would have seen the space along a given course as of the latest readings in his charts. He declined the option because he considered the information too old to be accurate at that level of granularity.

Jacobs moved the tiny gryphon now because he needed to change course. Pushing the Deception Drive had put him ahead of schedule. Jacobs sat back for a moment and smiled. His crew had handled the emergency well, and his chief engineer and ship's mage had been able to maintain a high speed for an extended period of time without damaging the hull or straining the system.

Unfortunately, the speed and the zuglodon attacks had taxed both magicians further than was safe. Jang and Machado rested now, and would be down for several hours. In the meantime, Jacobs wanted to put the *Horizon Cusp* back on schedule without risking pursuit by returning to his previous flight plan. Paranoia, perhaps, but a ship with better scanners might have followed him without tipping its presence. Someone had sent those zuglodons. What if that someone were not a passenger?

Jacobs charted a path past a site where a series of asteroids had collided a few hundred years ago, leaving their rubble adrift to form "space garbage." If the helioship cut an arc close to the perimeter of the garbage in a yawing spiral, Jacobs could force any pursuit into scanner range along one of three axes and come out along a vector that would leave open space around the *Horizon Cusp* for more than a thousand clicks.

If anyone followed them, Jacobs would flush them out while giving the *Horizon Cusp* a slingshot head start. If not, the move would still connect his course with one of the cargo routes, where no one would look for a passenger vessel. As a side benefit, he would have a flight plan heavily trafficked enough to ensure current chart data: much safer in terms of hazards and travel times. It would also increase the possibility of finding aid, should the unthinkable happen.

Typical cargo vessels traveled at three-quarters the cruising speed of commercial liners, so Jacobs could slow his ship to maintain their scheduled arrival without drawing attention. Jacobs shook his head. He would not be able to give Jang the treat he promised. Their high-speed escape would have to suffice.

Jacobs rehearsed five different flight plans, each time pulling the ship's marker through a slightly different route and double-checking the scarlet trail that followed. He assessed the paths, scribbled a series of notes, explored a few emergency escape options, and finally settled on his selection. He chopped his hand through the display to clear it of his tests, pulled the miniature *Horizon Cusp* along his chosen route, then placed his left hand upon the updates pad and said, in a clear voice, "This is Captain John Jacobs. Update course."

The rubbery pad sounded a low gong that would also notify the helm and ex oh's stations. The scarlet trail turned bright blue, then faded and the tiny *Horizon Cusp* returned to its current position. Jacobs did not know how the system confirmed his identity. He tried not to think about it. At least it was a dumb system, leaving navigation entirely in his hands. It tracked the orders, fed changes to the helm, but all decisions were Jacobs' own.

Some of the newer ships now used "linked" navigation. They bound a lacuna, a space elemental, into the navigation and scanners systems. The lacuna could sense and track its location, as well as direct the ship to whatever destination the captain selected. Salesmen claimed that the elemental picked the safest, most efficient route.

Trust the safety of his ship and crew to a spirit's judgment and priorities? Jacobs would fly into a star first.

"Captain," called Jefferson, "Mr. Goldberg is asking to meet with you in his office."

In his office? Did we finally catch a break? Jacobs cleared his displays.

"Tell him I'll be right down."

Jacobs turned the bridge over to Tunold, took the sloping passage from the bridge down to Crew Deck One, walked past the break rooms and recreation areas, and took the personnel-only bubble to the Security Deck. Conspirators had infected his ship, but at least Jacobs could feel some confidence that they could not endanger it from the inside. All sensitive areas of the *Horizon Cusp* - engineering, security, command, and crew quarters - were separated from the passenger decks by bulkheads as strong as the hull. It was as though the original design of the ship had been a cylinder forty meters across that was later inset into the body of a giant gryphon. Passenger areas surrounded the cylinder, but the layout kept most passengers from even noticing that they did not have access to the whole ship.

The Security Deck was the main point of connection between the crew decks and passenger decks. It stretched beyond the cylinder and partway into the body of the gryphon. It also included one of the public bubbles, although the undines had been commanded to restrict access to ship personnel. If any passengers got around this restriction, they would still have to go through more wards and the heart of the ship's watch to get anywhere important.

There were the access ladders, of course, but those were easily defended and would not allow any kind of speed. No, if the murderer had any designs on the *Horizon Cusp*, he would find his task difficult.

Goldberg's office was in the center of the Security Deck, near the core of the ship. When Jacobs reached it, he found Goldberg at his desk, filling out a duty roster. Three members of the watch slumped in chairs against one wall and crammed snacks in their mouths as fast as they could chew. Jacobs stood in the open doorway and knocked on the door frame.

Goldberg chuckled. "Door's open, Captain."

"You laugh, Saul, but at least you knock when my door is open."

"I like my job."

"Smart man," said Jacobs with a smile. He closed the door behind him and joined his chief at the desk.

"Don't mind them." Goldberg pointed his chin at the hungry men. "Double shifts. No one ever gets enough sleep or food. Best to grab both when you can."

"So what have you learned, Chief?"

Goldberg grimaced.

"We've got fanatics on our hands, Captain. They see themselves as serving a cause, so they won't talk."

"What's the cause?"

"Mancuso and al Rashid weren't just making a business deal, they're forging a Great Evil that shall devour all mankind blah blah blah." Goldberg pumped his fist in mock masturbation.

"Did we catch them all?"

"I don't think so, and only one of them has done any talking." He picked up a notebook from a stack behind him and flipped a few pages. Apart from official records, Goldberg, like Jacobs, kept his secrets and opinions on paper. "But from the way they look at each other, three of the eleven we have in the brig are part of their conspiracy." He tossed the notebook down. "I'm betting at least twice as many are still out there."

"Only eleven got locked up? I heard it was a big brawl."

"I tried to keep it to those who looked like they'd done real fighting."

Jacobs weighed that decision, then said, "Probably a good political move, though I wouldn't mind having all the brawlers behind bars." He looked sideways at the diners. "So you say there are more conspirators out there?"

Goldberg shook his head.

"We have too strong a screening process for any of them to be among the watch. But it does look like the conspirators have allies among both Mancuso's and al Rashid's guards."

"Terrific. Any resources we should be aware of?"

"Cromartie says that one of the ones we caught is a caster, a Neophyte. Not good enough to require a license, just someone who has had enough classes to cast a few spells and activate some toys."

"Could be dangerous enough. What's to stop him from casting spells in the brig?"

"One of our cells can be tuned to shut down a 'caster. Cromartie took care of it."

"Good." Jacobs sighed at a realization. "But if these guys have one magician, we have to assume he has a backup."

"Since he's just a Neophyte, he probably is the backup. But either way there's probably another 'caster out there with bad intentions. To make matters worse, we took commercial Pacifiers off of a couple of these guys, and I don't know how they smuggled the things aboard."

Jacobs grew still, willing himself to save his anger until it was needed. Tunold had pushed his customs contacts to check out these passengers. If they had managed to smuggle weapons aboard, it meant one thing.

"They had inside help."

"Maybe. Not from the watch though." The chief cracked his neck. "I'll go through the personnel records and look for candidates."

Jacobs felt every muscle in his body tighten at the thought that someone on his crew had betrayed him. He needed to work out this anger. A trip to the crew gym to pound the heavy bag would help. For now, a deep breath through his nose would keep him from wrecking the chief's office. He made that two deep breaths.

"All right. Run your possibilities past the ex oh. Kris should be able to help you narrow down the list, and you don't want me involved until you've found the guilty party." Jacobs forced his fists to unclench. "Also, get word to Mancuso and bin Zuka: dinner tonight will not be at Ambrosia. They each get one bodyguard of their choice. The rest of the security will be ship's watch, who will escort them to and from dinner. Any other passengers out of their cabins during the dinner hour are to be arrested and thrown in the brig for the rest of the voyage. I've played their game long enough. I want this out in the open and dealt with."

"Where do you want dinner?"

"Crew's Mess Hall. It's out of the way, and should be easy to defend. Unless you have a better idea?"

"Works for me."

"Good. Don't go public with that, just get them there when the time comes." Jacobs started for the door. He had to get back to the bridge and relieve Tunold, so the ex oh could handle his side of the investigation. A thought stopped him about halfway to the door. He turned back to the chief and said, "Oh, and I want the courier there too. His life is as much at risk as ours. He has a right to know what's going on."

As Jacobs left he noted that the diners had fallen asleep in their chairs. He wondered if he would get any sleep that night himself.

DONAL COULD FIND LI HUA EASILY ENOUGH. FIONN ONLY NEEDED twenty minutes to determine that she had to be in one of four sets of warded cabins: one was Donal's own, signs marked another as crew quarters, and guards in Transterran Properties outfits eliminated a third. The last had to be Mancuso's group. She would be there.

"I still think this is a mistake," said Fionn. "Your first priority should be rest. You can barely stand." The *cú sidhe* tilted its head as it examined its master. "You aren't prepared to meet with anyone. You hardly make a good impression in your current state."

"I need to talk to her. There's so much I don't understand."

"And if she has answers, will she share them with you?"

A ball of red light appeared at head-height, one meter in front of Donal. It had a corona, giving it a solar look. A servitor. Donal could not explain how he knew, but he knew. Every magician he had ever met could distinguish a custom-built spirit from one that had independent existence. Professor N'Kembe described it as looking at a realistic painting. No matter how good the artist, some quality would make it seem artificial. So Donal knew that the half-meter wide red sun before him had been created by spells, but he could not tell more without further examination.

When it spoke, its voice was hollow, an imperfect copy of a voice Donal had heard at Ambrosia the night before.

"Donal Cuthbert, you are confirming the location of Tai Shi Li Hua, a prominent 4M employee tasked with Mr. Mancuso's safety. We ask you not to pursue this."

So they've set a watchdog on me. That means it might have teeth. Donal saw Fionn shuffle a couple of steps sideways. Donal gave the tiniest nod he could manage. He needed to buy time for his familiar to move behind the servitor. The position would give them a slight advantage in a fight, if the servitor did not perceive in a three hundred sixty degree arc, which it might. Still, they could attack it from opposite sides. If Donal, exhausted and spent, could manage an attack.

"You expect me to sit alone in my cabin for the whole trip? The only people I have to talk to are part of some group that opposes you."

Fionn reached its mark without the servitor showing any sign that it had noticed.

"What we hope you will do," said the hollow voice, "is consider our plan, and not reveal our location. If you refuse, then we hope you will remove yourself from harm's way."

"Suppose I want to go collect the papers—"

"Donal Cuthbert, we have determined that it is unlikely you have hidden the package. Interplanetary and Intraplanetary Express' insurance requires them to prohibit their couriers from storing a package within an uncontrolled area, and they stipulate that a courier's wards alone are insufficient protection. You have not hidden it on your person or in your stateroom. Therefore, the only other likely location for the package is inside the ship's safe.

"Due to anti-piracy regulations, retrieving an object from the ship's safe while outside of port requires the approval of both the ship's captain and either the chief of security or the executive officer. If we are to hope that you will assist us, we cannot prohibit you from going to Captain John Jacobs."

Donal decided that a servitor this verbose had to have been created by a magician with aspirations in either politics or law. Donal lost the thread of its oration and realized that Fionn was right: he needed rest. But since his quarters no longer felt safe, the purser would have to find him another room, somewhere away from that droning ... wait, what?

"What was that last part?"

"Following the conclusion of the reasons we cannot and would not interfere with any attempt on your part to speak with ship personnel, I explained that if you attempt to approach either of the two companies at issue, I would be forced to stop you by any means necessary."

Fionn growled and bared its long fangs, emerald fur standing on the spirit deerhound's back.

If the servitor heard the growl, it ignored the sound.

"We would prefer not to harm you unless you give us no choice, which is why I am currently executing the basic form of prevention—"

"Filibustering," said Donal.

"—asking you not to do it."

Donal rubbed his face, ran his fingers through his hair. He could not muster the focus for an analytical spell that would reveal the scope and capabilities of this Red Sun servitor. He hoped he did not have to fight. He could barely shift enough awareness to spot its signature and tell that it had more power than it needed to follow him around and talk. Enough power that the servitor might be able to destroy Fionn, if Donal could not provide magical support. It might even be able to kill Donal.

"Fine."

"Thank you, Donal Cuthbert. We are confident that you will make the right decision. After all, the extent of the threat they represent endangers Earth as much as Mars."

"I'll find something else to do. Now leave me alone."

The servitor slipped through the wall and into the bulkhead. No wonder Donal had missed it. Even though a magician could sense magic through physical objects, walls and doors presented a psychological barrier — Donal did not perceive through them because he did not expect to. Perhaps if he had been more awake....

Donal pulled the lever to summon the bubble then turned to Fionn.

"What's your excuse?"

"I have already explained this, master. I think you would be better served to not try to repair the rift between yourself and Tai Shi Li Hua because she appears to share the imperialist goals—"

"Not that. I meant, why didn't you notice the servitor before it popped up in front of me?"

Fionn tilted its head, which Donal had come to think of as the canine equivalent of a shrug. "I did."

"And you didn't warn me about it because..."

"I stayed aware of its location and activities, and did not deem it an immediate threat until it spoke of stopping you 'by any means necessary.' Until that time, it appeared to be an ordinary watcher, or perhaps a messenger awaiting mandated circumstances to deliver its message." Fionn cocked its ears. "Do you wish me to inform you of every watcher?"

"Yes ... wait ... are they common?"

"Today alone three others observed you. Two were sendings from the ship's mage, following you to the bubble after each encounter with the deep space spirits. The third carried a signature I did not recognize, and it approached three times while you slept earlier. All three times it ascertained that you remained in your cabin and left."

"Point taken."

The bubble arrived.

"Will you please go rest now?"

"I'll do better than that." They stepped into the bubble's cage. To the undines, Donal said, "Main Deck, please." As the bubble descended, Donal turned to his familiar and said, "I can't relax in my cabin enough to sleep. Red Sun isn't going to let me talk to Li Hua. But surely there is no one on this ship who would stop me from getting a massage."

THREE HOURS.

Tunold stomped his disgust into the deck as he stalked from the cargo hold to the nearest bubble. Three hours of interviewing deckhands and dockhands without a single lead to show for the effort. Three hours of looking into frightened, innocent faces and questioning their loyalty. Three hours wasted.

Goldberg should have been doing this. Finding smuggled weapons was a job for the ship's watch, not the executive officer. But Goldberg had his hands full, and Tunold knew he had to take charge or the Old Man would do it himself. It might not be the ex oh's job, but it sure as hell was not the captain's.

Tunold paced as he waited for the bubble. It never came fast enough. Ever. He should have an override. He should, and the captain and Goldberg. Probably Tunold's fault they did not. The Old Man probably thought his ex oh would abuse it. But was it abuse if he used it in the line of duty?

His bubble ride from the cargo bay to the Security Deck took too long. Maybe Machado could do something about that. Possibly Jang. Tunold jogged the length of the Security Deck to the crew bubble.

Tunold had not yet covered the cleaning and cooking crews, but he doubted that anyone among them was the smuggler. He had initially ruled them out entirely, but on flimsy grounds. Now that he gave them further consideration, he decided that any of the cooks or the cleaners might have snuck a crate of contraband aboard under the guise of "supplies." Tunold would have to investigate those crews as well.

Hell.

Those crews could wait. Better for Tunold to finish this thread first, following from the workers to their supervisors. The boatswain, Olmega, ran the deckhands and dockhands. He could have had them moving contraband without their knowing it. The purser, Joffries, handled all the purchases. He could have dummied up an invoice and a label.

The crew bubble responded in proper time, but Tunold still growled that it took too long, as did the ride to Crew Deck Two. Once the he reached that deck, Tunold would need only a dozen steps to enter the office shared by the purser and the boatswain.

When the bubble stopped the cage opened. Tunold stepped down the hall and threw open the door without knocking. The office was three meters square and dominated by the purser's and boatswain's desks, the air above them busy with displays of duty rosters, planning calendars, files and forms. He found the two young officers at their desks, laughing at some shared joke.

At Tunold's abrupt entrance, the two men leapt to attention. He held them still with an evil grin. While the *Horizon Cusp* kept its chain of command clear, it did not stand on ceremony to the extent that junior officers should snap to attention at the sight of their ex oh, no matter how he might have surprised them. Tunold had caught them at something.

"Gentlemen, I believe we have a problem."

He closed the door behind him with a soft click.

"MR. CUTHBERT?"

The voice of the Swedish angel startled Donal awake. He lay stretched out, face-down on a massage table. He yawned.

"Mr. Cuthbert?" Her wonderful fingers were back, but this time they jostled Donal's shoulder instead of pressing deep into his tense muscles. Not that he felt tense anymore. Donal wished he could remember her name, if only out of respect for her skill. She continued, "Some men from security are here for you. I'll tell them you'll be out as soon as you're dressed."

Donal frowned.

Security? What did I do this time? Aloud, he said, "Thank you. Sorry I fell asleep. How long was I out?"

"That's all right, we could spare the room for a couple of hours and you needed it. Leave the towel in the basket, if you would."

Donal sat up after he heard the door close. His clothes were on the chair against one wall, where he had left them. He stretched, rolled his neck and shoulders, and reveled in feeling rested. He could think clearly again. He knew he still needed sleep, but now he felt as though he had stayed up late to study, rather than as though he had been beaten unconscious.

The setting probably helped him sleep too; the room was decorated in gentle blues and greens, pastoral scenes on the walls gently lit the room to the edge of dimness, with ferns in each corner producing soft guitar music. He enjoyed the tune for a breath, then turned his thoughts to the ship's watch. As he dressed, Donal called Fionn.

The emerald deerhound paced once around its master.

"You look much better, but do not press yourself hard or you will need days to recover instead of one night." Fionn nodded. "More sleep now would be best."

"I don't intend to pick a fight." Donal pointed at the door to the lobby. "Ship's watch is waiting. Go check them out. I need to know if I should expect trouble. Maybe those Red Sun fanatics filed a complaint because I took down two of their people. Don't look at me like that. They're hiding in plain sight and they want to cut me off from the other passengers. I doubt they're above setting me up."

As Fionn left, Donal tossed the towel into the wicker basket beside the door. Even his slacks and flannel shirt felt more comfortable. He checked his watch. It was almost six. Donal had slept for three or four hours. The Swedish angel was very patient.

His familiar returned through the closed door and said, "They are at their ease, and neither holds a ready weapon nor practices the Art. I do not think they mean you harm."

"Thank you. You better vanish, just in case."

The *cú sidhe* faded from normal vision before Donal walked into the lobby, where two watchmen flipped through a sports magazine. They looked up from discussing the pitfalls of interplanetary expansion for professional baseball.

"Mr. Cuthbert," said the tall one, "we are here to escort you to dinner."

"Thank you for the thought, but I can make it on my own. Ambrosia isn't more than thirty meters from here."

"Change of venue by order of the captain. If you'll come with us, please."

Donal felt his shoulders tighten.

TUNOLD LET HIS JUNIOR OFFICERS WORRY FOR A MOMENT, THEN SAID, "Both of you, front and center!" He pointed to a spot on the deck where they would feel exposed, would lack the safety of desks between themselves and him. Despite the cramped office, they had space to stand in front of the folding visitors' chairs.

Tunold prowled around the purser and boatswain as though he were still in the Navy. He could not afford to savor the feeling though. They would soon question this level of formality. He stopped in front of them, where he could see both of their faces at once.

"I'm here because I've discovered *contraband*." He snapped the word out with a jut of his chin. Joffries stared straight ahead, while Olmega's brow came down in confusion. Tunold held the silence, squeezed it until it seemed sure to burst.

A drop of sweat trickled down the side of Joffries' face.

"Mr. Olmega!" Tunold said.

"Sir?"

"Take a walk!" Tunold waited until he heard the door close behind him. He kicked a folding chair at Joffries, who caught it. Tunold folded his arms, a slow, deliberate movement. "Have a seat."

The purser sat. "Sir, let me explain."

Tunold gave him a crisp nod.

Joffries sputtered, then forced his words out in their proper order. "I didn't think there'd be any harm, sir. The tariffs have gotten out of control lately, and that can be hard on an independent businessman. So—"

"Mr. Joffries, what did they tell you you're smuggling?"

"Sir, we are talking about the Martian cognac. Aren't we?"

Tunold rubbed his temples. There couldn't be two smugglers on the ship. Could there? "Martian cognac."

"Yes, sir. From the first batch made on Mars."

"Did you actually see the cognac?"

"They gave me a bottle, sir."

Joffries hurried to retrieve it from a desk drawer. The seal was still intact. Tunold extended a hand and the crestfallen purser turned it over. The label looked legitimate.

"This will be tested by the ship's alchemist, and if she confirms that it's safe, the crew will share it at the end of the voyage."

"Safe, sir?"

"Show me the crate."

Joffries led him back to the cargo hold, then to the section usually reserved for the crew's oversized stowage. One of the crates, labeled and marked as though it were furniture, sat open and empty.

The purser's jaw bounced off his collarbone and his eyes opened so wide that he might have been able to see in the dark. He clawed and scraped inside the crate, but came up with nothing more than handfuls of paper packing material.

"I can't even find bottle dividers." Joffries' brow wrinkled in confusion. "This crate never held cognac. Well, no more than one bottle."

"No, it did not." Tunold sighed. "Congratulations, Mr. Joffries, you have smuggled weapons aboard this ship."

"Sir!" Joffries snapped to attention, tears running down his face. "I swear I didn't—"

"You did." Tunold shook his head. Joffries was a stupid kid, but a smuggling charge might smarten him up. He might even become a spacer someday, but not on this ship. "Now, tell me everything."

"A change of venue?" said Donal. "Am I in trouble?"

The guards laughed in what sounded to Donal like honest surprise, and the shorter one said, "Nothing like that. You did us all a favor when you gave Machado and Cromartie a hand. It's just that we've had one murder on this trip already and the captain wants to avoid a second."

"I might be a target?"

"I don't see why you would be," said the taller guard with a shrug, "but then you did help foil the attack on the ship. That might put you on the list. Anyway, the captain doesn't want to take chances."

"Who was murdered?"

The guards told him the story of the big brawl and the stabbing of Mr. al Rashid. Donal felt a sudden chill start at his cheeks and creep down his neck and back. He sat on a nearby padded bench. Mr. al Rashid was dead. The Red Sun agents had claimed it, but Donal had not really believed them. Maybe exhaustion had been playing tricks on him, but they had not seemed that competent. Still, they had started a brawl, arranged to have two creatures attack the ship, and murdered one of their targets. They might have been fanatics, but Donal had underestimated them.

Their leader said that they wanted Donal's help, but the watchmen were right: he had foiled them once already. Did that make him a target if he refused to do their bidding? They warned him that no one was neutral. If he refused them, Donal needed to be ready for a fight.

Well, sitting here would do Donal no good. He might learn something at dinner, and whether he did or not, he needed food. Even Fionn would support that.

Donal stood and followed the watchmen to the bubble while Fionn guarded his back. They rode the bubble a short way, then took a passage to a second bubble that took them up the water tube to the top levels of the ship, where the passages narrowed to two meters instead of three and shortened by a half-meter or so.

Ship's watch personnel were everywhere. Four patrolled outside this bubble, and Donal spotted two more standing sentinel beside another bubble and others by the access hatches.

Donal felt wards chime as he was escorted down the passage past the crew quarters. The first wards he crossed felt like detection magic, similar to the ones cast on exam rooms at U.C. Santa Cruz. Those triggered when someone tried to cross them carrying cheating aids. Donal suspected that these wards looked for weapons, or even violent intentions if the magician put enough time and effort into them.

Detection wards often doubled as a magic circle, a first line of defense against any incoming spells or spirits. The split purpose inhibited their protection aspect though. If the ship's watch were serious about keeping outside influences out, there would be another ... ah, there. Donal saw a line drawn across the threshold at the end of the hall. The corners of the open doorway also had small, painted symbols.

Donal shifted his awareness and sighed in relief when the adjustment came easily. He saw a serious ward attached to that threshold: strong, straightforward, and difficult to cast. It would allow access only to a predetermined group of people. Donal did not need further analysis to recognize it as the work of the ship's mage.

Donal could also see that every member of the watch carried a Pacifier and a small defensive charm that looked as though it guarded against mental manipulation.

Donal muttered a quick prayer to Lugh as he crossed the wards. He of the Long Arm must have been listening, because Donal felt his *cú sidhe* enter the room behind him. Fionn was on the guest list. The first to arrive, Donal could choose any seat he wanted.

Looking around the large mess hall, Donal felt a twinge of nostalgia for his college dormitory. That dining hall had been laid out the same way: many round tables surrounded by uncomfortable chairs, a buffet setup at one end - empty in the ship's case - and an opening in the wall where dirty dishes could be handed to the dish-washers. The décor distinguished the mess hall from its college equivalent. Duty rosters, maps, and ship regulations lined the stark walls, not paintings or windows. Also, the dorm cafeteria did not have the Starchaser Spacelines logo, done five meters wide and three meters tall on one wall.

Six members of the ship's watch, split into groups of two, formed a triangle perimeter around the dining area. A seventh, the Initiate Cromartie, examined the room's wards. Donal could tell that Magister Machado had cast them, and if Cromartie checked them, then the spells must have been rushed.

The Initiate looked pasty and exhausted, much like Donal had felt before the massage. Was Magister Machado as badly off? Perhaps the ship's mage would need Donal's help after all.

16

THE DINNER HOUR APPROACHED, AND JACOBS TOOK THE SLOPING passage from the bridge down to Crew Deck One. From there he rode the bubble to Crew Deck Three and the mess hall. As he strode across the deck he wondered how much grief Mancuso and bin Zuka would give him over his plan.

Tunold hailed him from further down the hall. "There you are, Captain. I'm glad I caught you."

Jacobs stopped. The diners could wait a few minutes. "What have you learned, Ex Oh?"

"Our purser is an idiot. He smuggled Pacifiers aboard thinking they were bottles of Martian cognac. The crate he showed me was empty, so the conspirators must have them all. From the size of the crate, twenty would be my guess."

"If he didn't inspect the goods, why did he think it was Martian cognac?"

"They gave him a bottle."

Jacobs smacked his fist into his palm. "Keep it away from me. I might break it over the dunce and waste the cognac."

"It's with Fredrickson for testing, and I confined Joffries to quarters. He knows he screwed up, and we might need the brig space before all this is over."

"Strip his quarters of all personal possessions and disable the entertainments. We may need the brig space, but he smuggled weapons aboard my ship. He doesn't get a soft sentence. Anything else?"

"I'll have a full report to you by morning."

"Thanks, Kris." Jacobs sighed, then pointed down the hall. "How do my dinner plans look?"

"Stiff, but functional. All the guests have arrived, and security is in place, but Cromartie looks like he's been pulling double shifts on the Flying Dutchman. I don't know what he'll have left if anything goes wrong. Any chance Mash could help?"

"None. Between the attacks, the escape, and the dinner wards, he's finished until he's had some sleep." Jacobs shook his head. "I'll tell you, Kris, I'm starting to think all our ships need an assistant mage on the payroll. The first time we've had anything major go wrong, systems problems aside, and even Machado could not have handled it all on his own."

"Think that's what happened—"

"No more *Beamrunner* talk. We won't know anything until we see the final report." He puffed out a breath. "How'd Mancuso and bin Zuka take the news about the change of venue?"

"Bin Zuka just nodded. Mancuso made a snide remark, but didn't bitch about it."

Jacobs snorted. "Their guards behaving themselves?"

"All still in their cabins as of two minutes ago. Pity the magicians are down."

"Yes, this would be a perfect time to find the conspirators. Which reminds me, if Goldberg asks while I'm at dinner, my answer is still no; he can't go in without magical support. We don't know the full extent of their resources."

"I still say we should throw all the bodyguards in the brig, just to be sure."

"Lovely thought, but we're getting enough bad press lately."

"Anything I need to know before I take the bridge?"

"Five by five right now. Space is clear around us, and engineering and maintenance have gotten all systems back to full capacity. Franklin's going to be up late brewing replacement alchemical supplies, but you should have an easy shift."

"That makes one of us. Good luck, John."

DONAL TOOK A SEAT ALONG THE PERIPHERY, NEAR AN EMPTY SECTION OF wall, with a clear line to the door in case anything went wrong. No sooner did he sit than Cromartie said in a deep, tired voice, "Mr. Cuthbert? The captain has ordered that all guests sit at the same table. Any of the inner tables."

"But I'm not part of their negotiations."

Cromartie shrugged. "I have my orders."

So they wanted Donal to sit at the adults table. He considered his options, and took a chair with an unobstructed path to the door at the closest of three inner tables. He dismissed Fionn rather than risk raising the tension level by having a familiar present. Doubt crept in within seconds. What if the other magicians had familiars out? Maybe even visible to the naked eye?

Donal had seen no familiars at the previous dinner, but tonight someone was dead. Donal wished he had paid more attention to the familiars unit of his Thaumaturgic Etiquette class. He shifted in his seat, toyed with the silver faun on his pendant. He needed backup. He should call Fionn back. But if he did, he would have nothing up his sleeve.

Focus, Donal. The ship's watch is here. Let them handle any problems. Like Dad always says, 'Don't go looking for a fight, especially when a fight might come looking for you.' All the big targets are going to be in one room soon, this room. Donal looked around the room. The watchmen and women looked fit and ready for action, except Cromartie who appeared two spells from unconscious. *And Machado isn't here, so he may be down. If the mages are weak right now, maybe this meeting isn't so safe. Maybe I should call Fionn back.*

The representatives from Transterran Properties arrived: a magician and a businessman by the look of them, both middle-eastern. Donal noted with interest that the magician was in charge, not a security agent like Li Hua. Most mages focused on their craft to the exclusion of other major disciplines. This man was an exception.

"You must be Donal Cuthbert, the courier," said the magician. Donal recognized him now: the man he had thought of as Swarthy at dinner the night before. "My name is Imenand bin Zuka, and this is Omar el-Sawy, my assistant." He paused as both men offered their hands to shake; Mr. bin Zuka's grip was firm but without challenge, while Mr. el-Sawy seemed to have something to prove. Donal rubbed his aching hand under the table. Mr. bin Zuka continued, "I am pleased that they allowed us our familiars. I do so dislike being without mine, don't you?"

"Yes." Donal wondered if everyone knew about Fionn except the two pseudo-guards he fought earlier. A quick shift of awareness told him that Mr. bin Zuka's familiar was concealed within its base, a bracelet literally up the man's sleeve. Donal finished, "I feel positively naked without him."

Mr. bin Zuka's mouth straightened in apparent distaste at the image, but the arrival of the 4M party spared Donal from an impulsive attempt to cover the awkward moment. He stood as soon as he saw Li Hua, and the Transterran Properties representatives followed his example.

"Standing for a lady? This *is* going to be a formal dinner," said Mr. Mancuso. "Perhaps I should have worn my tuxedo."

Even more than his counterparts, Mr. Mancuso wore a suit that Donal was sure had cost more than his college education. For the price of the three ties present, Donal could probably have paid for a semester of graduate school.

But Donal noticed these details only as shadows beside the radiance of Li Hua. While he had no sense of how much her sapphire blue dress must have cost, it shimmered and clung in ways that other dresses aspired to. Accenting her outfit she wore a simple silver neck-lace and matching earrings whose magic Donal knew extended beyond drawing male admiration.

"Good to see you, Cuthbert," said Mr. Mancuso as he and Li Hua joined the party at the table. "Glad you survived the day's chaos. Wish more of us had. Imenand, have you met Cuthbert? He played an important role in saving the ship from whatever that thing was. What did you call it, Tai Shi?"

"A zuglodon," said Li Hua who had not yet stopped smiling at Donal, even when she looked at her employer. "Two of them."

Does this mean I'm forgiven?

"Hell of a thing, hell of a thing. I told you, Tai Shi, he's one to keep an eye on. And if I'm not mistaken, he'll keep an eye on you too. But in that dress, who could blame the boy?"

Donal felt his neck begin to warm, but subtle breathing exercises helped him stave off an embarrassing blush. Mr. Mancuso shook hands with everyone at the table, and they all sat down. Mr. Mancuso's grip was tight, but not as though he made it a contest. Donal's guess was that the businessman knew how strong he was and did not care if you knew it too.

"Where's the captain?" continued Mr. Mancuso. "I thought he was supposed to be dining with us. Something about 'getting to the bottom of all this' or something. Imenand, do you know what the hell he's talking about?"

"I understand that the good captain believes some of our own guards to be conspiring against us."

"That's right," said Captain Jacobs from the doorway, cutting straight across whatever Mr. Mancuso might have said. As the captain approached the table, Donal noticed something: Misters Mancuso and bin Zuka had walked like confident men who knew themselves and their places in the universe. They had taken solid strides and their feet had clicked with certainty at every step. Captain Jacobs walked like he was in charge. Command hung about him like an aura, suffused his movements with a sense of priority. The thunk of his boots on the ceramic deck sounded like a metronome, establishing the tempo for everything around him. No wonder he held his own with these men.

AS HE SHOOK THEIR HANDS, JACOBS WISHED HE HAD THE WALNUT-crushing grip of his youth. These days he could barely match the testing handshake of bin Zuka's aide. They all sat. Jacobs considered the assembly. How far could he trust any of them? As accomplished businessmen, both bin Zuka and Mancuso could have lied to Goldberg and Tunold. Either of them could have ordered the death of al Rashid and might be planning to murder at least one person at this table, including Jacobs. Nor could Jacobs ignore the possibility that the culprit was Tai Shi or el-Sawy. Jacobs had to pay close attention to all of them. At least the courier's actions made him an unlikely candidate.

"I've got a murderer down in the brig who claims to be acting alone, but who has at least two accomplices down there with him. I've got a chief of security telling me that he thinks this conspiracy has more helpers among both sets of personal guards, and that at least one of you two is a target." The captain pointed at both bin Zuka and Mancuso. "Maybe both."

"The other target is Mr. Mancuso," said the courier.

EVERY EYE AT THE TABLE TURNED TO STARE AT DONAL. THE CAPTAIN scowled. Mr. Mancuso raised his eyebrows in amused surprise. Mr. bin Zuka adjusted in his seat as though waiting for a story. Mr. el-Sawy picked up his dinner knife and glared at Donal. Li Hua's eyebrows crinkled in thought, but even she had one hand toying with her enchanted necklace. The silence began to crumple, and Donal filled it before it could collapse.

"I'm not one of them," he said. Donal spread his hands wide on the table in the acknowledged "not casting" gesture, grateful that he remembered that much from etiquette class. He closed his eyes and sought confidence in a breath. He knew he was taking a big chance. This was no subtle approach to the captain. The entire ship would know that he told. Red Sun would kill him for this. But Donal could not just sit by and let those fanatics murder a man. A second man. He opened his eyes and spoke slowly. "They grabbed me this afternoon and asked me to help them. I turned them down."

"I would ask you to repeat that," said Mr. bin Zuka. He drew a small magnifying glass out of his pocket and held it up to one eye like a monocle. The others at the table now watched bin Zuka while Donal repeated his statement. "He tells the truth, or believes he does."

"I can't believe you brought a Veracitor to a business dinner," said Li Hua.

Donal agreed with the thinly veiled disgust he heard in her voice. Veracitors had not been used by respectable businesses for ten or twelve years. They were considered an insult these days, and a person who needed one presumably dealt with untrustworthy people.

"That they are not permitted during negotiations does not preclude carrying them," said Mr. bin Zuka as he put the Veracitor back in his pocket. "And you cannot deny that they come in handy."

"Did you also bring an Oathbinder?"

"They are not illegal in interplanetary space." Mr. bin Zuka held a patient tone, as though he had expected the question. "Nor is transporting them a customs violation. But no, I do not carry one on my person. Shall we discuss what you carry, Ms. Tai Shi?"

"Enough," said the captain.

"I did not bring you here to fight," continued Jacobs. This conversation had veered perilously close to off-course. Too much pride at this table. He needed to make these people focus on the current problem, not hunt for others. "And I don't want any more magic during dinner. I could have told you that Cuthbert was telling the truth, because if he wanted any of us dead, all he had to do was nothing. He risked his own life to save the ship this afternoon, and he had no obligation to do so."

"Actually," said bin Zuka, "he did. That is, presuming that Mr. Cuthbert is a licensed Journeyman in either New Leningrad or San Francisco, the two ports of call for this voyage. Thaumaturgy licenses in both places stipulate that a practitioner who is not otherwise engaged must offer aid against any clear and present magical threat. Rather like an off-duty doctor being required to assist at the scene of an accident. I was otherwise engaged with my duties, as was Ms. Tai Shi. Mr. Cuthbert, however, was available."

"That only applies," said Tai Shi, "if the threat is one that the magician could reasonably address. Good luck finding a licensing board that will agree that a Journeyman fresh out of college with no space certifications could stand against a zuglodon."

"A Journeyman under the direction of a Magister?"

Jacobs slapped an open hand on the table hard enough that several darting hands steadied their water glasses. "I said enough. We have a very real threat to face right now, and I won't have this discussion descend into accusations, loyalty tests, or other bullshit." Jacobs turned to Cuthbert, who still had his hands splayed on the table. The boy's eyes darted back and forth, but lingered on the girl — great, another complication. "Mr. Cuthbert, why don't you tell us about this kidnapping, and why I'm just hearing about it now."

"I was trying to get back to my room after the helping with the ... zuglodons?"

Li Hua nodded, a smile lighting her eyes but not yet touching her lips.

"Probably a good thing I didn't know what they were." Donal shook his head. "Anyway, I was worn out, and when guards dressed in 4M uniforms grabbed me, I didn't have the strength to get away." Donal saw Mr. Mancuso's eyes narrow. "I woke up tied to a chair. The kidnappers told me some story about how the big corporations were teaming up to take over all known space, that only they could stop the takeover, and that they needed my help. They wanted me to hand over the package I'm delivering. I think they wanted to use your signatures for magic."

"That might work with most contracts, but ours are protected against such applications," said Mr. bin Zuka. "The inks are a special blend. No one can use those signatures to form a link without the right alchemical key."

"Why doesn't everyone do that?"

"Because," said Mr. Mancuso, who regarded his counterpart with one eyebrow arched, "coming up with the formula in the first place required the resources of more than one corporation, and we have agreed not to publicize it until *after* this deal goes through."

"I hardly think this qualifies as alerting the press," said Mr. bin Zuka.

Mr. Mancuso glared at Mr. bin Zuka. Donal cleared his throat.

"Then either they don't know that or they have the key." Donal shrugged. "Anyway, they worried that I would go to you guys, so they had me tailed and threatened by a servitor."

"What was the threat?" asked the captain.

"They couldn't stop me from going to you, but if I made any move toward 4M or Transterran Properties they would stop me 'by any means necessary.' They also said that if I told you what they were doing, the situation would 'get very ugly.'"

"Why wouldn't they stop you from going to the captain, then?" said Mr. Mancuso.

"I would guess that they had already searched his quarters and could not find the package themselves," said Mr. bin Zuka. "They must have presumed the package to be in the ship's safe, which would require..."

"Me," said Captain Jacobs. "Why am I only hearing about this now?"

"I was still wiped out from my encounter with the zuglodons." Donal shivered as he said the word. He began to realize how close he had come to death today, not once, but twice. No wonder the ship's mage had been furious. "I fell asleep. Sorry."

"Trying to take over all known space," said the captain. "That matches what the murderer said."

JACOBS COMPARED THE COURIER'S STORY AGAINST THE NOTES HE TOOK during his meeting with Goldberg, then spoke directly to Mancuso.

"The murderer seems to think that whatever deal you and Mr. al Rashid were working out was intended to make you the de facto rulers over Earth, Luna, Mars and Venus."

Mancuso laughed. Bin Zuka furrowed his brow. Jacobs glowered. How could Mancuso laugh about this situation? It had cost one man his life already, and threatened dozens more including his own.

"I take it you deny this?"

"Of course!" said Mancuso, "Hell, Imenand, at least Hassan didn't die for some small reason." He chuckled. "We're trying to take over the solar system. That's a good one."

"An understandable conclusion," said bin Zuka, "based on incomplete information." He focused on the captain. "I assure you, Captain Jacobs, that the only empire 4M and Transterran Properties intend to build together is corporate. Hassan al Rashid, may he remember every proper answer from the *Book of the Dead*, had no interest in politics, and would never have aspired to such a goal."

"And that's all either of us will say about it," added Mancuso. "Look, Captain, we can give you all the assurances you want, but we're paying a great deal of money for this private," he glanced at Cuthbert, "semi-private trip, and the exact nature of our business arrangements is not your concern."

"There is no need to be abrupt," said bin Zuka. "Captain, I assure you that while the agreement between Transterran Properties and 4M will greatly expand the wealth and influence of both companies, it will also be a boon to space travel and interplanetary relations. It represents a step forward for the human race. We are not creating a darkness that would cast mankind in shadow."

Sincerity seemed to come off of bin Zuka in waves. Jacobs kept his face neutral, but noted to have Goldberg watch bin Zuka.

"I'm glad to hear it," said Jacobs. He picked up a bottle of merlot from the center of the table and signaled for dinner to be served. The wait staff consisted of more ship's watch. Goldberg's idea. Jacobs continued speaking as he circled the table and poured the wine. "But these people seem to think your agreement will trigger Armageddon, and that presents us with our problem. We don't know exactly how many of these zealots are aboard the ship, or the extent of their capabilities."

"There are at least eight, including an Initiate, and they have Pacifiers," said the courier.

ALL EYES TURNED ONCE MORE TO DONAL. THE CAPTAIN PAUSED HIS pouring long enough to finish some thought, or maybe reach some conclusion, then filled the remaining glasses and returned to his seat. Donal continued.

"This was before the kidnapping. I was resting from my ... ill-considered experiment, when I became aware of a second assault on the ship, and that this time the zuglodon brought reinforcements. I wanted to help. I opened my cabin door, and two people attacked me with Pacifiers."

"Clumsy," said Li Hua with a snort. "I take it you dispatched them?"

"I left them pacified in the hall. I didn't take time to do anything else about them because I wanted to find Magister Machado."

"How do you know they were part of the conspiracy?" asked the captain.

"They were wearing 4M uniforms." Donal shrugged. "I didn't think Ms. Tai Shi would have ordered that sort of attack." Li Hua's smile reached her lips.

"Well," said Mr. Mancuso, "they sure as hell didn't act on any order of mine or hers. I like you, Cuthbert. You're a sharp kid. And you're delivering a package for me. Why the hell would I attack a courier I hired? Bad disguises if you ask me."

"Not disguises," said the captain. "The same uniforms they boarded with. They had to have infiltrated your groups on Mars. But that doesn't tell us who we're dealing with."

"They called themselves Red Sun," said Donal. "And among the kidnappers I saw 4M and Transterran Properties uniforms, but no ship's watch. And one of the kidnappers was an Initiate. I thought it was a woman, but before I left I spotted the illusion magic disguising her face and voice, so there's no telling."

"Red Sun?" said the 4M magnate. "Dissidents, from what I hear. They aren't just pro-Mars, they're anti-Earth. They try to pressure Martian citizens to support only Martian-owned and operated businesses, like theirs. Any company with ties to Earth, like 4M or Transterran Properties — hell, like Starchaser Spacelines or IIX for that matter — would be boycotted and forced to withdraw if Red Sun had their way."

"It isn't quite as bad as that," said Mr. bin Zuka. "They consider themselves Martian patriots, true, but the problem is more that they wish to compete with both our companies in interplanetary trade, despite their having only one-tenth our resources." His head snapped a tight shake, left-right-center. "I suppose they wish to make up the difference in death."

"I suspect that Mr. bin Zuka is closer in this case," said Li Hua, drawing a raised eyebrow from her employer. "Most attempts at corporate and industrial espionage directed against us in the past year have come from Aetheric Dynamics, a Mars-based corporation whose business interests cross 4M's in a number of places. Over the last several months, I've been hearing more and more about overtures toward a merger between Red Sun and Aetheric Dynamics. They may well have been working toward the same goals that we are, only without our scale or financial base."

"Could be," said Mr. Mancuso, "but if they are then they're still idiots. Even we aren't big enough to pull this off. We're not here representing two companies, but six. They would need—"

"It doesn't matter," said the captain.

<hr>

JACOBS REMEMBERED SERVING AS AN ENSIGN ABOARD THE U.S.S. IOWA, when he got between two chief petty officers who squabbled over engine parts. Both men were proud, accomplished engineers, and such salty sailors that they bled seawater. Jacobs could still feel the clack of their skulls slamming together from when the time came to make them listen to reason.

Jacobs' knuckles popped for want of that sensation now.

"It doesn't matter what their strategy is. It doesn't matter what forces brought them together. I'm not even sure that it matters if they're right." Jacobs had all the attention now, and Cuthbert almost dropped his wineglass. "What Red Sun is doing right now threatens the safety of this ship and everyone aboard. We need to contain the threat, and to do that I'm going to want your full cooperation."

"What will you do with them when we reach Earth?" asked bin Zuka. He and Mancuso looked at each other, seemed to reach some understanding between them.

"Turn them over and let the port security sort it out."

"Press nightmare," said Mancuso. "Hassan was Terran, so Earth will claim jurisdiction. The killers are probably Martian, so Mars may try to extradite them for local prosecution."

"Depending on Red Sun's political pull," added bin Zuka.

"Either way, they'll use the attention to smear us. Drag it out as long as they can." The 4M magnate shook his head and picked up his wine. "Wish there were another way."

The conversation paused while the salads were served, tossed greens mixed with sweet fruits and berries, served fresh as the hour they were picked and flavored with subtle dashes of spice. Jacobs waited until the watch stewards had finished before he spoke again.

"I trust you aren't suggesting we throw the murderers overboard."

"I do not believe that either of us would suggest such a thing." Bin Zuka picked up his fork. "And certainly, the conspirators should be remanded to the custody of the proper authorities at the first opportunity. For my part I simply find intolerable the prospect that a technicality might free the man who murdered my friend and employer, Hassan al Rashid, may his name and memory live a thousand years and a year."

"The courts are not my concern. The press is not my concern. The safety of this ship is. I will not have it endangered by fanatics." Jacobs fixed a scowl on both businessmen. "Or mob justice."

"Of course not, Captain," said Mancuso, "nor should you. Grisly business, executing a man, and it would cause an even bigger uproar than a trial." Mancuso tried to catch bin Zuka's eye again, but the other was too busy with his salad. "I think they should be turned over on Earth, where they'll be away from any Martian sympathy votes they might hope for. That's probably why they hit so close to Mars. They must have been hoping that Martians committing a crime in Martian space would fall under Martian law, where homicide can still be justified."

"That only works," said Tai Shi, "if a clear motive can be proven that would move a reasonable man to murder. It's not that easy."

"It. Doesn't. Matter," said Jacobs. Corralling green spacers on their first shore leave was easier than keeping these people on point. "This is not a debate. This is not a court of law. This is a helioship and I am the captain. I am the law here, and I will direct what happens. Are we clear?"

Bin Zuka's face smoothed to impassive. "I think we need," started Mancuso. Jacobs spoke over whatever was coming.

"I didn't ask. Gentlemen, I brought you here to be certain you understood the situation. I have a murderer in custody, and he will stay that way until we reach Earth. That murderer has accomplices among your guards who threaten your safety and the safety of this ship. They need to be thrown in the brig until we can turn them over on Earth.

"Now, I can accomplish this with your assistance or without it, but with will be easier on all of us. What will it be?"

Jacobs focused on Mancuso and bin Zuka, but kept Tai Shi and el-Sawy in his peripheral vision. Mancuso set his jaw. Bin Zuka stilled to a near statue. Jacobs reached up and scratched behind his right ear, signaling the ship's watch to be ready. The two businessmen locked eyes and some sort of agreement seemed to pass between them.

DONAL TRIED TO TAKE A NONCHALANT DRINK OF HIS WINE, BUT THE glass was empty. How could the others eat through so much tension? Not that anyone ate at the moment. The three leaders held a standoff. No one spoke or looked away. Donal wanted to rattle his utensils, or break into song. Anything. He snuck a glance at Li Hua, who had set down her knife and fork to finger her necklace. Mr. el-Sawy gripped his table knife like he contemplated cutting more than lettuce. The businessmen yielded first, at almost the exact same moment.

"Very well, Captain," said Mr. Mancuso.

"We will assist your search in whatever way we can," said Mr. bin Zuka.

"But you must understand," continued the 4M magnate, "that you're telling us our corporate security has been violated, and our business secrets are in jeopardy — a lot of risk to us, but even more to all of our contracts and holdings. Right now we have no idea who these infiltrators are, how they slipped in, or what they might have learned."

"He's quite right, Captain," said Mr. bin Zuka. "Great as the danger might be to us, we must consider the billions of dollars, hundreds of shareholders, and thousands of jobs at stake."

These people had actually begun eating again. Donal forced himself to try a little fruit, and hoped he could keep it down. He also switched to water, though a steward had refilled his wineglass.

"What do you propose?" asked the captain.

Donal had heard that tone of voice once before. The dean of alchemy at U.C. Santa Cruz had asked Donal just what exactly he had been trying to accomplish when he stole those reagents. The dean did not like his answer.

"Trust me, Captain," said Mr. Mancuso, swirling his wine, "we don't want to interfere. You have the authority here, and we want to give you room to do your job. But with so much at stake, we need to make sure this is done right. Properly. The last thing we want to see is a corporate secret splashed onto the headlines because your men didn't know what they found when they searched a room for weapons."

Donal wondered if the captain were aware that he was flexing his fingers. And his jaw, for that matter. Perhaps this was why all magicians studied meditation. If Donal allowed himself to get as angry as he suspected Captain Jacobs was, he might work a spell on the target of his ire without conscious intent. The corners of Donal's lips twitched as he imagined Li Hua calling it 'clumsy.'

"And so, Captain," said Mr. Mancuso, "we would like to send observers to the arrests. Two should be enough, wouldn't you say, Imenand?"

"Yes," said Mr. bin Zuka, in a tone that left Donal unsure the man had known what his counterpart was going to say. "Two observers each should give us both the chance to protect our interests while your men are protecting our persons."

"Fine," said the captain.

Soup was served.

"Two observers each." Earlier in the day Jacobs had considered a trip to the gym, but now he planned to make it happen before bed. His fists urged him to pound a heavy bag until his arms could no longer move. Yes. A heavy bag. "No weapons. No questioning anyone until they are in custody, and every crew order will be followed. I will oversee the investigation. The two of you stay in your cabins, under guard entirely by the ship's watch. Oh, and with your assistants."

"Never mind that," said Mancuso. "I'll want Tai Shi there as an observer. She should be able to help you smoke out the Red Sun agents, too. Knows which of our guards have been around the longest. Hell, she hired most of them. Did you hire all of them, Tai Shi?"

"No, sir. I was making arrangements about the courier matter when you requested additional security. They would have been hired by Pete or David."

"So we're all agreed then?" said Jacobs. "You help us separate the loyal employees from the Red Sun conspirators, while your observers make sure your interests are protected." Both men nodded. Jacobs was surprised, but knew better than to push his luck.

"I can help," said Cuthbert. Jacobs was so surprised that he almost signaled the watch to move in. The intensity of the conversation had made him forget the courier. "I'm sure Magister Machado can find something for me to do."

"No," said Jacobs in a tone that brooked no debate. "Thank you for the offer, but I don't want you involved in this."

Everyone went back to eating, but Jacobs did not like the thoughtful look on Cuthbert's face. Perhaps a night with ship's watch outside his door would make sure the boy took the situation seriously. This was a job for professionals.

"I must say, Captain," said Mancuso between spoonsful of soup, "I will not forget what you're doing for us today." He gave Jacobs a level look. "Or how you're doing it."

The captain's spoon started bending in his fingers. He clenched his teeth until he worried his jaw would crack. He forced himself to think of future contracts, of charting a course to Venus, of retirement in Mazatlan, of straightening his spoon without drawing attention. Lost cause there. Everyone at the table must have seen him do it. He unbent the spoon anyway.

Jacobs turned his attention to the soup. Too thin. He would have preferred a gumbo, or maybe a beef barley soup, but this was one of the chef's creations. No doubt the man would say that it "prepared the way for the main course." As though soup could not be an end in itself.

At least Mancuso and bin Zuka seemed to be following Jacobs' lead, albeit under duress. He had no doubt that they had plans of their own, but as long as they did not oppose him, Jacobs should be able to find the conspirators and get them into the brig. From there, the San Francisco Spaceport could deal with them.

A clatter across the table drew Jacobs' eye, but it was just Cuthbert dropping his spoon.

DONAL DROPPED HIS SPOON, BUT PICKED IT UP WITHOUT LOOKING AWAY from his soup. The others stared, but they did not matter just then, not even Li Hua. Donal understood. Something had bothered him since he recounted his kidnapping, and Donal finally put the pieces together.

At the time, Donal had been looking for Li Hua, and based his search on the four warded cabin areas he could find: his, the ship's, 4M's and Transterran Properties'. He should have counted a fifth: the conspirators. They had told him their story behind wards. Even in his weakened state, Donal felt the tingle of wards when he left their cabin. That cabin was on a passenger deck, so Red Sun could not have been behind the ship's wards. Red Sun's quarters were nowhere near either 4M or Transterran Properties, so they could not have been within either of the other two sets of wards. So where were they?

Donal did not believe for a moment that Red Sun had taken him to their real base of operations. More likely it was a loyalty check — if the ship's watch showed up, they would know Donal had decided against them and they would implement whatever contingency plan they had in mind. Such as killing him. No, the conspirators were somewhere else, safe behind wards that defied casual detection.

That meant that they had concealed their wards, which meant that their real base of operations would also be similarly concealed.

That required camouflage spells, part of the magic of deception, one of Donal's two specialties.

So the captain had forbidden Donal from assisting in the official ship's search. He had not barred Donal from conducting a little search of his own.

17

After dinner, Cromartie held Donal behind until everyone else had left, then escorted him down one bubble and across the Security Deck to another. Donal had just stepped alone into the cage when Pinyin-Lung formed in the air before him.

"Greetings, Donal Cuthbert. My mistress requests the honor of a conversation, if you would be so kind as to meet her on deck Promenade Four."

"It would be my pleasure," said Donal.

"Thank you," said the spirit dragon with a slight bow. "I shall so inform her."

Pinyin-Lung faded through the floor and Donal realized that the bubble had not closed. "P4 please," he said and the undines sealed the bubble and began to slide the cage through the watery tube. Donal paced, tugged at his collar, checked his breath. Li Hua wanted to talk. Did this mean he really was forgiven? He touched his silver faun pendant three times, almost calling Fionn each time but changing his mind.

Donal's hand was on his pendant for a fourth time when the bubble halted and the cage opened onto Promenade Four. Li Hua stood before him, radiant in her blue dress. Without the distractions of the dinner, Donal could appreciate just how beautiful she looked in the gown. She smirked and said, "Would you like to step out of the bubble before it gets called away?"

Donal closed his mouth and joined her in the hall. Out of the corner of his eye he saw Pinyin-Lung fly past on patrol.

"I heard about how you stopped the zuglodon. Excellent work. It's not easy to pull together that complex and potent a spell that quickly. You must be even better than I thought."

Donal wanted to savor the admiration in her eyes, but he had to be honest. "It wasn't easy. I knocked myself out in the process. Magister Machado lectured me about pushing too far."

"It was a rush, wasn't it? Pushing yourself to the limit, risking yourself for others."

"I didn't have time to notice."

She laughed, and this time it carried an undercurrent of intimacy. Donal's breath caught. He moistened his lips. Had she drawn closer?

"That's how it is the first couple of times," she said. "You're scared and shaking, but you can't tell because your head is in the moment. But then you learn to recognize and enjoy it. Magicians have more presence of mind than anyone else. We have to."

Donal could smell her jasmine perfume. Every nerve in his skin tingled. She was beautiful and she was right and she was oh, so close. Was she really that different from him? Donal aspired to push himself in his research, while she pushed herself against ... other people. And killed them.

But the people he saw her kill were trying to murder her and Donal, and they had already slaughtered several innocent bystanders. Were there right reasons to kill? Was saving lives enough, or did the cause have to be noble?

How noble was her cause?

Donal closed his eyes, took a deep breath, and said, "What did you mean when you said, '4M will be the only name that matters?'"

"What?" Li Hua took a step back.

"On Mars. When we toasted the package I was carrying."

"Oh, Donal, you don't believe Red Sun."

"It's not that—"

"I don't believe this." Li Hua spat something in Chinese and pulled the lever for the bubble.

"Li Hua, wait."

She boarded the bubble. Donal watched it slip away.

DONAL RETURNED TO HIS ROOM TO FIND HIS DINNER ESCORTS FROM THE ship's watch standing guard. The tall one said, "We're your babysitters tonight. Chief's orders. We don't need to come in, so we won't get in your way."

Donal shrugged, offered them coffee, which they declined, and pulled out his tuning fork. He ignored their curious glances as he struck it against the doorknob. Knob, door and tuning fork flared fluorescent green for a moment, which was proper, but the tones of the harmonics were off. An overtone had been added that was not Donal's.

He took a step back, shifted his awareness, and spotted a slight orange discoloration in a spot along the wall. Something had tested his wards, but not penetrated them.

"Trouble?" asked the short watchman.

"No, thanks. I have all I can handle." The watchmen exchanged a quick glance, so Donal added, "Just something odd. Nothing to worry about. Thanks for asking."

Donal entered his room and called his familiar the moment he was alone.

"Check the wards." Donal slipped the tuning fork into his pocket and gave the room a quick scan, but saw no signs of physical tampering. "Someone tried them earlier and I need to know where their signature is strongest."

Fionn checked the perimeter, then centered on the discolored spot while Donal knelt in the meditative pose of analysis. He sat on his crossed feet with his knees directly in front of him and thighs resting on his calves. Hands on his knees, he leaned forward, nose first. Donal had begun to accept that these poses, like the breathing patterns, were crutches, training tools. They were slight of mind tricks to help a magician focus. One day he would not need them. Right now, he needed their certainty.

"I have it," said Fionn.

Donal opened to his familiar. The *cú sidhe* enveloped his mind like a shadow, but a shadow that clarified Donal's senses instead of dimming them. He could feel Fionn tug his attention toward the signature. Donal did not see the discoloration as orange now, but as the color of an overripe tangerine. He also heard a quavering trill pulse through the affiliated overtone.

Donal followed that trill toward the signature itself, his body forgotten behind him. He knew that he did not truly separate his consciousness from his physical form, but he was so absorbed in his work that the distinction might have been academic. Along the edges of his mind, Donal felt Fionn lend strength and guidance.

Donal's wards looked to him now like a bubble woven from the web of a spider, with each strand formed by a parameter of his spell: here he saw the rules of detection, there the conditions that would activate defenses against spirits, and over there he saw the sticky overlay that would trap details about anything trying to breach the wards. If Donal inspected the joins and junctions in his spell work, he could figure out its rate of decay, which would tell him when he needed to recast the wards to maintain their full strength.

But right now Donal needed to follow the trill along the sticky overlay to the spot where someone had left a mark: the interloper's signature. What magicians called a "signature" was the distinctive style of each individual's approach to spell casting: the precise timing and logic underlying a spell's structure, which aspects were emphasized, how the parameters joined, and so on. If Donal had time and a complete spell to study, he could have learned a great deal, but the echo left in his wards could take him only so far. He needed to wring out all the information he could.

The signature before Donal lacked the grace of Li Hua's, the sangfroid of Master Machado's, or the workaday practicality of

Cromartie's. It had an almost freehand look, like a smooth circle drawn without a compass: perhaps as accurate, but not as uniform in thickness. Donal thought it resembled the signature of the Red Sun servitor. If only he had gotten to study that construct.

Deeper now.

Donal could tell from the way this spell caster coordinated resonance that he or she could muster as much power as a Journeyman, but the magician lacked precision at the junction points, as though he or she had not pursued technical excellence.

Why would that be? All my classes stressed technical excellence. Could this Journeyman have undergone an old fashioned apprenticeship? Those are rare these days.

The shape of the component elements had a teetering quality that implied a specialty in spells of disharmony. *Good specialty for causing a big brawl.*

Donal yearned to push further, but fatigue wore at his focus. He eased himself back, back from the signature, back from his wards, back from his familiar, back to where his legs had grown numb.

Donal clambered to his feet and shook his prickling legs awake. He had a fix on a signature that had to belong to Red Sun. One more night's sleep and Donal would be ready to hunt for hidden wards.

18

RIGHT. RIGHT. LEFT-RIGHT-LEFT COMBINATION. JACOBS HAD NO TIME for speed bag work tonight, nor running on the small track, nor swimming in the pool. He had not come to the empty crew gym for exercise. He had come to pound the heavy bag.

"A smuggler." Right cross. Left. Right uppercut. "On my crew." Left. Left. Left. Right hook. "A smuggler!"

Left. Right. Left to set up two quick rights, low, body blows on a person, but a heavy bag had no ribs for Jacobs to avoid, no organs for him to bruise. Left cross now, and a reminder that he had seen more than eighty years since his birth. Half a lifetime ago, Jacobs' left cross would have strained the chain, yanked the bottom of the bag up like a man knocked off his feet. Now Jacobs could feel the hit, solid, perfect, and the bag only swayed off-line.

"Observers," he spat. "As if this clusterfuck weren't bad enough."

Right. Left Jab. Right. Right. Straight, solid punches, a little slower than they used to be, but they still felt good to the muscles.

Jacobs did not want to run an investigation around potential hostages. He had meant to leave the whole cleanup in Goldberg's hands. Lord knew the chief did not need his captain over his shoulder. But involving VIPs meant a senior officer had to fly escort. If

Jacobs left it to his ex oh, Tunold would end up putting one of the observers in the med bay or the brig. Jacobs had to run this circus himself.

He blinked sweat out of his eyes. "When the hell did I become a diplomat?"

Left elbow slash across the middle. Right jab once, twice, three times followed by a left hook.

"You'll see, Johnny," Captain Nemeth had warned him. "When you get a command of your own, they'll make a diplomat out of you. No more leading with your fists. You'll have to use your head for something more than smashing noses." Jacobs grinned. He had won more than one fight with his forehead.

Jacobs did not know if his old captain ever believed that his young hellraiser of a helmsman would last long enough to hold his own command, but Captain Nemeth treated all his junior officers as though they might one day be his peers.

Left. Left. Grab and knee strike. Another. Again. Fake the head butt.

The last time Jacobs followed through on a head butt on the bag, he paid for it. "What the hell are you doing?" Ramirez had yelled. Jacobs had not known his soft-spoken doctor *could* yell until that examination. "You're not a kid anymore! You think your head and neck are just going to forgive you for this kind of abuse?" Ramirez got right in Jacobs' face then. "You do this again, even one more time, and I won't give you anything for the pain. If you won't listen to me, I'll let your body remind you just how old you are."

Even Jacobs listened to that threat. The heavy bag hurt a lot worse than a nose.

Right cross, right eye-flick combination followed by a decisive left. Jacobs wiped away more sweat. Exhaustion trembled through his hands and knees. *Duck, old man, don't get lazy.* He forced himself to mix ducks and blocks back into the routine. Not as satisfying, but Jacobs had a word for fighters who slacked on defensive drills: unconscious.

At least Mancuso and bin Zuka agreed to stay in their cabins, protected by the ship's watch. Not the suites they were used to, though. At six hundred hours, Goldberg would move them both to new quarters without telling anyone their location except Jacobs and their respective aides, Tai Shi and el-Sawy. That should help. Perhaps Jacobs should have pushed further and insisted on Machado warding the new suites. Mash said that none of the passengers were as good as he was. Mash might have been arrogant, even for a mage, but he did not boast about magic. He was just that good.

Still, leaving part of their safety in their own hands had relaxed the businessmen, and Jacobs understood the need for control.

Right elbow slash, back fist, left cross, block, right hook to the body, duck, left cross, right jab, duck, left jab, left jab, block, right to the body. Jacobs grinned as the bag swung back a half-meter before returning on its arc. Not quite the young hellraiser anymore, but Jacobs' punch could still have broken a rib.

The difference was that now, Jacobs might break a knuckle on that rib.

Fatigue finally overrode will, and Jacobs collapsed onto a nearby bench, drenched as though he had been bailing water in a sea storm. Another way he knew he was old: he never used to get tired. Not like this. Five minutes with the heavy bag, only two of them serious, and now he felt as though he had pushed the *Horizon Cusp* all the way from Mars to Earth. His lungs struggled to pant. Half the muscles in his body burned or cramped.

Jacobs remembered another time he sprawled exhausted on a bench. Fifteen rounds it took him to beat that Marine sergeant, on points. *Jarhead bastard wouldn't go down. What was his name?* Then, after the fight, Carl jumped up and down on his daddy's chest before Rhonda could grab him. *He couldn't have been more than four, big smile and tight curls like his old man.* Carl would not stay away, jumping around and singing, "Daddy won!" until Jacobs picked him up and held him.

Jacobs managed a misty smile at the memory. He almost wiped it from his face, shoved the moment to the back of his mind, but realized he was in the crew's gym. No one would find him here except someone under his own command, and Tunold said that the crew respected their captain's workouts. No one would bother him. Jacobs could rest for a while before he showered and returned to his quarters. Tomorrow would be a long day; at least he would sleep well tonight. Perhaps Benny Sugg would join him, purring supervision from beside Jacobs' pillow. Carl and Rhonda would have liked Benny.

19

THE NEXT MORNING, JACOBS ARRIVED AT THE MAIN DECK SECURITY office ahead of schedule and found most of the ship's watch prepared for a fight. They were decked out in safety skinsuits the color of adobe, with hoods covering everything but their eyes, and goggles to protect those. Yoshi once said they looked like "ninjas, as interpreted by a ballet company" and the image had always stuck with Jacobs.

Invented to aid in riot suppression in the early days of the Rise of Magic, the skinsuits had defensive charms designed to reflect the force of anything stronger than a light pat. The modern version not only protected its wearer but also doubled her striking strength. They were quite effective, but too expensive to maintain on an everyday basis. The *Horizon Cusp* kept a dozen available in case of emergency.

Goldberg himself had once again opted for his uniform over the safety of a skinsuit. He insisted that he did it to make one more available to his people, but Jacobs suspected his chief hated wearing tight clothing.

"What's our status, Chief?"

"We're just about ready to move. Machado and Cromartie have laid the groundwork with some detection spells, and right now they're warding the exit routes off of P2 and P3 to help with containment. If anyone leaves the 4M or Transterran cabins, we'll know who and where. Machado and Cromartie will join us on P3."

"Mancuso and bin Zuka?"

"On P10 and P11 respectively. Tai Shi handled Mancuso's wards, and bin Zuka cast his own."

"What about the courier?"

"He's already out of the way, so I left him where he was."

"The rest of the ship's watch?"

"Everyone's on shift right now. If they aren't part of the cleanup, they're either with the VIPs, on the bridge, in engineering, or roving, in case of the unexpected."

"What about our observers?"

"Due any minute or we go in without them."

"We should be so lucky."

The universe must have heard Jacobs, because Tai Shi, el-Sawy, and their attachés took that as their cue to arrive. All four observers wore business suits, as though attending a meeting.

Jacobs recognized the blonde woman with Tai Shi as Stevens, Mancuso's business assistant. He recognized el-Sawy's aide from dinner the first night, but had not been introduced to the tall, solid man. None of them wasted time on pleasantries. Everyone seemed to want this search resolved as much as Jacobs did.

"Remember," he said, "you four are only here to witness and provide information. Stay out of the way and let the chief do his job. Chief?"

"Okay, ladies and gentlemen," said Goldberg to the ship's watch, "one Pacifier each. Let's make this quick and smart." He gave his captain a wry glance, then tapped the comm pad on his desk with a single finger. Jacobs scoffed: comm pads were made to be slapped. When Jefferson's image appeared, the chief said, "Bridge, this is Goldberg. We're ready to go in. Kill the bubbles."

"No bubbles?" asked el-Sawy. "How will we get there?"

"Access ladders, mostly." Jacobs grinned. "Hope you aren't afraid of a little exercise."

Donal started his morning with meditation to find balance and cleanse his mind of stress and doubt. He began in silence on his bed, but after half an hour he rose and showered with ritual slowness, his thoughts empty of all but the basic actions of cleanliness: fresh body, fresh mind, fresh day.

Donal toweled dry, dressed, and cast an enchantment on Fionn to let the *cú sidhe* penetrate deception magic. He sent Fionn to find any spells that matched the signature they had analyzed the night before, anything that might lead them to the wards. Even traces of expired spells would help.

Donal then ordered a simple room service breakfast: fruit and a bagel, with water.

When his food arrived, Donal noticed that his babysitters were gone, probably to bed unless they were going to be part of "the fun," as Mr. Mancuso had called it.

Fionn returned as Donal finished eating. "I have found a ward that matches the signature. The one we seek is two floors above us." The *cú sidhe* twitched its ears. "Are you certain we should not report this...."

"The ship's watch is busy enough right now, and I'm sure not going to tell 4M or Transterran Properties." Donal shook his head. "You should have heard them last night. The captain is trying to keep us alive and they're worried about trade secrets and stock prices. Maybe they're no better than Red Sun. Maybe they're even worse."

"They do not wish to kill you. The Red Sun does. They as much as said so."

"I doubt that, or they would have come after me last night when I was exhausted. I would have been easy prey, especially if they took any blood, hair, or skin yesterday while they had me unconscious. With even one of those as a link, they could have put together a spell that would cut through any defense I could have mustered last night. But here I am." Donal stood. "I don't know, Fionn, maybe they'll target me and maybe they won't. But I do know that they are going after Mr. Mancuso, and they're willing to kill us all to get him. I refuse to sit here and do nothing while they try."

"Could you not enlist Tai Shi Li Hua? Their target is the man she is paid to defend."

"We're not exactly on the best of terms right now."

"This cause could be reason enough to set aside your differences."

"I also don't want to kill them. There's been enough killing."

"You think she would murder?"

Donal stopped and sighed.

"I don't think so, but I don't *know* she wouldn't. If I were to bring her into something like this, I'd have to *know* it."

"Can you afford to go in without an ally?"

"I can't afford to go in conflicted." Donal took a deep breath that reached down to the soles of his feet and into the deck below him, then let it out as slowly as he could, eyes closed. By the time he finished, he had found his balance again. "Besides, I have an ally. I have you." He stuck his tuning fork up his sleeve. "Let's go."

Jacobs chuckled as he reached the access panel to P2, behind the bulk of the security team but ahead of the observers. The whole group had climbed down five meters or so from the main deck. If the observers complained, he could send them to wait with their employers. Of course, that would mean another twenty to forty meters by access ladder, depending on whether they returned to Mancuso or bin Zuka. Jacobs chuckled again.

Promenade Two had only the expensive cabins: large rooms and suites with fancy furnishings, combination shower-bathtubs, and thick carpets everywhere, even in the wide, tall hallways. Jacobs came out of the access panel and found Goldberg organizing the team, including Machado, Cromartie and another five watchmen and women who were dressed in regular uniforms instead of skinsuits, to minimize their implicit threat of violence. Goldberg, Cromartie and those five would lead the way, while Machado and the remainder of the team stood ready.

The whole motley gathering passed the first two doors of the 4M-occupied section. Two skinsuited watchmen peeled off to stand rear guard while the group moved to the third door. 4M's Initiate was behind this door, and Jacobs had insisted on dealing with the magicians first.

"Anything we need to know?" asked Goldberg.

Jacobs looked at Tai Shi, who shook her head.

"I understand the need to check everyone," she said, "But Claire has been with us for years. She's a good Initiate. She won't have been involved."

Goldberg knocked, and a middle-aged woman opened the door. Her skin had the perpetual sunburn of a Martian. "Yes?" she said.

"My name is Saul Goldberg. I am chief of security for the *Horizon Cusp* and I have permission from your employer to ask you to identify yourself and repeat a prepared statement under the confirmation of a Veracitor, to be witnessed by two 4M employees of Mr. Mancuso's choosing." Goldberg gestured to Tai Shi and Stevens, and continued, "The statement is this: 'I have not been working or conspiring, through action or inaction, against the continued health and well-being of Donatello Mancuso or Hassan al Rashid or both.'"

During her recitation Jacobs watched Cromartie study the woman through bin Zuka's Veracitor. She looked nervous, like a cadet before a stern instructor. When she finished, Cromartie nodded.

"Thank you very much," said the chief. "We appreciate your cooperation and ask that you remain in your cabin for the next two hours. I'm afraid that room service will be unavailable during this time."

Claire nodded stiffly and closed the door.

"Finish this floor first?" asked Goldberg.

"Sorry, chief," said Jacobs. "We deal with the greatest potential threats first, and that means 'casters."

The group marched back to the access ladder and began their ascent two floors to Promenade Three, on the other side of the main deck. Two skinsuited watch members stayed behind to guard the access ladder, in case the conspirators had plans of their own.

DONAL TRIED TO CALL A BUBBLE, BUT IT DID NOT ANSWER ITS LEVER. HE scrounged around, found an access hatch, and began the climb to P11. As he crawled up the cold metal ladder in the cramped channel, he considered the magician he was going to see. Donal believed that this person had not studied collegiate magic, but had trained as an apprentice. Donal had heard that apprenticeship carried some advantages, such as specialized training that could reach graduate level at times, and custom lesson plans that emphasized the talents of the student. It did have limitations, though: the scope of study was said to be narrower, and the teacher passed on his weaknesses alongside his strengths. The breadth of Donal's education might give him an edge if it came to a fight.

By the time Donal stepped back into a hallway, he had decided that climbing was almost as good a workout as swimming. He could feel a pleasant soreness through the muscles up and down his arms, as well as in his shoulders and calves. Perhaps he should take access ladders to and from meals aboard the *Horizon Cusp*.

Donal closed the hatch behind him, called Fionn from his pendant, and started down the passageway. He soon spotted the wards his familiar had found. The hall was quiet, unoccupied. *Shouldn't someone be standing guard?* No deception on the wards either....

A foreboding chill crept up Donal's shoulders. "Fionn, did finding the wards give you any trouble?"

"No. No attempt had been made to conceal their presence."

Something was wrong. These people had infiltrated both sets of company guards. They had already hidden their wards once that Donal knew of. They had been hiding all through the trip. Why would they not conceal themselves now?

Donal double-checked the signature before him. Yes, it definitely matched the remains of last night's attempt to breach his wards. It also matched, so far as Donal could tell, the signature of the Red Sun servitor. Whoever defended that cabin was definitely involved in one or more attempts at murder.

"Fionn, you've seen all the wards on this ship, right?"

"I've seen official wards cast by Ronaldo Machado and Aaron Cromartie. I have seen 4M wards cast by Tai Shi Li Hua, and also those protecting Transterran Properties."

"Cast by?"

"Unknown. Presumably they would have been cast by Imenand bin Zuka or someone in his employ."

"Considering their importance, he probably cast them himself."

"A reasonable assumption, but without more personal information, it is conjecture."

Donal stared at the signature and thought back to the dining room on the first night, when all the passengers had been present. He had checked out each of the mages: one in the ship's watch, Cromartie, two at the captain's table, Li Hua and Mr. bin Zuka, and two among the company guards. Magister Machado had been absent.

Since Donal had eliminated Li Hua, Machado, Cromartie and bin Zuka, that left the two guards, but Donal had thought that they felt like Initiates. They could have been weak Journeymen, but he was pretty sure they were Initiates. That fit with the one who spoke for the kidnappers. From what Donal had seen of her magic circle, she was not good enough to have passed the Journeyman exam. Since she had held about the same amount of power as the other guard magician, that one had to be an Initiate as well.

But the Red Sun servitor had looked like Journeyman work, and it bore the same signature as last night's breach attempt. Donal could read that signature again in the wards before him with only a casual inspection.

He had two Initiates as suspects, but the culprit was a Journeyman. Perhaps Donal had overestimated the breach and the Red Sun servitor. He knew he had not gotten enough sleep recently.

"Fionn, based on the signature, what do you think of the magi-cian we're going to see?"

"He, or she, is your equal in power, though with a different focus. His or her experience is more difficult to gauge."

Could there be another Journeyman running loose on the ship? Someone Donal had not seen nor sensed?

"I've missed something."

"We should leave."

Fionn was right. Leaving now was the smart move. Donal's profes-sors had always told him: a magician acts when he is ready, not before. He had not prepared enough before sending his mind into space, and it had nearly gotten him devoured by a zuglodon. Donal should find Magister Machado and tell him everything he knew and everything he thought he knew.

But Donal had survived two encounters with that zuglodon. He escaped it the first time, and tricked it the second. Everyone said that Donal's help had saved the ship. The safe course of action was to retreat before this unknown magician, but perhaps Donal had played it safe too long. If he had fought the black mark on his college record, he might have been in graduate school right now, carving a name for himself as Bran was. And look what taking chances had done for him. Donal took a risky off-world delivery, and as a direct result he had bound a familiar and developed the confidence needed to drive off a zuglodon with no preparations and almost no remaining resources.

Donal could seek help, but the authorities had their hands full rooting out the rest of the threats on this ship. Donal was a licensed Journeyman with a Bachelor's Degree in Thaumaturgy. This risk, he could handle.

"We're not leaving."

Donal knocked.

"One moment," called a man's voice, and Jacobs sucked in a long breath. He checked the formation around him: Goldberg and Cromartie up front with the uniformed ship's watch, while the skin-suited watch fanned out around them and encircled Jacobs, Machado and the observers. Everyone had taken position. Jacobs let that breath out in slow silence.

A young man opened the door, dressed in a bathrobe and toweling his hair dry.

"Abdul Nassar?" said Goldberg.

"That's me," said Nassar. He tossed the towel over a chair and slid his hands into the pockets of his robe. "What can I do for you?" Goldberg went through the official statement, and Nassar got confirmation from el-Sawy. The Transterran Properties Initiate sighed, rolled his neck, and said, "I have not been working or conspiring—"

"Enchantment in his pocket!" yelled Machado. "Stop him!"

What Nassar pulled out of his right pocket did not look to Jacobs like a threat. It looked like a chicken egg, hollowed out and painted gold with red lettering. Goldberg did not wait to find out. He dove forward and drove his shoulder into Nassar's guts like the prow of a ramming ship. Nassar's air whuffed out of him. The Initiate managed to throw the trinket as he fell, but his shot must have gone wide. He missed everyone by at least a meter.

The egg shattered against the wall.

"Oh, hell," said Machado. "Incoming!"

Half the doors in the hall burst open, and guards from both 4M and Transterran Properties flooded the hallway.

Donal had to wait all of ten seconds before the door opened, just wide enough to let the occupant see who had knocked.

"Oh, it's you," said Imenand bin Zuka. He poked his head out and craned his neck to look up and down the hall. "I suppose you had better come in." Mr. bin Zuka turned his back to Donal and walked into the room, a ship's watch Pacifier dangling from his right hand.

No sooner had Donal stepped through the door than it closed behind him. "Part of the ward," said Mr. bin Zuka over his shoulder. "Keeps itself sealed that way. It is an easy trick if you want to learn it."

Donal stepped past the closet and bathroom and into a stateroom the size and layout of his own. Two men of the ship's watch lay unconscious on the floor. A round table and its two chairs, which should have rested against the far wall under the porthole, had been moved to one side, next to the dresser. On the carpet in their place, a circle had been drawn in charcoal, with hieroglyphics sketched around the outside in a configuration Donal did not recognize. He could tell, though, that the power contained within the circle held a half-ready spell, tied off as though with a temporary latch.

Mr. bin Zuka tossed the Pacifier onto his bed, and turned back to face Donal. "I should be angry with you for interrupting me, but better you than Machado. How did you know?"

"The signature of the Red Sun servitor matched your wards." Donal wished he felt clever just then, but this meant, "You've been working with Red Sun all along."

"Odd, the servitor did not notice your check. You must be better than I gave you credit for." Mr. bin Zuka sighed. "Will you listen, or will you make me regret not killing you last night while you were weak."

Fionn took up a guard position between Donal and what was clearly an enemy. Donal frowned. Mr. bin Zuka was right. Donal could not have stopped him last night, and yet Donal lived.

"So why didn't you?"

"I do not want to kill anyone. I do only what I must."

Donal could not keep the incredulity off his face. "You murdered Hassan al Rashid."

"And I will kill Donatello Mancuso in a few minutes. I have puzzled my way through the wards of Ms. Tai Shi, so I can move ahead with or without the signatures." Mr. bin Zuka implored Donal with his eyes. "You must understand, Mr. Cuthbert. Red Sun may be full of zealots, but in this case they are right. This deal would have created a shadow government to rule the whole of our solar system.

Not because 4M wished it, nor Transterran Properties, nor any of the affiliated companies, but because Hassan al Rashid and Donatello Mancuso orchestrated the agreement out of a lust for power."

"That's not what you told the captain."

"If I had told Captain Jacobs the truth about Hassan, Mancuso would have deduced that I killed him, and I would not have lived long enough to complete my work. Ending Hassan, may Anubis judge him fairly, is not sufficient to stop what they have begun. Mancuso is too clever. He plans too well. Do not be fooled by his bluster. The oral contract was real, and witnessed, and he will find a way to persuade the companies involved to go ahead, in Hassan's memory if for no other reason. If I sign the written contract, but oppose Mancuso's goals as his partner, he will outmaneuver me." Mr. bin Zuka slapped the palm of one hand with the back of the other. "Mancuso must die. Before we reach Earth. Before he can set his plans in motion. His partner on Earth will take his place, but no single business can countenance two men like Donatello Mancuso. The partner will either prove more reasonable or less able, and I can handle either."

Mr. bin Zuka gave Donal an appraising look. He nodded.

"Mr. Cuthbert. Donal. I can guide this arrangement into a golden age for all humanity: Terran, Lunar, Martian, even Venusian. Just imagine: unprecedented sharing of resources among the planets, while respecting the sovereignty of each. Economies will boom. The possibilities for space research and travel will make the discovery of carterite look like a catalyst instead of an event. But if Mancuso lives, he will hoard the benefits and dominate us all from the shadows."

Mr. bin Zuka looked at his circle and the spell half-cast within it. He looked back at Donal.

"You could help me. Not just with this small matter. You have displayed talent and ingenuity, as well as a strong moral sense. You could work as my assistant and see to it that we make our dreams a reality that historians will laud for time beyond time." Mr. bin Zuka extended his hand. "Help me, Donal. Help me create a golden age."

Donal looked at that hand. Could he do that? Could Donal guide the fate of the entire human race? This could be an accomplishment beyond any Enochian discovery. Donal imagined the smiles on his parents' faces, proud of their youngest boy at last.

But at what price? Certainly he could not stand by and let a tyrant assume a shadow throne, but murder? Donal might not kill Mr. Mancuso himself, but he would be as much a murderer for doing nothing while Mr. bin Zuka did the deed.

Donal considered the waiting murderer.

Red Sun claimed they had evidence, and what Donal had seen of Mr. Mancuso made it easy to believe. Suppose this were the only chance to end the threat. Suppose that the moment they reached Earth, Mr. Mancuso ascended his shadow throne. Donal could stop him right now.

All he had to do was take a life.

And this single murder would accomplish more than stopping a tyrant. "A golden age," Mr. bin Zuka promised, with Donal's help to guide it. Of course, Mr. bin Zuka could have lied. He had lied to the captain. But even if he told the truth, did it justify murder?

Donal looked at his *cú sidhe*, standing ready guard. The words that sealed their bond returned to him: my tears, my blood, my sweat, your life. Those words were the final step, but they grew out of the chants that preceded them, and the song that only Donal and Fionn would share.

Magic grew out of the smallest details, built up clarity and gained power until it could not be stopped, until it must achieve its task. Every stage of any spell built on the one before it. Every final result reflected the steps taken to reach it. Donal looked at Mr. bin Zuka, and spoke.

"You may be right about Mr. Mancuso. You may even be sincere about this 'golden age.' But you are also a magician, so you should know that if you taint the process, you taint the outcome. If you want to stop Mancuso, you need to find another way. I will not let you commit murder."

20

Ship's watch clashed with Red Sun agents. Tight quarters for a skirmish. Just what Jacobs wanted to avoid. Friend and foe Pacifiers clacked all around him. Pacifying enchantments crackled like dry wood in wildfire, unable to slip past each other. No clear battle lines, both sides were everywhere. Jacobs counted uniforms and polo shirts: ten conspirators against thirteen watchmen and two magicians, including Tai Shi. Both sides had Pacifers, but the watch had eight skinsuits.

Two uniformed watch lolled on the deck, already out of the fight. Eleven good guys left then. Too close to even odds. Too close to out of control. Good thing the captain was on deck.

"Tighten those ranks," Jacobs snapped. "I expect a wall of watchmen between me and the enemy." He turned back to the observers. "Tai Shi, help Machado. You three, flat against the wall."

Jacobs rolled his wrists and flexed his fingers, in case he had to take matters in hand, and tried to see how Goldberg was doing. No good. The chief, Cromartie and Nassar were out of sight in the cabin.

El-Sawy and Stevens flattened against the wall, out of the fight and safe in the gap wedged by the watch's forming defensive lines. Tai Shi joined hands with Machado and chanted. Where was that other one? El-Sawy's aide? There: Jacobs saw the big man stab a conspirator in the gut. Who gave that damned fool a blade? His target dropped to the deck, squirming and moaning in his own blood.

Jacobs grabbed the aide's knife arm and tested his right cross against a jaw for the first time in ten years. Sharp pain jolted up the captain's knuckles, but the aide dropped his knife and staggered back a step. Jacobs picked up the knife in his left hand, shook out his right, and turned back to see the fight under control. The watch had stopped relying on Pacifiers alone, and started taking advantage of their skinsuits. Jacobs saw one watchwoman parry a Pacifier, then twist her hips and drive an elbow into her opponent's midsection, popping him backwards with twice her normal striking force. A quick wave of her Pacifier and that foe was out of the fight. Red Sun agents dropped quickly now, and the watch surrounded them, leaving the enemy fighting back-to-back.

All six of the remaining conspirators collapsed to the deck. Machado and Tai Shi must have finished their spell.

Jacobs strode into Nassar's cabin where he saw Goldberg and Cromartie bind the Initiate's hands and feet. The wet towel Nassar had used to dry his hair had been shoved into his mouth as a gag.

"Cromartie," said Jacobs, "finish binding him. Goldberg, I need you securing the hallway. And get a med team up here ASAP."

"I want every Pacifier collected," bellowed Goldberg on his way to the hall. "Nagy, that's on you. Johnson, get Doctor Ramirez up here now. I want the rest of you gathering prisoners. Going to be a tight fit in the brig, boys and girls."

"Why did you hit me?" said a voice behind Jacobs. The captain turned to see the knife fighter.

"What's your name?" said Jacobs.

"I am Fahd Zamal," said the aide, still rubbing his jaw.

Jacobs resisted the urge to rub his own knuckles. He held up the bloody knife.

"What did I tell you to do, Zamal?"

"They had superior numbers, I thought—"

"Learn to count. What did I tell you to do?"

"I do not work for you, sir."

"El-Sawy!" Jacobs froze Zamal with a glare until el-Sawy entered the cabin. "Did you send this man into the fight against my orders?"

"No, I did not, but—"

"I don't have time for this. I agreed to allow observers, *unarmed* observers, and you agreed to follow my orders. Zamal, you're done." Jacobs pushed past the two men and into the hall. "Chief, I want Zamal here confined to this cabin for the duration. Stow his knife and give it back to him when we dock."

"This man is my bodyguard," said el-Sawy, right behind the captain and trailed by Zamal.

"Share his confinement then."

"He was protecting me."

Jacobs turned to face el-Sawy. He held up one finger.

"One more word and Zamal spends the rest of this voyage in the brig. Sharing a room with you."

Jacobs sighed as he remembered that Starchaser Spacelines needed more business contracts like this one. Well, not quite like this one. He turned his threatening finger into a gentle, open hand.

"Let me explain something. We have limited medical resources. We don't outfit the ship expecting mortal combat. We're not police and we're not military. Our security personnel are trained to take people down while minimizing the risk of permanent damage. Pacifiers and combat training can handle most of their work, and magic makes up the rest. That," he pointed at the writhing, bloody man on the deck, "is a major problem. One slash of your man's knife and my doctor is going to have his hands full for the rest of this flight. Two or three would mean at least one death."

Jacobs shook his head. The watch had almost finished the round up.

"And I'm burning time here. Behave and tag along. Don't and go to the brig. Either way Zamal stays here in Nassar's cabin." Jacobs turned and saw that all the Red Sun agents were on their feet, still dazed, their hands sealed behind them. Good. "Chief, I want all of them moved into that cabin." He pointed to a random open berth. "I want them locked inside and two guards posted. Machado, Cromartie, ward the cabin to keep them in. Nassar gets the same treatment in any empty cabin."

"Captain," said Goldberg, "is there a reason we're not taking them to the brig right now?"

"It was too easy, chief. This was a diversion. They must have known we were coming."

Tai Shi snapped at the air in Chinese. Jacobs stared at her.

"I've sent my familiar to check on Mr. Mancuso."

"How long will that take?"

"Perhaps a minute."

Jacobs looked back at the prisoners, still standing in a wet noodle of a line despite his direction to Goldberg to detain them. "Chief, did you want to bring those prisoners with us?"

Goldberg ducked his head. "Move it people, get them into that cabin! Cromartie, get started on those wards. Mash, would you mind?"

"I've already finished Nassar's wards. Cromartie can handle the other set."

Jacobs considered a private reprimand for Goldberg, but decided against it. His deference was Jacobs' own fault for assuming command of the investigation. He could not expect Goldberg to act like a chief when he had to serve as a lieutenant.

"Mr. Mancuso is secure," said Tai Shi. "All safeguards are in place, and he assured Pinyin-Lung that all is well."

"The wards are still intact around bin Zuka," said Machado, "but *Saravá* tells me someone was granted passage."

"We head for bin Zuka then," said Jacobs. "Let's go."

"*Comórtas Draíocht*," said Donal, using the formal title.

"It has always irritated me," said Mr. bin Zuka, "that Gaelic grew to such prominence in magic. Such an ugly language. Like choking on the bones of a pheasant."

"Do you accept?" The pressure of the moment ground away at Donal's nerves, but he held himself steady. He had issued the challenge with what he hoped would sound like confidence born of experience, but in truth he had never before fought a duel. He strained to remember everything his self-defense professors had taught him, the tricks he had learned in classes and tested in casual games with friends.

"And is that Irish or Scots Gaelic? I can never tell."

"Do you accept?" Tension stretched Donal until it almost bowed his back. He had challenged and called twice for an answer. A third demur would constitute surrender. Mr. bin Zuka would then have to yield to Donal or violate the sanctity of a formal duel. That would break the oath of licensure every magician swore and jeopardize whatever agreements the man had with bound spirits, starting with his familiar. Even declining the duel would be better, because he could still choose a dishonorable fight without becoming an oath breaker in the eyes of his spirits. And if the servitor was any indication, bin Zuka had bound several spirits.

"Yes, yes," said Mr. bin Zuka. "I accept your challenge to the contest of magic. I just wish you had issued it in English." He frowned. "Not that English is much better. No music to it." He shook his head. "Pity you rejected my offer, but I suppose you think you're right." Bin Zuka clapped his hands and from somewhere up his sleeve came a djinn. From the waist down the djinn was a half-meter of whirlwind, but it had the upper torso of a muscled man the color of slate. Its talons, rough beard and snarled hair were black as the crack in a tomb, but its eyes shone like amethysts. Donal did not need a closer inspection to identify it as Mr. bin Zuka's familiar.

Donal offered a prayer of thanks to Lugh, Brigid and the Dagda for his *cú sidhe*. The two familiars would describe the boundaries of the duel and act as seconds. Without Fionn, Donal would have been at a fatal disadvantage.

Donal locked eyes with his foe to match his timing, nodded, then together they recited the formal commencement, each infusing his words with a touch of power: "I declare that this matter binds us. No escape, no interference, until I yield or prove my mastery by spell alone." Each turned to his familiar and said, three times, "Guard. Guide. Witness."

Cú sidhe and djinn began to circle in a slow pace around the duelists. Donal offered and received the formal salute, given with the first two fingers of the right hand: point down to acknowledge those who have gone before, touch the core of the self, the solar plexus, touch the link to the universe, the forehead, point up to acknowledge those who will follow, and sweep a final gesture of respect to Those Who Watch.

With these simple rituals, Donal committed himself to the task. He and Mr. bin Zuka were bound until one of them yielded: each had a direct link to the other, but neither could affect anything outside the duel. Mr. Mancuso was safe for a while. Now Donal needed to save himself.

Jacobs winced as his right hand gripped what felt like the five thousandth rung on this thrice-damned access ladder. "Let me handle this, John," Tunold had said. "It's not right to risk the captain on a security action." Technically, Tunold was correct — if they were still in the Navy. But they worked in the private sector now, and Tunold needed to understand that if he ever wanted to hold his own command. A naval captain might have been able to let his security chief or ex oh take care of rounding up troublemakers, but a private captain had to keep his clients happy. Now more than ever, Jacobs could leave no doubt that Starchaser Spacelines had given its passengers everything they might reasonably expect for their money, and maybe a little more. Even if it meant picking up an ugly, painful swelling in his hand. Even if it meant climbing too damned many rungs. Even if it meant talking to imbeciles like el-Sawy as though they had any sense at all.

At least Tunold had been smart enough not to make an issue of Jacobs' age. If he had, the executive officer would have pulled ship integrity detail for a month: searching the hull for cracks. From the outside. Still, Jacobs had to admit that a younger man would have moved faster up this ladder, would have taken down Zamal without half-crippling his hand. Then again, Tunold would have put Zamal in the med bay over that stabbing. Dr. Ramirez would not have been grateful.

More rungs. Jacobs might be red-faced and marinating in sweat, but at least he could take some small consolation in the heavy breathing he heard from others on this eternal ladder. His workout regimen might not have been as rigorous as it once was, but it kept him in reasonably good shape.

This climb should not have been necessary. Red Sun should not have known they were coming. Jacobs should have had the foresight to start with the VIPs. He should have checked on the targets before hunting the killers.

He should have let Ramirez look at his hand.

SLIPPERY BASTARD, THOUGHT DONAL AS BIN ZUKA TWISTED HIS WAY OUT of a recursive trap. Donal had almost caught his opponent in a loop, continually beginning the same spell but never finishing it.

Bin Zuka retaliated with a fast Arabic chant and swirl of his wrists one over the other that sent a trio of impulses whirling at Donal. Donal pushed his hands out with his breath, reached toward the spell. It felt like an auric strike that would daze Donal and render him defenseless for crucial seconds. He incanted through an indrawn breath and twirled his hands toward his body in a movement syncopated against his opponent's. Donal braided together the power of all three impulses, pulled them in, then swung his body around with his arms out like an Olympic hammer thrower and hurled the combined power back at bin Zuka as a new effect, a bewilderment.

Bin Zuka began a counter spell of his own, but the rewoven structure of Donal's new spell collapsed under the pressure of his added layer of magic. The spell's power splintered between them.

Donal panted from the apparent effort. He hoped that if he faked weakness, bin Zuka would go straight for the kill and make a critical mistake. The theory sounded good, but his opponent had yet to cooperate.

"Not much of a counter spell." Bin Zuka raised an eyebrow.

"Kept your spell off of me."

"I suppose it did at that." Bin Zuka's voice was full of disdain, but he made no move to continue his attack. Once more he had declined to press an advantage. Donal's eyebrows came up in amazement. Was bin Zuka waiting his turn? Did he think this was a formal tournament, with judges present and some spells forbidden?

If that were true, Donal might forfeit his turn if he hesitated any longer, but he needed time to think. He whipped together a basic deception spell: a bolt of illusory fire that would explode on contact into gas and scramble his target's sense of direction. Bin Zuka might misstep out of the dueling circle, which would be an automatic loss.

What spells are banned from tournaments? Anything that controlled or directed the decisions of another was out of bounds, but those spells were far too slow and difficult to be practical in a duel anyway. If Donal could think of a useful but forbidden spell, perhaps he could catch bin Zuka unprepared. Donal might be able to win this duel yet.

He threw his illusion. Bin Zuka waved a hand to redirect the bolt of flame, which triggered the explosion into gas. Bin Zuka spun his arm in a wide circle, then rapidly tightened the circumference to no more than a dozen centimeters, sucking together the gas until it formed a tight cone. Donal expected it to come back at him as a funnel, but bin Zuka kept it there, in the area described by his spinning arm.

Bin Zuka smiled and raised his other hand, a ready spell on his lips.

***

EVERYTHING LOOKED QUIET TO JACOBS AS HIS TEAM APPROACHED BIN Zuka's cabin. No sign of any intruders. No watch personnel, but they would be inside the cabin so as not to draw attention. Only the magical defenses should have been visible from the hallway.

"Mash?" he said.

"Wards are still up," said Machado. "And they look intact. They admitted someone, but I doubt anything more has slipped past them."

"Positions," said Jacobs, standing poised to knock.

"Captain," said Goldberg, "aren't you supposed to be back there with the observers?"

"Not this time. Everything might be all right in there, which means I'll have to do the talking."

"And if there's a problem?"

"Fine. You stand here next to me. Machado too. But if anyone has to explain this to bin Zuka, it will be me."

Goldberg arranged the uniformed watch in a ring around them, then the skinsuited watch as an outer ring, then the observers and Cromartie.

Jacobs raised his right hand without thinking, but his purple, swollen knuckles throbbed before he could close his fist. He knocked with his left instead.

No answer.

Jacobs drummed his good fingers on his thigh. The door should have opened by now. He knocked again....

"This is Captain John Jacobs," he called in a voice that had once carried across a deck over the roar of a winter storm two days south of Hawaii. "Open this door at once!"

Nothing.

"Ladies and gentlemen," he said to the group as he took a step back, "I need to be inside that room right now. Make it happen."

Machado started on the wards while Goldberg organized work on the door. Perhaps nothing was wrong. Perhaps the wards muffled sound and no one inside even knew what was happening. Jacobs knew his luck better than that. He had used up all his good fortune years ago, in a ship floating dead in space. The universe owed him no more favors. If anything had gone wrong for bin Zuka, Jacobs would be too slow. He might already be too late. Bin Zuka might be lying dead on the deck right now and it would be on Jacobs' watch.

I'M GOING TO DIE, THOUGHT DONAL. EVERYTHING HAPPENED TOO FAST. Donal could barely breathe, no faking necessary. Bin Zuka needed no pause. No sooner did Donal cast a spell than bin Zuka countered it. He retaliated as swift as a spirit escaping a mis-drawn circle. Donal could not keep pace; the effort strained his attention and frayed his confidence, and with his confidence went his repertoire. Donal's attacks had gotten simpler, his defenses less elegant. He settled for mere deflections instead of counter spells.

Bin Zuka fired off a series of jarring, discordant tones that could shatter concentration. Donal longed to shift them into harmony, and slip a counter-attack into the tune. But stress and speed kept him from even budging half of the tones out of phase to produce an active silence that could carry a counter spell. Not enough time. Not enough focus.

He picked a pleasant tone and added resonance until it drowned out the other notes and neutralized bin Zuka's spell. Ugly, but it worked.

Donal had to answer with an offensive spell, but what more could he do? He had already run through most of the deceptions he could customize: intense pleasure and pain, false certainty that Donal had surrendered, fake heart attacks, and illusions of jungle cats, demons, rains of fire and ice, an invasion of ship's watch, a zuglodon, even the phantom of a risen Hassan al Rashid after revenge. Donal had conjured fire and earth elementals, spirits of longing and failure, even an avatar of justice. That last one might have gotten bin Zuka, if only Donal had had time to instill enough strength.

Now Donal pushed beyond his experience: he had to improvise effects or give up and fling raw power. If he fell to that, bin Zuka would smell victory. Raw power had no art, it was little more than one mage's attempt to batter away the spirit of another until damage seeped through to injure the mind or the body. Worse, that sort of assault would exhaust the attacker quickly, and could be countered by even a talented high school student.

Donal needed to find a weakness while he still had the strength to attack it. There had to be some hole in bin Zuka's defenses Donal could exploit and survive this conflict. Bin Zuka came out of the apprenticeship system, not a university. He would have exceptional knowledge in a few areas, but gaps in others. Bin Zuka also followed the formal rules of the *Comórtas Draíocht* as though it were a tournament, taking turns with Donal, not pushing for victory the way Donal had seen in a duel back in Santa Cruz. Then again, perhaps bin Zuka held back to stay fresh for Mancuso's murder.

Donal had to find some way to win, any way, or soon bin Zuka would wear him down.

He took a deep breath and conjured an astral serpent to swallow bin Zuka's power. Two meters long and white as cirrus clouds, the winged snake flapped only once before its target spat out two words and cut the air with his fingers. Donal felt his connection to the creature sever, and with it his control. The serpent whirled and hissed as it bore down on Donal.

"Ladies and gentlemen," said Jacobs, "that door is still closed."

The ship's mage hummed noncommittal interest, the kind of sound that provided no useful information. Machado had about fifteen such sounds and applied them interchangeably. This hum was short and flat.

"What is it, Mash?"

"I've double-checked my work, but if I read this ward right, it will collapse if it I hit it just so. Right ... here." Machado punched the air, mumbling something Jacobs could not hear. The pudgy magician shook his head in disgust. "Yep. Whoever cast this thing locked it, but left the key under the doormat."

"How did you spot that?" said Tai Shi.

"It takes a delicate, sensitive touch," said Machado. "Perhaps I could show you over dinner."

"Flirt on your own time," said Jacobs. "Goldberg, is that door open yet or do we need a fire axe?"

"Got it, Captain. Master key works now that the wards are down." Goldberg stared pointedly at Jacobs' swollen purple knuckles. "Mind if I take point again?"

"First positions," said Jacobs, and the team fell back to its original formation, with Goldberg, Cromartie and the uniformed watch at the door.

Goldberg shoved the door open and said, "What the hell?"

From his spot near the rear, Jacobs would have sworn that he saw a huge, hazy sphere in the middle of the cabin.

"*Comórtas Draíocht*," Cromartie said with reverence.

"Right," said Goldberg. "Put them both down, boys and girls, and we'll sort it out afterwards."

"No!" said Machado, Tai Shi and Cromartie all at once. Machado spoke first. "That is a formal magical duel. Anyone who tries to interfere risks injury or death at the hands of one or both familiars."

"I thought familiars didn't have that kind of power," said Jacobs. Familiar spirits were an accepted part of society. If every 'caster were running around with a lethal weapon at the ready....

"They don't. Usually. This is part of the magic of the duel. The duelists are bound within their own world until one of them wins. The familiars are empowered to prevent interruption, and that power grows with each spell that gets defeated." Machado frowned and furrowed and bobbed his head back and forth as he studied something the captain could not see. "Those two would be lethal right now."

"Two watch down in the room," called Goldberg from inside the cabin.

"Circle up, spell ready. Assault of some sort. Signature isn't Cuthbert's." This was from Cromartie, in the room with Goldberg. Machado went to investigate.

"Donal tracked down an unfinished assault spell?" said Tai Shi.

"And he's dueling bin Zuka?" She folded her arms, stared at the sphere and muttered, "Donal, you sly sorcerer, you're just full of surprises, aren't you?"

Jacobs could not decide if he heard amusement or admiration in her voice.

"What happens to all that power when the duel is over?" he said.

"It dissipates," said Machado, coming back from the doorway. "And Cromartie's right. That's not Cuthbert's attack spell. It's bin Zuka's. And I'll give you odds that the target is Mancuso."

"I did not know, sir. I swear," said a pale el-Sawy. "I will cooperate in any way you wish."

"For right now just stay out of the way." Jacobs turned back to Goldberg and the watch. "I want that spell dismantled. And surround the duelists. I want bin Zuka down the second we have a winner. He can sit in the brig until we straighten all this out. And, Chief, if you think of any questions for el-Sawy here, he's available."

The watchmen and —women leapt to their positions while Machado started on the circle.

"You can take him, Donal," whispered Tai Shi.

COVERED IN THE SWEAT OF HIS EFFORTS, DONAL FOCUSED ON HIS SILVER pendant, drew support from its touch of alchemy. Bin Zuka's latest spell worried away at Donal's connection with Fionn. More magic of disharmony. The man leaned on his specialty. Almost every offensive and defensive spell he threw was based in disharmony. Something nagged at Donal about specialties....

Of course! He saw the key to his foe's defenses. A mage who studied under one master would not have had electives, much less mandatory classes in secondary areas of magic. Bin Zuka had one clear specialty, but Donal had two: deception and conjuration. He could combine them into a dual-core spell. Tournament rules forbade dual-core spells because the United International Thaumaturgy Committee of Earth determined that not enough schools taught interdisciplinary magic to allow the practice. It would give an "unfair edge" to a handful of advanced countries. Bin Zuka might not know how to defeat a dual-core spell under pressure.

Donal's revelation carried another gift in its wake. Bin Zuka's latest attack wore away at Donal's connection to Fionn, but the spells of the contest had shunted a great deal of power into the *cú sidhe*. By attacking the connection, bin Zuka had permitted Donal to draw on that power, at least for this one defense. Bin Zuka must have sensed immanent victory, and in his haste he had erred.

Donal tapped that extra power to reinforce the harmony of his connection to Fionn, and bin Zuka's spell overloaded and fizzled. Donal pulled on the resonance of this counter spell to form his next attack. The time had come to blend deception and conjuration.

Donal remembered the first rule of magic: fear devours. He drew on the fear he felt from the spaceport explosion and the terror of the crowd around him, and channeled those emotions to conjure a powerful spirit of fear. He wrapped the summons in an illusion that bin Zuka had lost control of his spirits, so that they all turned on him at once. Donal launched the combination at his foe, exhaustion quivering his hands, making his gestures frantic. *Another desperate, unplanned attack. Honest.* Closer to the truth than Donal wanted to admit.

Red haze threatened Donal's vision. He knew he could not last long. He could barely watch his spell take hold. While bin Zuka began to counter the illusion, the fear spirit rode the link and embraced him. Terror flooded bin Zuka's eyes, squeezed a tiny sound out past his flapping jaw. His fingers shuddered through what Donal assumed was a second attempt at a counter spell, but no power supported it.

Phantasmal spirits roared their attack: the red sun servitor seared bin Zuka with rays of light, the djinn hurled thunderbolts and the dueling circle appeared to collapse. Other spirits, which Donal had never seen, joined the fray. A cat pounced, clawed at eyes while a rat assaulted someplace lower. How many spirits had the man bound?

Bin Zuka screamed and collapsed unconscious on the floor.

Donal felt the magic of the *Comórtas Draíocht* dissipate, and about a hundred watchmen swarmed over his fallen foe. Was this part of Donal's final illusion? Did the fear spirit carry the image forward?

Then the foggy realization came that he saw reality again. The released power and tension overwhelmed the spent Donal. He dropped to all fours, threw up, and passed out.

21

Three days passed, and Jacobs began to believe that he had all his troublemakers in the brig, where they belonged. Well, Joffries was only confined to quarters, but under the circumstances that would suffice. There had been no more zuglodon attacks, no more brawls. So far as Jacobs could tell, his entire complement of passengers had stopped trying to kill one another. He might be able to relax and enjoy this flight yet.

At his station on the bridge, Jacobs checked the latest system updates: five by five. As of thirty minutes ago, every system reported operating at full capacity, even if the *Horizon Cusp* would need more maintenance than normal once it reached port. That zuglodon attack had been hard on his ship.

"Sir," said Jefferson, "I have Chief Goldberg for you."

"Link him through." When Goldberg's face appeared, Jacobs said, "bin Zuka again?"

"Got it in one. He still wants to talk to you."

"I don't have time for rhetoric, Chief, I have a ship to run."

"And I have a headache from passing along his requests. I'm not a messenger service." Goldberg hesitated. "Just give him five minutes, so I can have some peace."

"No time. I have meetings set up with Tunold, Machado, Fredrickson and Ramirez. I have to get a feel for how much Red Sun has eaten into our profits for this voyage and whether or not we can afford to pursue more charter work, considering the risks."

"Don't make me remind you that legally—"

"Are you about to quote regs to me, Mr. Goldberg?"

"I never served in the Navy, Captain, and we're talking about laws, not regulations. Bin Zuka knows his interplanetary law. He knows he has a right to plead his case to you, and I can't deny him or I become accountable."

Jacobs pinched the bridge of his nose during a long, slow breath.

"Fine, I'll come talk to him."

"The pounding in my temples thanks you, sir. Security out."

Goldberg cut the connection. Jacobs turned the bridge over to Tunold and went to save his chief a headache.

The *Horizon Cusp* had only one cell designed for 'casters, and Machado said that the cell's magic would not restrict two magicians at the same time. From the way Machado had explained it, every magician's spells had the same identifying characteristic, like a magical fingerprint. Since the anti-magician cell was occupied, Machado enchanted a pair of wrist-sealers to shatter any forming spells that matched bin Zuka's "fingerprint." Machado had done the same thing for Nassar.

So Jacobs found bin Zuka in a regular cell, seated on a bunk with his legs folded underneath him and his wrists in his lap, bound together by Fenrir-brand sealing ribbon.

"I understand you have something to tell me," said Jacobs.

"I did not want to kill him."

"I have four magicians, one a Magister, who say otherwise and are willing to testify."

"Excuse my imprecision. I would of course have killed Donatello Mancuso, and would do so this very moment were I not restrained."

Jacobs smiled at those restraints through the bars of the brig. He would definitely give Machado a bonus when they reached Earth.

"What I meant," continued bin Zuka, "was that I did not wish to kill Donal Cuthbert. I might have had to take his life to defeat him, but that would have been regrettable."

"Why tell me?"

"I wish my official goal on the record as clearly and completely as possible. On this voyage I sought only the deaths of Donatello Mancuso and Hassan al Rashid, may the good he has done outlive the evil."

"The courts will decide that." Jacobs raised an eyebrow and added, "Even beating you took a toll on that poor kid. He's been under the care of Dr. Ramirez and Mr. Machado ever since." Jacobs ran a finger along the bars of the cell, relying on his left hand since his bandaged right was recovering from two broken knuckles. Machado had probably placed a second layer of spells on these bars. He preached redundant systems to handle anything important. Good man. Jacobs looked at bin Zuka again. "Is that all you wanted to say?"

"It's enough. You must understand, Captain, I do not wish to kill any innocent persons. I am not an evil man, but a good man tasked with a difficult job..." and on he went again. The danger of Mancuso and the shadow government, and how only bin Zuka could stop it. Goldberg had already ordered his men to check on this prisoner in pairs, to make sure no one got caught up in the rhetoric.

"I have a ship to run," said Jacobs. "Tell it to Earth."

Jacobs made his way past the other cells, each overflowing with bin Zuka's co-conspirators.

"Captain," called bin Zuka behind him, "You must believe me! Ask him! Ask him about ... regulating competition!"

Jacobs shut the brig section door behind him with a firm left hand.

THREE DAYS OF ENFORCED BED REST. OR AS DONAL THOUGHT OF IT, solitary confinement. He was in a private room with the lights kept low and the shelves empty. The bed was white. The table beside it was white. The carpet and walls were beige. The only variation was a lightened spot on one wall. Donal had long since decided that a painting had been removed just before they brought him in. He had spent hours speculating what the painting had been.

No books to read, no games to play, no shadow plays to watch, no entertainment at all. Donal was not even allowed visitors. No stimulation of any kind, just rest here in the medical bay while Donal's mind and spirit recovered. They even fed him bland food. All the marvelous dishes available on this ship, and Donal had been eating sliced turkey, mashed potatoes and green beans without a hint of seasoning anywhere near the plate.

To make matters worse, Magister Machado had done something to the room so that Donal could not work any magic. Donal had called for Fionn several times, but the *cú sidhe* remained in its pendant.

None of this had mattered much on the first day, because Donal slept through it. But for the past day or so, he had felt more and more himself and boredom set in, then grew, then squeezed, until now Donal considered kicking down the door and escaping.

True, Magister Machado had had a point. Donal overextended himself in that duel, strained himself somehow. He had pressed past the point of fatigue for too long, or perhaps pushed that point while he channeled too much power through his mind. Donal was unclear on the distinction because he had still been hazy when Magister Machado explained it.

Donal stared at the door. How thick could it be? He sat up. If Donal kicked near the handle....

The handle turned, and Dr. Ramirez came in. He consulted Donal's chart with steady patience. Donal half-expected that the paper was blank. After all, he had no real injuries.

"How are you feeling today?" asked the doctor with his perpetual smile.

"I've got to ask. What painting was on that wall? It was four dogs playing poker, wasn't it? With the hand we can see being aces and eights?"

"Painting?" Dr. Ramirez looked around where Donal pointed.

"Oh, that was an eye chart. Mr. Machado thought your mind would make magic symbols of the letters, so he asked me take it down."

"Can I leave yet? Aren't three days of this enough? I feel fine, and I've been able to shift my perception normally for over a day now."

"Let's take a look at you." He gave Donal a brief medical examination. "You seem to be recovering well from that initial exhaustion. I'll sign the release as soon as Mr. Machado gives you the all-clear. If you don't mind a recommendation, though, I'd suggest you avoid casting spells for the rest of the voyage. You're on a cruise ship. Try to enjoy yourself."

Donal blinked.

"Without magic? Impossible. Magic is part of me. It's in everything I do. You might as well ask me not to breathe."

"Then at least try to relax." Doctor Ramirez shrugged. "If you don't, you'll be right back here before you know it."

Dr. Ramirez left, and now Donal sat, stuck in limbo without so much as a single spell available. This felt worse than when he had to wait for the results of his licensing exam. If Donal had failed that, he would still have been allowed to practice magic, even if he could not have done so for money.

He threw himself back on the bed and stared at the beige ceiling.

Jacobs heard the yeoman's sharp knock on his office door. He set down his notes. The meetings with his officers had gone well. Even with the all the trouble bin Zuka and his cronies had caused, plus Cuthbert's foolishness, the bottom line for the voyage looked good. Jacobs needed to run a few more numbers before he met with Zoltan though. He wanted to project the costs and benefits of hiring an assistant ship's mage.

The knock came again. Jacobs set down his pen. "Yes, Mr. Kelly?"

Kelly opened the door the precise distance necessary to lean past it at his trademarked crisp angle. Jacobs mused that Kelly never spoke about his parents because they were a ruler and a sextant.

"Mr. Mancuso to see you, Captain. He says the matter is important."

"Very well. Send him in."

Perhaps Jacobs should do all his work on the bridge. No one ever "happened" to show up looking for a word or two when he was at his duty station, however much his office seemed to be fair game.

Mancuso came in the door talking and did not stop even when he took a chair that Jacobs did not offer.

"Ah, Captain Jacobs, thank you for seeing me. Short notice, I know. Idea just came to me and I had to come talk to you about it. I won't take long though. I know you must be busy, even though all the criminals are behind bars. I know the second I set foot at the office I have to answer a thousand questions and sign a million papers. Must be much the same for you." He cleared his throat. "First thing I want you to know is that 4M appreciates the way you've handled this trip. Most of it, anyway. You've been flexible in the arrangements and decisive in dealing with threats from inside and outside the ship. Can't say it's been a great trip, but it looks like I'll survive it, and I have you to thank for that. And Cuthbert, of course. Must thank the boy properly when I get the chance. If that doctor of yours ever lets him go."

"Is that what you wanted to see me about? You want me to speak to Doctor Ramirez?" *Did you want to get anywhere near a point?*

"No, no, nothing like that. Never interfere with a professional at work, that's my motto. The doctor will let the boy go when he's ready, I'm sure. No, I wanted to let you know first and foremost that I think, which means 4M thinks, that Starchaser Spacelines has done an excellent job with this whole affair, and we'll keep that in mind for our future travel."

Suddenly Jacobs felt better about this meeting, but Mancuso was not finished.

"I also have a small request, if possible. I know that Hassan arranged for this to be a ten-day trip, in case the negotiations went long, but obviously that's no longer necessary. I feel like I'm on a vacation I don't have time for. Is there any chance you could get us to Earth on the normal seven-day schedule?"

Must not slap the customer, especially when he wants to be a repeat customer.

"We are on day six of ten," said Jacobs in a slow, even voice. "Are you asking me to make this ship cover four days' worth of space in *one day*? Even if the *Horizon Cusp* could do it, the risk level would be beyond ridiculous."

"Well, when you put it that way, it does seem like a lot to ask." Mancuso heaved a sigh that almost lifted him out of his chair. "Tell you what: for every day you shave off our travel time, 4M will add ten percent to the contracted fee."

"Fifteen percent," countered Jacobs, "to cover the additional risk."

"Make it twelve and a half and you have a deal."

"Fine, but we round up to the nearest four hour increment."

"Done," said Mancuso, and the two men shook hands. "I'll have Stevens bring the amendment for your countersignature within the hour." The businessman stood and gave his cuffs an unnecessary straightening.

Jacobs thought of bin Zuka's warning. Curiosity pushed words out of his mouth. "Oh, before you go, I've been hearing rumors that Earth wants to regulate competition in space transportation. What do you think about this?"

"Politicians should stick to what they know best: how to drain public money for their own use. Not one of them has any business sense, much less any idea how to run a country. We'd all be better off...." Mancuso shook his head. "Don't get me started. We'll be here all day and I won't have covered half of what's wrong with the government."

As the door closed behind Mancuso, Benny Sugg poked his face out around the corner of the couch, ears cocked and head at a quizzical angle.

"I don't know what to make of him either, Benny, but at least we should get a few more commissions out of him."

MAGISTER MACHADO CLEARED DONAL FOR RELEASE ABOUT TWO HOURS later, though it felt to Donal like two days. The ship's mage also gave him a warning that sounded too much like the doctor's advice: "Simple spells only until we dock. You hear me? Do anything stupid and I'll shut you down for a month. Don't think I can't."

Donal must have looked crestfallen, because the Magister gave him a lopsided smile and said, "I didn't say 'no magic.' I said 'simple spells.' I suspect that gives you a lot of leeway. Just play it smart."

Donal ate a quiet lunch in his room, but had no interest in the ship's games or entertainments. Instead he called Fionn and took the bubble to the Observation Deck, to enjoy the cascade of colors that flowed among the stars. He arrived to see Li Hua standing aft, where they had spoken the last time they were here. She was dressed in the style of shirt and slacks combination she had favored on Mars, this time in yellow and tan.

Donal walked toward her. Fionn glanced between them, back and forth, but said nothing. Donal had not yet reached her when she said, still facing the stars, "I can't figure you out. You think bin Zuka is right, you even think I'm involved, but you risk your life to stop him."

"I never said he was right."

Li Hua turned to face Donal and noticed Fionn.

"You told me you didn't have a familiar."

"I didn't. I took your advice."

"Nice work." She examined Fionn with an appraising eye. To the *cú sidhe* she said, in Gaelic, "What made you decide to answer this one's call?"

Fionn glanced at Donal, who nodded. "His heart leads him," said the emerald deerhound, also in Gaelic. "Such a one must have trustworthy advisors."

Li Hua sucked in her lips as she thought about that. Then she said to Donal, in English, "Good thing you listened. Without a familiar, bin Zuka would have killed you in that duel."

"So that's twice you've saved my life."

"That's right," Li Hua said with a smug smile. "You owe me."

"How about I buy you dinner when we reach Earth?"

"Does this mean you don't think I'm a murderer who's plotting to take over the galaxy?"

"You have to admit, that after hearing Red Sun's claims, your toast sounded pretty bad."

"4M is about to send its competition into the red, to stay. That's all I was toasting." She raised a sardonic eyebrow. "But by all means, run everything I say past the ramblings of lunatics." She gave Donal a level look. "What about the murderer part?"

Donal looked at his feet. "During that duel, I realized that bin Zuka would kill me if I didn't find some way to beat him. I was desperate. I would have done anything to stay alive." He rubbed the back of his neck. "My talents are deception and conjuration, so I didn't have to kill him, but I would have." He looked up at Li Hua. "I'm sorry I judged you. You don't murder. You just try to survive, the best you can."

Li Hua grabbed Donal's face and kissed him, and they shared between them all the excitement and fear of the past week, and perhaps a little hope for the future.

JACOBS WORRIED AS HE SAT AT HIS DUTY STATION. THE MEETING HAD lasted two hours. Jang had assured Jacobs that the Deception Drive could handle shaving two days off of the trip. Machado had been cautious, but all of Jacobs' officers approved the increase in speed. Still, Jacobs worried. He had already done everything he could do. He had ordered Machado to help Jang keep an eye on the Deception Drive until they were satisfied that the engine could hold this speed safely. He had ordered the crew to prepare emergency supplies and quarters in case something went wrong. Jacobs had even gone to threat rotation with Tunold, so that one of them would always be on duty and the other sleeping to ensure a fresh mind in command.

Now he could only watch.

Jacobs poked the ship's image in the engineering section again, but Jang had not updated her reports. The numbers he saw floating above the gryphon were over an hour old. He drummed the fingers of his left hand on the console. If the *Horizon Cusp* had been one of the seagoing vessels from before the Rise of Magic, he would have known what speed it could handle and for how long. In those days a good captain had to know his ship's full capabilities, how far its engine could be pushed, how much strain the hull could take, what effect the seas had on its performance. Nowadays Jacobs did not even know how fuel worked. Everything came down to spirits and spells. All that stood between the crew and vacuum were a few tons of ceramics and a bunch of chants.

If space were still a vacuum.

Jacobs had come to understand how the HK Drive would react under ordinary conditions and how it would respond under pressure. From the bridge he could even pretend the *Horizon Cusp* ran an old fashioned electro-mechanical engine. At least, when he could forget that the hum was missing. But now with the new Deception Drive, Jacobs would have to start over, re-learn his ship.

At least that sort of challenge kept the job from getting stale. Still, the Deception Drive would be his last such change. Jacobs had to admit that he was almost ready to retire. This trip had taken too much out of him. Besides, he had begun to reminisce too often. Jacobs always promised himself that if he started seeing more ghosts than crewmen, he would hang up his captain's hat. Also, he was sure that Benny Sugg would like to live out his remaining years someplace with grass, and maybe a few birds to chase.

But Jacobs yearned to see Venus first, to captain the first commercial passenger flight to the morning star that had guided so many sailors. Then he could retire on a final great accomplishment.

If he lived through this one. Jacobs checked the engineering and damage control reports: no updates. Jacobs drummed his fingers. All the readings he could see looked right. The Deception Drive maintained a speed the HK Drive could not even have achieved. Not as fast as their escape from the zuglodon, but the hull could not have withstood that strain for so great a distance. For that matter, neither could Machado and Jang.

Jacobs activated the comm and spoke before Jang's head appeared.

"Engineering, how is she doing?"

Jang took longer to answer than Jacobs would have liked. When she did, her face was sweaty and her hair in disarray.

"Same as last time, Captain. Mash and I have her under control."

"Stow that tone, Chief. If anything does go wrong, I expect an update five seconds later."

"Aye aye, sir."

Jang's cheek twitched and Jacobs felt the hair on his neck stand up. Was she covering something?

"You two have to sleep sometime. You're sure that won't be a problem."

"We know how to do our jobs, sir."

True. Jang could be a pain in Jacobs' backside, but he could count on her to keep his ship flying. She deserved a chance to fix whatever she had tried to hide. Besides, Machado was there to help.

"That's why I hired you. Bridge out."

Everything Jang and Machado had said during the meeting meshed with the reports Jacobs had demanded every trip about the Deception Drive's performance. That Jacobs had already taken them to a major shipping lane helped because any course corrections would have a wide margin of error. The numbers all lined up.

That was what worried Jacobs. The theory might have been sound, but if something went wrong in practice, he could not help. In the old days he could have grabbed a wrench to lend a hand. What could Jacobs do now, grab a wand?

Magic.

Jacobs went over the reports again.

DOWN IN ENGINEERING, MACHADO WIPED SWEAT FROM HIS EYES AS HE sketched rapid binding symbols in the air. He would not let the Deception Drive's lacuna escape.

"Under control?"

"Shut up, Mash!"

Jang swung her censer on its chain like a weapon, though the incense would not spread any faster. Machado would not make an issue of her technique, not so long as she covered the corners of the room in time for the next phase of the ritual. But her tone was another matter.

"Don't forget I'm bailing your ass out. I warned you about those harmonics. You never listen."

"It was fine until we had to hold this speed. And we're fixing it!"

The lacuna slithered around edges of the spell they were assembling. Its song grew urgent, rapid notes rising in pitch.

Machado hated singing spirits. He always thought they lied with their songs and hid truth in the silence between notes. And now this one sounded almost excited....

Machado swore. It must have spotted a way out. It might not slip the outer safety binding, but once past its primary binding, connections would sever and take their speed with them. The *Horizon Cusp* would end up drifting on its carterite. Worse, when that primary binding unraveled, other systems might follow.

No. Not on Machado's watch.

"Finish the incense, then double check the binding connections and reinforce them with oil." Binding oil would not lend strength for long, but it would clamp the spells in place while he and Jang worked. "I'm going to hold this thing myself until you finish."

"No way you can—"

"Now, Jang!" She might have replied, but Machado could no longer hear as he threw himself into his task. He could not even spare a thought to wish that *Saravá*, his familiar, were with him and not on patrol.

Chanting, Machado spread his arms wide and stretched his will around the lacuna. The space elemental felt to Machado like a chorus of whispered echoes. The lacuna noticed his efforts. Its melody took on a curious quality. It probed at him.

Let it look. Only the binding matters.

Machado felt it taste his shape, not his plump build but the area it filled, the space his body kept the lacuna from touching. A look must have been all it wanted, because now it tested Machado. A high note pierced his ears, rattled his teeth. A second note joined, off-key, and ached his jaw, sliced down his back like tearing muscle. Still Machado held to his will. He slipped into a simple breathing pattern — not one taught in the schools, nor used by anyone else, but tailored to his body and mind.

A third note joined, and the hellish chord buffeted his ribs and pelvis. Intense pain cracked a hairline through even Machado's will. As it had to. Even a Hierophant could not have held so powerful a lacuna for long. Will alone could not bind such a force.

Chugging breath like a steamboat, Machado fell to one knee, arms still outstretched and fingers locked forward in a mountain climber's desperate cling. Fatigue trembled through his limbs.

Machado felt a touch on his mind, not thoughts but the breath of another's power. Jang must have finished preparing. He tried to let go and failed. He had pushed so hard to hold the lacuna that he could not relax his will.

Machado had to release the lacuna. This was his last chance. If he failed, the lacuna would break him, splinter him. He would not survive, though his body might.

Machado felt a gentle nuzzle of psychic fur against his will. *Saravá* must have felt its master's need and returned. The panther joined with him, relieved enough pressure that he could ease himself loose.

He forced his weary, half-dazed eyes open and saw Jang in position for her part.

Machado drew on the last of his reserves and began the formal chant that would renew the binding. He reinforced key symbols as he paced the circle while Jang harmonized on the opposite side and fortified different symbols.

Seventeen passes completed the spell. Nine more solidified it. One final pass, while clapping a certain rhythm, keyed the drive's link to the other systems of the ship.

They finished, and Machado flopped on a chair while Jang slumped against the wall.

"I can't believe you held that thing," she said.

"Don't ... ask me ... to do it again."

They shared a moment of spent silence. Machado wondered whether he could make it back to his cabin.

"See?" said Jang with a weary chuckle. "Under control."

22

TWO HOURS IN A HOLDING PATTERN AND JACOBS PACED THE PERIMETER of the bridge for every second of it. Spaceport control was making him pay for arriving two days ahead of schedule. He was sure of it. Then again, perhaps not. The port traffic at San Francisco grew worse every flight. If it continued at this pace, he would have to move the Starchaser Spacelines offices. Perhaps Mazatlan? No, Zoltan would never agree to it. Too many business reasons to stay in California.

"Captain," said Jefferson from the communications station, "I have the go-ahead to begin docking procedures."

"About time," muttered Jacobs. Aloud, he said, "Send the codes, Ms. Jefferson, and tell all stations to prepare for remote landing."

The boatswain's whistle sounded less than a minute later. Not that anyone would need the half-hour warning on this flight. Jacobs suspected that his passengers would already have gathered to wait for the shuttle if security allowed it. Standard procedure said they had to wait until the five minute alert, and Jacobs upheld it.

The half hour warning did bring a smile to Jacobs' face. In only thirty minutes, he could get bin Zuka and his accomplices off the *Horizon Cusp* once and for all. Which reminded him....

"Ms. Jefferson, alert Port Security that we have prisoners to turn over. And send them Goldberg's report." Goldberg had covered the situation well. Jacobs expected a smooth exchange.

"Sir?" said Jefferson. "Chief Goldberg is on the line for you."

"Link it through to my station, then get right on Port Security." Jacobs climbed his stairs and felt a sigh of relief from the bridge crew: the Old Man no longer hovered with one eye on their work. Jacobs smiled again. Good to know that time had not eroded his authority. As he reached his station, Goldberg's sour face greeted him. "What's up, Chief? Everything ready for the hand-off?"

"Five by five, sir, but bin Zuka is asking for you again."

"Why should I care? In less than thirty minutes he will officially be someone else's problem."

"I'm not saying you should, but technically he is your problem for another twenty-eight minutes. He does have the right to give a statement for your ears only."

"Damn it." Jacobs thumped the arm of his chair with his right hand and got a jolt of pain for his effort. He needed to remember that the knuckles would not be fully healed for another week. "All right, I'll be there in a minute." He leaned down to Tunold, who had arisen early to be on shift when the *Horizon Cusp* docked. "Kris, watch the bridge for me. I have to go talk to an assassin."

Jacobs grumbled through the passages, down the bubble, past Goldberg in the watch headquarters and into the brig, until he stood again outside the cell of Imenand bin Zuka. The prisoner meditated on his bunk in the same position Jacobs had last seen him, legs crossed beneath him and sealed wrists in his lap.

"Well, what is it?"

"Thank you for coming, Captain." Bin Zuka opened his eyes. "I will not see you again, so I wished to thank you. Obviously I did not achieve the result I desired on your ship, but you and your crew have been fair, reasonable, and professional in every aspect of your work. That should be acknowledged."

Jacobs scowled, expecting an ambush. "You're welcome."

"I know you do not believe me about Mr. Mancuso, but perhaps you yet will. Follow my case. I expect to be murdered before ever reaching trial. Donatello is a powerful man, and he will not want the truth to become news for fear that even a few would believe. Easier to make of me a footnote."

"Murdering you would draw attention to him."

"Not if it does not look like murder." Bin Zuka smiled. "I asked Doctor Ramirez to give me a full medical examination, and Chief Goldberg permitted it. My health is now a matter of record on your ship. Remember that, and contact Red Sun when you believe."

"I'll keep it in mind," said Jacobs, not bothering to hide his scorn. Zealots. He left without a goodbye. The conversation had reminded him that Tunold's report on the weapons investigation awaited his attention, forgotten in the aftermath of the accelerated trip.

Donal stepped into a suite more than three times as large as his own berth, perhaps four times as large. No bed in this room, but two interior doors, not counting the bathroom and closet. Make that five or six times the size of Donal's berth.

He looked around at the half-dozen guards scattered about, but did not see Li Hua. She had not had much free time in the last day or so. Donal had hoped to see her here, and felt surprised that Mr. Mancuso was willing to meet with a magician without his own magician present. Donal took the invitation to mean that he had proven himself trustworthy.

Mr. Mancuso sat in a huge recliner next to a small table arrayed with fruits, cheeses, and chocolates. A matching recliner sat empty on the other side of the table. Mr. Mancuso wore dark suit pants with a white shirt and dark green tie, but without the matching jacket.

"Thank you for seeing me, Donal."

Donal froze at the sound of his first name coming from the man's lips. Mr. Mancuso had never called him anything but Cuthbert. Mr. Mancuso waved Donal to join him in the recliner's match. "Help yourself to anything. Been meaning to send for you for days, but too much business to take care of. Big merger underway."

Mr. Mancuso caught Donal surveying the room.

"Hope you don't mind that I've got Tai Shi running a few errands. Stevens too. I know they're much nicer to look at than I am, but they're also damned important and they both have last-minute matters to take care of. Security, of course. Tai Shi's worried that there'll be another attempt on my life as soon as we touch down. Probably paranoia, but I don't tell her how to do her job.

"And speaking of attempts on my life, I hear they only stopped Imenand because of you. I owe you, which means 4M owes you. Hell, Transterran Properties owes you too, but I can't speak for them. At least, not officially. Not yet."

Mr. Mancuso paused for a sip of coffee. It smelled rich, with hazelnut. The scent suited the appetizers on the table, but Donal's mouth grew dry at the thought of snacks or coffee. His stomach shuddered agreement. Some quality of this meeting reminded Donal of his grandmothers' stories, as though Mr. Mancuso were an unseelie *sidhe*. Eating his food might be a big mistake.

"So the question is," the magnate continued, "what can I do for you? You've got too much potential to waste as a courier." Mr. Mancuso focused his full attention on Donal, who fought the urge to squirm as though trapped. "Want a job working for me? It could be security, maybe working with Tai Shi, or something else if you prefer."

"While I appreciate the offer, sir, I don't feel ready to begin a career—"

"That's right! You're the bookworm type." Mr. Mancuso gestured with his coffee cup. "And I mean that in a good way. We need the bookworms of the world or we wouldn't be having this conversation in space. You were telling me on Mars that you wanted to go to grad school and study ... some damned subject that wouldn't make any sense to me anyway. Well, you got it, Donal. 4M will give you a full ride anywhere you want to go. Hell, become a Hierophant twice over if you want. As long as you're studying something in school, we've got you covered, and when you're ready to do private research, 4M will be there with funding."

Full funding? Two doctorates? More? Donal whirled at the possibilities.

"Mr. Mancuso, I—"

"You saved my life, boy, call me Donatello."

"Donatello, I—"

"If you're going to say anything but 'thank you,' then save your breath. I know you're the modest type, but I'm not going to let you undervalue yourself. I know you want to go to graduate school, and I owe you my life. I'm paying for your education if I have to pay the schools directly on your behalf. Let's do this the nice way."

Donatello stuck out his hand. Donal looked at it and thought again of stories about human bargains with the Fae. Donal could still get out of this. He would have to insult his would-be benefactor, but he would remain free. The man might yet be the tyrant bin Zuka described. But the offer meant all the education Donal dreamed of, research funding, and more. This could be the path to everything he ever wanted. Besides, refusing the bargain would not halt Donatello's machinations, but accepting it would keep Donal close as he rose in power himself.

Could Donal reject this opportunity on the word of a killer? Could he accept it even though his instincts said not to trust Donatello?

Play it safe or take a chance?

Donal reached for his hand and said, "Will you put that in writing?"

Machado looked up from taking notes in his zephyrpad. The knock on his office door was sharp, rapid and persistent. Had to be Jitters. Not that Machado would ever call Jang that to her face. "Come in, Chief."

Jang threw open the workshop door. Her eyes darted to the three magic circles inscribed in the deck, to the small alchemy lab at the back, and to the library along one wall before finally alighting on Machado himself, at his desk along the other wall.

She started toward him with hate in her eyes.

"Thought you could hide from me?"

"I don't need to hide from you, *Initiate*." Machado stood and set his zephyrpad on the desk. "And unless you are looking for a duel, I suggest you remember your manners."

"Oh, forgive me, *Magister*," she said with a sneer and a mock curtsey that Machado would have found laughable under other circumstances. "I just got my copy of your damned report!"

"And?"

"Two weeks in port? Two weeks, you bastard? We don't—"

"Call me a bastard again, Initiate. See what happens."

Jang seethed while she either thought it over or got control of herself. Machado waited with spells dancing on his fingers and tongue. Jang was a great engineer, but that would not save her.

"We don't need two weeks," she said through gritted teeth. "Three days. Five tops."

"We need two weeks. Three would be better."

"I can have this ship—"

"You couldn't get this ship home. We would be dead in space if *my will* hadn't been strong enough to hold that lacuna while you made the final preparations." That shut her up. "We were going far too fast for the HK Drive to maneuver if the Deception Drive went down, and who knows where that would have put us? You should never have tried to maintain that speed."

"The speed was fine! It was a fluke of the bindings."

"It wasn't a fluke. We both knew it could happen, and you still pushed the lacuna too hard for too long. That pressed the bindings, and the stress..."

"... left them vulnerable to those bad harmonics." She grimaced. "But we handled it, and the fix will—"

"We got lucky that the captain ordered us both to keep an eye on it. We have no business going back to space without overhauling and testing every binding in every system on this ship."

"Every system? Oh, the zuglodons." She deflated in a sigh.

"The zuglodons, and I have a few ideas for emergency wards that might save lives in case of a breach."

Jang scratched her cheek. "The Kupferberg Theorem?"

"A derivation. I suspect that if we divide the ship into sections along the hull meridians—"

"I blew it, didn't I," Jang made it a statement. "I almost let my enthusiasm get us killed."

"I prefer to think that you assumed I could get us out of anything you got us into."

"I can't believe I'm saying this," she said through gritted teeth, "but maybe you should remind me of this, the next time I don't listen to you."

"How you almost got us killed?"

"How I had to admit you were right."

Machado laughed, so loud and full-bellied that after a moment Jang joined him, though hers might have been a little bitter.

"So," said Jang, "you have anything to drink around this place?"

Donal clutched the package under his arm as he and Fionn awaited permission to board the hippogriff shuttle to the port proper. Comfortable seats lined the pale gold and sandstone-colored waiting area, but no one used them. Donal was not alone in his impatience to disembark.

He could apply to graduate programs as soon as he got home, but would have to make a few more deliveries before he could quit courier work. He needed to eat while he waited through the ice age that was the grad school application process.

Donal smiled at Li Hua where she stood with Donatello and his entourage. It felt strange to refer to the man by his first name, but Donal would have to adjust. He knew he would hear from his benefactor again soon. He already had a dozen 4M documents in his zephyrpad: an array of promises, contacts, and resources.

When Li Hua noticed and returned his smile, Donal put future worries on hold. He had a dinner date with her tomorrow night. With luck, no one would try to kill them. They might actually have time to sit and talk like human beings. Perhaps they could compare further notes on thaumaturgy. Perhaps they could do more than talk.

"Excuse me, Donal Cuthbert," said a voice near the deck. Donal looked down and saw a translucent gray panther: Magister Machado's familiar. Fionn exchanged a greeting with it that Donal could not understand. "I bear a message," it continued. "My master wishes you to know that he would be happy to provide you with letters of reference, should you wish to further your education."

"Yes, please."

Donal felt even more graduate school options open up to him.

"He shall provide them in the morning, and has advised me that they will carry additional weight at California Thaumaturgic University, San Luis Obispo campus, and the Massachusetts Institute of Thaumaturgy. He apologizes for sending me with this news instead of bearing it himself, but his duties require his attention. Fare well, Donal Cuthbert."

The familiar swirled away in a wisp of smoke. *Smooth.*

Members of the watch cleared a path through the waiting crowd. The doctor came through, wheeling the covered body of Hassan al Rashid on a gurney. He was followed by the chief of security, who led a procession of prisoners, all with wrists sealed behind their backs, and the three spellcasters gagged. A contingent of ship's watch moved with them on either side. The captain himself came last. The whole group boarded the shuttle.

"I guess we're taking the next one," said Donal.

"Nothing presses on our time," said Fionn.

"Hey, can you do that wisp-of-smoke trick?"

"Perhaps."

Donal had not known that his *cú sidhe* could smile.

The tall watchman who had guarded Donal's door came trotting out of the shuttle and up to Donal. "Captain wants you on this shuttle. Says he doesn't want anyone taking a pot-shot at you while the watch isn't there to keep you safe."

"The captain is a wise man," said Fionn, who followed Donal onto the shuttle to an isolated seat near the rear, with the tall guard beside him. The shuttle took wing and landed seconds later.

"You're last off the shuttle," said the tall guard. "Hang back until you see the prisoners leave with Port Security. Then you're safe to go your way."

"Thanks," said Donal, who distracted himself by reviewing the 4M paperwork on his zephyrpad. The complement filed out, and Donal at last came down the stairs and set foot once more on Earth.

AN ENTIRE SECTION OF THE PORT HAD BEEN CLOSED TO ENSURE SAFETY for the prisoner handoff. No civilians — apart from the courier who hung back as instructed — just Jacobs, Ramirez, Goldberg, his ship's watch, the prisoners, and a large contingent from port security. The turnout impressed Jacobs. The port security commander herself, Jane Caraway, brought forty men and women, plus two medical personnel to receive al Rashid's remains. It was more than necessary, in Jacobs' opinion, but he could understand the reaction, given the list of charges. Caraway stepped to the front and said, in a clipped business tone, "Captain John Jacobs of the *Horizon Cusp*, UNAS license number J8181073627F6?"

"That's right."

Jacobs handed over his identification, and the inspection took only seconds.

"I am authorized to accept responsibility for the remains of Hassan al Rashid, as well as your prisoners, charged variously with the following crimes, committed at high space: murder, conspiracy to murder, attempted murder, assault, assault with thaumaturgy, incitement to riot, reckless endangerment of a ship at space...." Jacobs' mind wandered as Caraway continued the list. He needed to talk to Zoltan about his idea for a passenger cruise to Venus. He had calculated that a Venus run could turn a profit, if Jacobs took out a smaller ship for the first voyage. So long as he carried at least ten paid passengers the trip would qualify as a commercial flight, and Zoltan could probably sell ten seats without leaving his desk. Then, on returning, perhaps Jacobs would retire at last.

Caraway had started on the roster of prisoners, confirming them one by one with Goldberg. No surprises there: bin Zuka, his conspirators, and Joffries. Jacobs grimaced. Damned fool of a purser actually took money to bring contraband aboard a ship without confirming the contents. The man was not even a good smuggler. He should have known the cargo was not Martian cognac, no matter what story they fed him about skirting the tariffs. Mars had yet to produce any grapes or wines of note. How could they produce a decent cognac?

But Joffries' criminal ineptitude did not matter. He had allowed passengers to bring weapons aboard Jacobs' ship, and those weapons had been used against both passengers and crew. If Tunold had not begged leniency for the man's youth and inexperience, Jacobs would have had the purser up on conspiracy charges alongside all the others.

Finally that business finished, and Jacobs dismissed his men. Goldberg would take them back to the ship to monitor the general disembarkation, not that he or the chief expected more trouble.

Before port security departed, Jacobs stepped up to Caraway. "Commander, has there been any word on the investigation?"

"Officially it is ongoing." She lowered her voice. "But I wouldn't be breaking any regs if I told you that the early reports look good for you, from a legal standpoint. They're finding independent confirmation of a couple of space anomalies around the right time and location to have caused it."

"Thank you." There were other reasons not to move the business to Mazatlan. San Francisco's administration had always been easy to work with. Jacobs turned to head toward the Starchaser Spacelines offices in port.

On the flight from Mars, Jacobs had worked up a good beginning toward a navigable route to Venus. The flight would take about five days, depending on the ship. He planned to err on the side of caution and take longer if it meant a safer trip. He would have a better idea about that when he picked up the most recent charts. He wondered how Benny Sugg would adjust to travel on a smaller ship after so many years aboard the *Horizon Cusp*.

A small commotion ahead of him drew Jacobs' attention. The port security crew looked flustered about something. Jacobs approached. Imenand bin Zuka lay motionless on the deck, with no visible wounds.

Port security buzzed about. Their commander shouted orders. Jacobs could only stare. Bin Zuka was dead, just as he had predicted. Had he been murdered? He had been willing to kill others for his cause. Perhaps he had committed elaborate suicide.

The man was a fanatic. Jacobs had no doubts of that. Bin Zuka would not have been above killing himself to accomplish his goal. But what if Mancuso had murdered bin Zuka to silence him? What if the fanatic were right all along, and Mancuso stood ready to become humanity's hidden overlord?

How could Jacobs tell? Either way, it meant bin Zuka had died by magic. Jacobs considered that. Bin Zuka had predicted that the spell would leave no trace, would be indistinguishable from a natural death. That was why he had asked for the physical from Doctor Ramirez, to prove he had been in good health. But a physical would not clarify the question of murder or suicide.

Jacobs would send port security a copy of that physical, of course, as bin Zuka had known he would. Did bin Zuka also assume Jacobs would tell Caraway of the fanatic's final prediction of murder? It was in Goldberg's report with the rest of bin Zuka's ravings, but if Jacobs raised the idea in person it would sound sane, would carry more weight.

What if bin Zuka had counted on Jacobs doing just that? What if he had tried to get a known, respected captain like Jacobs to bring up the possibility of homicide as a last attack on Mancuso?

Could that have been the truth, or was it what bin Zuka claimed — his last defense against a political plot by Mancuso?

Jacobs spat. He had carried bin Zuka's ravings far enough. He had carried Mancuso's politics far enough. They were on Earth now, and this was a problem for landlubbers, not spacers. Well the landlubbers could have it. Caraway already had Goldberg's report. Jacobs would send her the results of bin Zuka's final medical examination and let her draw her own conclusions.

Jacobs started walking again. Hard enough work saving a business. Humanity would have to tend to itself. And Jacobs had to find some local dirt for his landing ritual. After the voyage he had had, a moment of thanks sounded right.

———

THE PRISONER EXCHANGE SEEMED TO LAST FOR HOURS, BUT FINALLY Port Security turned to leave and the ship's watch began to return to the shuttle. Donal took that as his cue and started forward, Fionn by his side. After a few dozen paces, Donal felt a surge in the local magic: something powerful and nearby.

"Death magic," said Fionn. "We must have a circle, immediately. You might be next."

A commotion up ahead among Port Security. Captain Jacobs stared, lost in thought. Donal flung wide his awareness, stretched to find the caster...

Power slammed Donal back to himself like he had run headlong into a steel door. He turned to Fionn, but his familiar had been knocked back into its pendant. Donal knelt and touched the ground, waited for the world to stop spinning.

"Is your name Cuthbert?"

Donal looked up to see a Port Security officer standing over him. "Yes."

"Commander Caraway says to tell you that she read about you in the *Horizon Cusp's* reports, and that she knows you had nothing to do with Bin Zuka's death, but if you touch her crime scene again you're going to jail."

"Bin Zuka's dead?"

The officer did not grace Donal's question with a response, but turned and ran back to the cluster of investigation. Donal summoned Fionn.

"That spell killed Bin Zuka."

"Then you are probably not a target." Fionn paced a lap around its master, ears perked and checking for problems. "But what barrier did you strike?"

"Port Security. Apparently I don't need to try to solve every problem I run across."

"Prescription for a longer life."

"Let's go home, Fionn." Donal picked up his fallen zephyrpad and tucked it into his messenger bag. "The delivery can wait until tomorrow. We have a future to plan."

ACKNOWLEDGMENTS

They say that writing is a solitary profession, but the truth is that I could not have written this book without the following people:

My wife, Melissa Mears

My parents, Ed and Kay Mears

My wife's parents, Richard and Adrienne Oringer

My brother, Michael Mears

My brother in all but blood, Patrick Griffin

My thesis second reader, Sean Stewart

The workshop that dealt with my first draft: Wayne Ude, Erika Brummet, Sara Callor

All my professors and fellow students at Whidbey, each of whom taught me a great deal

Last but not least, my friend and thesis advisor, Bruce Holland Rogers

Thank you all so much.

SIGN UP FOR STEFON'S NEWSLETTER

Stefon loves to keep in touch with his readers, and loves to keep you reading. The best way for him to do both is for you to sign up for his newsletter.

Sign up at http://www.stefonmears.com/join

If you sign up for Stefon's newsletter, you get...

- Monthly updates about his publishing and travel schedules
- His latest news, in brief, and answers to reader questions
- A free short story for signing up
- List-only offers and occasional specials
- Plus a free short story every month!

ABOUT THE AUTHOR

Stefon Mears knows the dangers of courier work. Stefon has more than thirty books to his credit, and he never stops writing. He earned his M.F.A. in Creative Writing from N.I.L.A., and his B.A. in Religious Studies (double emphasis in Ritual and Mythology) from U.C. Berkeley. He's a lifelong gamer and fantasy fan. Stefon lives in Portland, Oregon, with his wife and three cats.

Look for Stefon online:
www.stefonmears.com
himself@stefonmears.com